BOYS OF FALL

Katie Gage

Book Formatting by Derek Murphy @Creativindie

Boys of Fall
Copyright © 2024 by Katie Gage.

All rights reserved. Printed in the United States of America. No part of this book may be used or reproduced in any manner whatsoever without written permission except in the case of brief quotations embodied in critical articles or reviews.

This book is a work of fiction. Names, characters, businesses, organizations, places, events, and incidents either are the product of the author's imagination or are used fictitiously. Any resemblance to actual persons, living or dead, events, or locales is entirely coincidental.

The body text is set in Open Sans. Header and footer text is set in Aleo. Title and chapter number text is set in Graduate.

For information contact : Katie Gage at katiegageauthor@gmail.com
KatieGageAuthor.com

Cover design by Copyright © 2024 by Destiny Gage
ISBN: 9798336731156

First Edition: October 2024

10 9 8 7 6 5 4 3 2 1

For Eli–
My brother and friend.

Nerd.

SOPHOMORE YEAR

Before we get started, we should clear some things up right off the bat. First: six man is just as real as "real" football. We still run, throw, block, tackle. Just because there are fewer men on the field doesn't mean it's any less difficult, exciting, or important as eleven-man football, so get your heads out your asses right now. Get it? Got it? Good.

Second: the field is only eighty yards long instead of a hundred. A first down is fifteen yards instead of ten. After a touchdown, there's a PAT (that's a point after try). When I say PAT, I'm talking about running it in, which gets us one point. A kick for a PAT, which is far more rare in six man, is worth two points. (Basically, the point values are swapped from the way it's scored in eleven-man.) A kickoff has to go fifteen yards for the kicking team to recover, and if it goes out of bounds, it's a penalty. It's way more common to kick onsides instead of trying for a deep kick like you see on TV. Clear as mud? Awesome. That about covers it, but don't worry if you're lost. You'll figure it out as you go along. I certainly did.

I played soccer all through middle school and freshman year, and then everything changed. Right after my freshman year of high school my parents made their divorce official, and split. My sisters would stay with my mom, back in Houston, and I went with my dad. Gendered parenting. Because obviously that made sense, that's what's healthy, that's what's best for your three children, instead of sticking it out and working it out. Obviously the best thing for your children is to split them up and send the quiet, introverted middle child off with the grouchy, withdrawn father. The father who didn't understand what all went into mixed hair care, and thought that me needing multiple styling products instead of a three-in-one was "girly." Separating me from the only other two people who knew exactly what it was like to grow up in our disjointed house, the only people who really seemed to understand me. And separating me from my mother, who had been the one support I could count on all through freshman year, the toughest year of my life to date. But I digress.

Dad packed us up and drove us six hours northwest, to Nothingville—to Terrytown Texas. Population 832. Or I suppose 834, now. Home of the Terrytown Soaring Comets. A town kept alive by oil, cattle, and very little else. It consisted of a four-way stop, a post office, a Whataburger/Exon combo on the highway, and a tiny strip center hosting Dollar General, a hardware store, and a Mexican restaurant. Oh, and a restaurant called "Mama D's," but evidently "Mama" had left town about twenty years ago and hadn't been back. There were other things in town, too, the school, for example, and the Methodist and Baptist churches. I'm not sure why such a small town needed more than one church. You'd think they'd all get together, but no. They have to be passive aggressive and give each other *looks* when meeting in passing at the grocery store. Dad and I moved into a little two-bedroom rental house, and he went to work at the oil field, and I did what any other self-respecting teenager would do in smothering heat (I'm talking, like, 110 degrees). I played video games, watched TV, and filled up my sketchbooks. In other words, I stayed inside. Alone. Lonely.

Dad would leave early, come home late. I didn't see him much that summer. I didn't really want to. I called my sisters a couple times, but it felt weird to call someone I'd formerly been able to interrupt by busting into their bedroom, farting, and turning off the light before leaving and not shutting the door behind me. I wallowed in my depression, letting myself be made miserable and comforted by the isolation in alteration. I basically subsisted on frozen pizza and Whataburger, and I missed my mother's cooking dearly.

This state of affairs lasted until the beginning of August, when I finally decided I should learn my way around. School would start soon, and I wanted to know if I could get myself to school on my skateboard or if I would have to take the bus. Throwing on a loose black Batman tank top and shorts, I coasted down the street, kick-push-gliding. It was hot. Coming from Houston, I was used to hot but this kind of heat hit differently. It was like opening an oven, the way it blasted into my face when I opened the front door. Even the breeze stirred up as I skated was more hot air buffeting me. Houston was humid. Terrytown was hell. I was sweating buckets by the time I made it to the school half an hour later.

Next to the school was a football field, surrounded by a chain link fence. There were metal bleachers on either side, the press box at the top of the home side, and a slightly dilapidated scoreboard at the south end. And about twenty-five boys doing planks in neat rows, all wearing orange t-shirts, all dripping sweat. A coach walked among them, loudly counting off. "Three, two, one!"

They dropped from their planks, panting.

I coasted to a stop, kicked my board into my hand, and walked closer to the fence. On the home side of the stands there was a tree, angled so at an evening game some of the fans could get a little shade. That was where I stood then, squinting at the sweating boys.

Back home, I played soccer. I had been pretty good, mostly dribbled the ball, protected it, and passed it to someone else to score. Midfieldman. Terrytown didn't have a soccer team and I knew I was going to miss it–the rush of the game, the thrill of a victory, the feeling of being unified and part of a team without having to struggle through immense amounts of social interaction. I let myself seem cool and aloof, but did my job as a team player on the field, laughed at all the right jokes off the field, and let the flow of community forged by sweat and victory carry me along. Without that in Terrytown, I wasn't sure how I'd fit in.

The boys disbanded on the field, moving to guzzle water from squirt bottles and squat for a minute in the little patches of shade. Their conversation drifted back to my hiding place, but I only heard indistinct mumbles.

To this day, I cannot tell you why I didn't leave right then. I didn't want to be noticed. I had no secret delusions of joining the football team. I didn't even know that much about football—and in Texas, that's a feat.

But one of them spotted me.

Broad-shouldered, square-bodied, he made his way to me slowly, almost meandering. I had plenty of time to run away. But I stayed in my spot, like my converse had put down roots.

He stopped on the other side of the fence, looking at me. His brown hair was buzzed close to his head, like a little boy's. He was at least four inches taller than me, and with his wide shoulders, he cut an impressive figure. He was solid in a comfortable way, a very grounded presence. "Howdy, neighbor," he said. Really, that is what he said.

"Hey," I said, hoping I didn't look too stupid standing there like a dweeb creeping on the football team.

Sometimes, when you meet someone who's going to be important to you for the rest of your life, you know. There's something in the air, the heavens open up, your heart skips a beat, something like that. That did not happen now. He was just a sweaty boy in workout wear and I was just an equally sweaty boy with a skateboard.

"Are you new around here? I don't recall seeing you before."

Ah yes, small towns. Where everyone knows most everyone else and anything different sticks out like a sore thumb.

"Yeah," I said. "Just moved at the start of summer."

His face split into an earnest smile. "Welcome! I'm Nathan." He stuck out his hand to shake, reaching over the fence, which didn't seem to strain his arm too much. I grasped it, and his handshake was firm and strong, that of a boy who lifted weights and threw footballs on the regular.

"Zed."

"Nice to meet you, Zed. You a freshman?" His smile never dropped, his eyes brown and friendly.

"Sophomore."

"Me too. Do you want to try out for the football team?"

And that's the thing about Nathan. He rarely ever has much on his mind, and when he does, there's a good chance it's probably football.

"No, I wasn't planning on it," I said, a little surprised. He'd literally just met me.

"Aw, that's too bad, man," he said, and he sounded genuinely disappointed. "Batman is my favorite." He indicated my shirt.

"Mine, too," I said, a smile tugging at my mouth, despite how awkward I found speaking to new people.

Another boy appeared in my periphery, chattering, "Nathan, where'd you go? Who's that you're talking to—?" He stopped short at the sight of me, saying sharply, "Who are you, then?"

"I'm Zed. Who are you?" I returned with equal sharpness, narrowing my eyes. I'd been picked on before, and I had no desire to keep up that trend in a new school.

"None of your effin' business, that's who." He was short, at least a head shorter than Nathan, but he puffed himself up like the big dog on the street.

"*Finn*. Be nice. Zed is new, just moved here, a sophomore like me. But he doesn't want to try out for the football team."

Finn gave me an appraising glance, an up-down scrutiny that made me conscious of my short stature and thin arms. Though he was not particularly tall or muscly himself, I got the impression I was being measured up and found wanting. "No. He doesn't seem like the footballing sort."

I bristled, raising my chin and tensing my shoulders. "I play—played—soccer."

Finn snorted. "Ah. The inferior football."

"*No*, it's the original football."

He shrugged. "Doesn't matter. Got a newsflash for you, man, we're in America."

"You're the one who called it football."

"Pssh. Poor excuse for it. Half of it's prancing around, acting like you're hurt. Bet you couldn't even make it through one of our games without giving up."

I huffed through my nose. "*Actually,*" I directed my words at Nathan, who had been watching us with a worried wrinkle on his forehead. "I think I would like to try out for the football team."

His face split into a smile. "Really? Come on in then, I'll introduce you to Coach."

I leaned my board against the fence and climbed over in quick movements. I landed squarely on my feet, sending a challenging look at Finn as I did so. He was unimpressed.

Coach turned out to be a square-faced man wearing a ball cap, who frowned at Nathan as though he'd turned up in his kitchen with a muddy stray puppy. Which wasn't too far from the truth, actually, but he looked at me for a few seconds before saying, "How old are you, son?"

"Fifteen."

"And you've played soccer?"

"Yes sir. I could probably be a good kicker, if you needed."

"There's not much kicking in six man, but I'd be happy to give you a try."

"Wait. Six man?"

"Yeah." He squinted at me. "You ever heard of it?"

"No, sir."

Behind me, Finn made a disparaging noise.

"Well, it won't take you long to catch up. Get out there and run a lap."

Soccer is mostly running. But after a summer of lazing about on the couch and in my bed, I was not in shape for running in the midsummer heat. I finished my lap, sweating and panting, but I did it. By the time I got back, Coach had sent the other boys out for more conditioning and the assistant coach was counting them through jumping jacks.

Coach, though a short man, was broad in the chest and shoulders. He frowned at me past his crooked nose. He jotted down my stats (Height: 5'9"; Weight 160lb; Shoe size 9;) and said, "Well, there's not much else to do except to let you play. Get out there and do some jumping jacks."

I raised my brows in surprise.

He glanced back at me and seemed surprised I was still standing there.

A third man, bespeckled and wearing a grimy white ball cap with a red cross on the front said, "You got cleats?"

"Yes," I said.

Coach squinted at me once more. "Bring 'em tomorrow." He glanced at the other guy then, gruffly, as an afterthought, he added, "Congratulations, you're on the team."

"What?" I shook my head to clear it. I thought he'd have me kick some field goals, maybe throw some passes, but that was it. Soccer tryouts were rigorous and involved, but clearly at a smaller school there was less dog-eat-dog mentality.

He shrugged. "Yeah, what's the worst you'll do? Sit on the bench and bulk up my numbers? Play as a route runner? Yeah, you're on the team."

When I tried out for the team to make a point to some asshole badmouthing soccer, I wasn't planning on staying. But I was in this mess now, so I might as well see it through. I joined the back of the line. It was too hot, and I was out of shape. I had no one to look at in companionable misery. I wanted to die.

***

After practice, Coach Carlson, the assistant, handed me an orange t-shirt with black lettering spelling *Comets!* "Wear this tomorrow. And some cleats—Coach said you played soccer?" I nodded. "Good. We start at four o'clock. We'll be done about supper. You got folks?"

I took the t-shirt, still dazed. My legs hurt. My arms hurt. My brain was so tired it was probably little more than painfully jiggling mush. "Uh. I have my dad."

"He planning on picking you up?"

"No."

Coach Carlson squinted at me over his glasses, making an assessment of that statement. No pity entered his gaze, I was glad to note. "Alright. See you tomorrow, Zed."

I heard Nathan, calling from behind me. "Zed. You need a ride?"

I turned around.

He stood there, shirtless and sweaty. He was smiling at me, looking sincere. He didn't even know he'd gotten me into this mess. I'd be mad, but he just seemed so dang *nice*. If he'd never said hello—if I'd never stopped to watch practice—

Finn appeared beside him, also shirtless. He was probably 170 soaking wet, built like a steel beam, lean and ropy. He pulled a gross-out face. "C'mon, man, he doesn't even have clean clothes. He's going to stink up my truck—"

"Finn," Nathan said firmly. "Your truck already smells. *You* smell. *I* smell."

The other boy huffed and rolled his eyes, but thankfully shut up.

"So?" Nathan prompted. "A ride?"

I hesitated. Cicadas hummed around us. A ride sounded nice. Sitting down, air conditioning. However my general annoyance at what I'd gotten myself into, plus the murderous look in Finn's eyes, deterred me.

"Thanks," I said, "but that's okay."

Nathan's smile slipped, just a bit, and I felt like I'd kicked a puppy. "Okay. See you tomorrow?"

"Yeah. Tomorrow."

Man, the ride home on my skateboard was the worst I'd ever taken, legs like Jell-O and lungs feeling sore. But there was something satisfying about it, you know? About using your body for a purpose and feeling good after. And football, even six man football, couldn't be that different from soccer, right? *Right?*

Katie Gage

Turns out six man football is pretty different from soccer. I guess the principle is the same: get the ball into the goal. The way it's accomplished is way, way different.

I slunk into practice on the second day toeing the line of late. I placed myself in Nathan's vicinity without greeting him specifically, not sure if I wanted to be noticed yet or not. I tossed my old soccer bag onto the bench. It held my cleats, water bottle, cooling towels, and old shin guards. Guess I wouldn't be needing those anymore.

"Welcome back!" Nathan smiled hugely at me, like an excited puppy. I could practically see his tail wagging.

"I didn't think you'd come," Finn said, giving me a once over. He offered me an approving nod.

"Well, I am back." I pulled out my cleats and started lacing them up with deft, practiced fingers.

"That's good," Nathan said, pleased.

"Hope you looked up the rules or something last night, can't have you looking lost and being useless," said Finn.

"I'll be fine." As a matter of fact, I knew I should have looked up the rules last night, but I'd spent time sketching instead—mostly useless doodles: a three-dimensional dodecahedron, eyes, a skeletal hand raising a middle finger. My own middle finger twitched with wanting to show this kid exactly what I thought of him.

Finn rolled his eyes.

"I'll catch up," I assured him. "I *will*." I don't think he believed me.

That first week, we did mostly conditioning, and switched over to drills and running plays, but without equipment. We'd be getting that on the first day of school. It was hell, hot and sweaty hell, but Coach kept saying we'd be the best in shape in the state, have the best endurance on the field; I kept wondering if it was actually worth it. I couldn't remember soccer training being quite this hardcore.

Coach taught me to swivel my hips, to cut the corner, to tuck the ball and run. I learned how to tackle low around the legs and not try and shove the man. All the footwork I'd learned in soccer came in handy, but it took on new shapes, molded into a different form. I was also informed about the mandatory participation in track and cross country, intended to keep us in shape. Coach supervised those sports, too. I didn't realize six man football came with a side of death-by-running, but here we were.

Doc took my stats for real that day, putting me on the scale. It turned out I'd gained a few pounds over my lazy summer. He still had on that grimy white cap with the red cross symbol.

"What kind of doctor are you?" I asked, as he wrote something down about jersey sizes.

"Oh, I'm not. Just the athletic trainer. And biology teacher."

"Oh. I guess the hat–" I indicated the cap.

"Gift from a student who graduated a few years back."

"Ah." The athletic trainer and a biology teacher. Weird, but it must be a small town quirk.

It was the same for the other two coaches. Coach, who didn't seem to have a real first name, who coached football, track and field, and basketball. I assume he didn't coach anything else because the school didn't offer anything else. Coach Carlson, on-field, was in charge of drills, sideline organization, and water bottles; off-field he taught P.E. and government.

On the second week, Coach kept me, Nathan, Finn, and three other boys late, specifically to run through plays with me. Though I'd seen the drawings on the whiteboard, I still didn't fully understand how it all worked. There were so few of us on the field, how could we even strategize?

Nathan set up as center on the fifty yard line, bending at the waist with his long legs wide apart, like a giraffe getting down for a drink. Finn stood ten yards behind him. They put me three yards in front of Finn and offset a yard to the left, some kid named Alejandro paralleling me on the other side. The other two boys set up on either side of Nathan, lining up their inside foot with his on the white stripe.

"This is a diamond spread," Coach said to me. "Our preferred formation. I want you to be able to run a diamond spread in your sleep. Savvy?"

"Yes, Coach."

"You," he snapped, "Catch it and pitch it to him." He jerked his head to Finn. "Run it like a sweep right," Coach said to Finn.

Finn nodded, called for the snap. The ball sailed straight to me, and even my unpracticed hands didn't have to move much to catch it.

"Now pitch it, pitch it!" Finn yelled, jogging.

I tossed it underhand, too short, and the ball fell to the ground.

"That's alright, you'll get it," Coach Carlson said.

"Again," snapped Coach, and we did it again. And again.

Just as I was preparing myself for another repeat, Coach swapped me and Finn. This time, Finn caught the ball and pitched it to me, and I, predictably, fumbled it.

We ran variation upon variation of that play. Nathan could snap it to any one of us three behind him, and we had to toss it, as I'd been doing to Finn. Then Finn could tuck it and run.

Sometimes he could pass it. Anyone is an eligible receiver, even Nathan. It keeps everyone on their toes for sure, opponents included.

Coach tried me in several positions, as halfback, linebacker, receiver, and even quarterback. I think he wanted to see how well I handled those positions, what skills I brought to the table. I liked being a receiver, liked sprinting ahead and looking back for the ball soaring toward me. I also liked getting the hand off and making for the hills, just absolutely dashing toward the end zone. I can tell you right now, I was not meant to be a quarterback. I don't have the arm for it. I also don't have the fortitude to withstand Finn's glares as I experimented with his position.

There were twenty boys on the varsity team, nearly a quarter of the school. There were also a handful of middle schoolers that would join us for practice after school started. They had their own team, but with a school so small it was effective for Coach to train both teams at the same time.

I assumed I wouldn't be playing much this year. I was a sophomore, brand new, and barely understood the game. Nathan played almost the whole game, offense and defense usually, because he was the most reliable snapper and could read the defense like a book, plus he was one of the biggest boys on the team. And Finn, though he was a junior, played mostly on offense. He was the best player on the team, hands down. He could juke any of us, throw further than the rest of us, and run *really* fast. As fast as me. That was my one skill, running fast. If I could figure out how to catch the ball, I'd be all set. I still wasn't used to being allowed to touch it with my hands, some long-ingrained instinct causing me to resist touching the ball as though it was hot, fumbling more often than not.

The other boys were nice, casually enveloping me into the team camaraderie. They tossed me water bottles and slapped my butt and back, easy as anything. I guess sports teams aren't terribly different no matter what sport you play: a bunch of dudes just having a good time getting sweaty with some friendly (or not so friendly) competition.

The one person I couldn't figure out was Finn. He just didn't seem to like me, and for the life of me I didn't know why. He kept throwing little verbal jabs my way, about soccer and how I didn't understand the game, which only served to make me work harder to get better. I liked Nathan just fine, liked his easy smiles and simple, solid presence. If he and Finn weren't joined at the hip, I would have liked him a lot more. But they were a package deal: easy, happy Nathan, and sharp, prickly Finn. They were so different. I didn't understand it.

And every day after practice, Nathan offered me a ride home. And every day Finn rolled his eyes. And every day I told them no.

After a week and a half of practice, it became apparent I'd need to tell my dad what I'd been doing. I hadn't mentioned it yet because: a) I rarely saw him, and b) I didn't think he'd care. But I needed to pay some dues for a practice t-shirt and new cleats. So I waited until Friday evening, when I figured he'd be mellowed out by some beer and the prospect of the weekend.

"Hey Dad?"

He grunted and glanced away from the TV only briefly, remote in one hand and a beer in the other.

"I need to talk to you about something."

"You'd better not be in trouble."

"What? No, I'm not. I do need some help though. Not like, bad help or something? I've just, um."

"Just spit it out," he said, sounding distracted.

I fell silent, jaw clenching.

"*What?*"

"I joined the football team and I need some money to pay for my gear."

He finally looked at me. "Money?"

"Yeah, money."

"How much?"

"About seventy dollars?" Cleats weren't cheap.

He sighed, heavy and put-upon. "Fine." After digging about in his pocket for his wallet, he counted out wrinkled bills. "I hope that's all." He was already turning away.

"It's fine."

"Don't go doing anything else impulsive, hear me?"

"Okay."

"I don't have the money or time to be following you around. Especially after last year."

I did not flinch at the reminder of last year's detentions, grades, or parent-teacher conferences. I was going to do better, I swore to myself. "Okay."

He rolled his eyes and returned to his beer.

I retreated to my room and my art supplies. For a brief moment, I sharply, painfully, missed my mother.

She would have been proud of me, would have pressed her hands to both my cheeks to look in my eyes. She would have driven me to practice, would have been at every game. She would have learned the rule book so she could yell at the referees. Her ruby red lipstick outlining her loud, joyful cheers, large hoop earrings swinging around her face. It was what she had done for soccer, never missing a game, even in the cold of January and the rain of February. She had bundled up in a felt peacoat and black scarf, a hat pulled over her heat styled hair, and when it would get sunny, she whipped out chunky sunglasses with little rhinestones.

Living with dad now, I understood why my parents did what they did, even if I didn't quite believe it was right. He was hardly ever home, barely spoke to me at all, and was always distracted. Our home was a dim animal's den, windows shuttered and the rooms sparsely furnished. Empty pizza boxes piled on the counter. Fast food wrappers overflowed in the trash can. I was just as guilty of hoarding my garbage, with styrofoam cups on my dresser and nightstand, and a mix of dirty and clean clothes littering my floor. In truth, it didn't bother me, but I couldn't imagine what my mother would say upon walking in. I could picture the repulsed face she'd make, her nose making her commentary on the smell without her saying a word.

At my desk, I took up my pencils, and again began to draw.

***

School started the third week of August, two weeks after I officially joined the team. I debated taking the bus, but decided to skateboard. The bus is for freshmen and those who live too far away to drive. So I skateboarded, wearing black skinny jeans ripped at the knee, and a black AC/DC t-shirt, in spite of the heat. I had an image to keep up. Besides, I knew I was going to spend half of my day wandering around looking lost. So I might as well look cool while I was doing it.

Here's the thing, first days of school are always awkward. There's no avoiding it. Everyone's trying to figure out where their classes are, whether they get to have lunch with their friends or if they have to endure the horror of eating alone, and whether or not the people they were friends with last year will still be their friends this year. I had to make sure my papers were sorted out and my football registration was all good, too. I stowed my skateboard in my locker, the remnants of a former student's sticker still leaving sticky white streaks on the front. I suffered through math, survived homeroom, and actually enjoyed English.

I already knew this school was small, because the town was small, but there were less than a hundred students at the school. I guess I wasn't expecting the football team to make up a fifth of the school. Or for there to only be six cheerleaders. Or for the band to be another quarter of the school. Everyone knew everyone, and everyone knew I didn't belong. There was only one school bus, and plenty of kids walked or drove themselves to school. All the trucks parked at the back of the parking lot, where they could smoke or chew in peace, and I later learned this was called "hillbilly row."

As I headed down the hall for lunch, I saw Nathan, Finn, and behind them the vague shape of a skirt I assumed was attached to a girl.

I was planning on seizing a quiet a table in the corner and drawing through my lunch period. I made to slip by them, not wanting to invade their little clique, but Nathan spotted me, and waved.

"Zed, hi!"

"Yeah, hi." I stopped, backpack hanging off one shoulder.

Finn looked at me across their little circle, and if looks could kill, I'd be very, very dead. Or perhaps nothing more than just a smoking pile of ash.

"Do you have someone to eat with?" Nathan asked.

"No."

"Good, you can eat with us, then."

The girl made a small sound behind him.

"Oh, introductions. Zed, this is my sister, Naomi."

Remember how I said sometimes when you meet someone who'll be important to you for the rest of your life, the heavens open up and angels sing? That's what happened. The heavens parted and Nathan stepped aside to reveal the most beautiful girl I'd ever seen., I know what you're thinking. *Oh, Zed, you just think she was the most beautiful girl you'd ever seen because you were fifteen and you'd never seen a girl with proper boobs before.* But no. That's not it. It was her face, her hair, her whole *being.* Her hair was curly, the curls as big around as a pencil, or maybe my finger, brown like Nathan's, falling past her shoulders. Freckles spattered across her cheeks and nose. She wore a loose purple shirt ripped horizontally at the arms and midsection, revealing a yellow tank top underneath. Her skirt, which fell almost to her ankles, looked to be made of what was once several other items of clothing. It was all sorts of colors, the fabrics cut into varying shapes, stitched together in a weird patchwork. She smiled, a bright, genuine grin, and stuck out her hand. "Hi, Zed. I'm Naomi."

I at least had the presence of mind to shake her hand, the softest, most delicate hand I'd ever had the pleasure to shake. "Hi," I managed stupidly. I tried to recover by sweeping a hand through my thick hair roguishly, but failed as my fingers caught on a tangle I'd missed that morning, and it left my fingers greasy from the curl milk.

She smiled again, and I trailed helplessly in her wake as we went to the cafeteria.

So, no, it wasn't just because she had boobs. Though the boobs did help.

***

I hate cafeterias. It's so sectioned, so divided. Everyone sits with their little group and hates everyone else who isn't in their little group. That's how it is in the big city, and it wasn't so different here, either. I wondered where I would sit without this ragtag crew—by myself, probably. Just pigeonhole myself into the quiet loner image before anyone else can do it for me.

Naomi, Nathan, and Finn made their way to a round table near the door to the courtyard. Finn sprinted ahead and skidded to a stop by the table, saying, "Ha, suckers. No one's stealing our table."

Naomi rolled her eyes in a fond sort of way.

Hoping to sit by Naomi, I followed her to the table, but Finn wormed his way between us, seizing the chair beside mine.

"Move over, Finn, that seat's mine," Naomi said.

"I've decided I'd like to be here."

"No you haven't, go sit down over there." She pointed to the other side of the table.

He sighed, but moved anyway, over by Nathan, poking him in the ribs until the boy shifted over to give him more space, almost reflexively.

So, I ended up sitting by Naomi, and that singular event made my whole day. They chatted about classes and schedules, teachers they'd known for ages. I listened, observing the comfortable fellowship between them. People kept stopping by to tell Naomi hello, and she knew all of them–knew all of their names, asked after bits of their lives. It was like she had a gravitational pull and no one could resist. I certainly couldn't. And then Naomi turned to me.

"So where are you from?" She fixed her eyes on my face, and I felt like I was the center of the universe for a moment.

"I just moved here from Houston."

"Oh, the big city! And are you liking it?" Not really, but in the face of her bright spirit, I couldn't help but nod. "So how'd you meet these two idiots?"

I glanced at where Nathan and Finn were laughing about something to do with the cafeteria's French fries. "Football. Nathan convinced me to join."

"That's not true!" Finn interrupted. "I convinced him to join."

"I think you made fun of me until I couldn't say no."

He sniffed. "Same difference."

"Do you like it?" Naomi asked, her attention never wavering from me. Her eyes were so very blue.

"Yeah, s'alright."

"Were you a footballer before?" One of her hands rested on the table, her pointer finger worrying at the cuticle of her thumb.

"Yeah, but like. The other kind. The kind where you can't use your hands."

"We don't have that kind, do we?" she said ruefully, like she was apologetic on behalf of the whole school.

"Nope."

"Shame. Well, I'm glad the boys are looking after you."

Nathan grinned at me, Finn glared at me, and I offered a weak smile in return.

"Trash?" Finn asked, hopping up and grabbing the siblings' plates. He left mine. Nathan gave him a disappointed look as he walked away.

"So you're siblings?" I asked.

"Yep. Twins."

"Oh really? Identical?" I said, and then could have slapped myself. "That was stupid." Naomi was busy laughing, a loud jubilant belly laugh that sounded nothing like tinkling bells and everything like joy personified. She scrunched her nose as she did so.

Nathan gave me a look that was probably meant to be comforting. "You'd be surprised how often we get that."

"I'm fifteen minutes older," she said, with a saucy tilt to her head. Her curls bounced. "And I'm never letting him forget it." He grinned at her.

Finn strutted back into view. "C'mon, Nathan, I want to see how many ketchup packets I can steal before the lunch monitor notices."

"That's a terrible idea," Nathan said, already getting up. "I'll help."

"Don't get detention, I need my ride home!" Naomi called after them.

I leaned over to her. "Why does he hate me?"

"Who?"

"Finn."

Her brows furrowed. "Hate you? What do you mean?"

"He's always looking at me like he wants to kill me or something. Can't figure out what I did to him."

Naomi sighed. "That's just how Finn is. He should probably come with a warning label. 'Warning: accidental jerk ahead.'" I laughed. "Sorry. He'll come around, you'll see."

"At least Nathan likes me."

She nodded. "That's probably part of it."

"What?"

"Nathan's always needed a little more…protecting than the rest of us." She shrugged. "He's always been hurt easier—more easily than the rest of us. And Finn, well, he just tries to save Nathan from himself."

I hummed, thinking a little about the way she'd changed the language to *more easily*, rather than *easier*. Didn't leave out the fact that they got hurt sometimes, too. "Nathan does seem very friendly."

"He is. And he means every bit of it. But that's come back to bite him more than once. Finn's seen that happen too many times, I think."

"He must be a good friend."

She smiled, giving me a nod in understanding. "He is. He really, really is. A little too intense sometimes, but otherwise all around excellent."

Looking back, that sums up Finn perfectly: a little too intense but otherwise excellent. A little too intense in football, in fear, in love. Otherwise excellent in working hard, in having fun, in being a friend.

Our first game of the season was a home game.

I was not prepared for the way a small town goes hard for football. People rolled up with their parents, their grandparents, their neighbors. Guys backed their trucks up behind the away goalposts or drove through the grass to park outside the fence, sitting off the tailgate with their boots swinging. I'd never seen so many cowboy hats outside of the Houston Rodeo. The concession stand sold the usual fare of hot dogs, nachos, sodas, and water. Our pitiful little band, fifteen students strong, sat on the bleachers and bravely played tune after tune. An announcer sat up in the press box, and, unless I was mistaken, he had someone from the local radio station there as well. I was used to students and family coming to games–I was not used to the whole town coming out for a high school six man football game. I guess in a huge city (read: very tiny) as sleepy as Terrytown, it made sense. I wouldn't have been surprised if local businesses shut down in favor of going to the game.

When we walked out from the locker room, the crowd was already deafening. Our six cheerleaders held a paper banner they'd painted with a soaring Comet and orange letters saying "Go Team!" We sprinted through it and the noise from the crowd escalated into cheering. I kept my eyes forward, on Nathan's number 75 in front of me. Game time.

Through the speakers, the announcer said, "Ladies and gentlemen, please stand for a moment of prayer and the national anthem."

The stands rumbled as the crowd stood, whipping off hats. Over the speakers, the voice of a child came cautiously. "Dear God, please keep our players safe, and let us have a good game. Amen."

A round of applause.

Around me, my team lined up and put a hand on the shoulder of the man in front of them. We faced the flag. A woman sang the anthem, heavy with country twang. I watched the flag ripple in the light breeze, less concerned with our country and more concerned with the game. As the song died away, the crowd cheered, and my teammates and I slapped the shoulder pads of the person in front of us, a clattery plastic sound. It was time.

"Let's play some football!" said the announcer, and we were off.

I was on the sidelines for the kickoff, eyes glued to the ball. My palms sweat inside my gloves, my heart thudded in my ears. So much depended on this one shot. The players ran. Matteo kicked it, it rolled. My team trotted after it, giving it a wide berth because we couldn't touch it unless it made it fifteen yards. When an opponent dropped on it, I exhaled. Time to play some football.

On our opening drive, Finn received the pitch and juked, scrambling. He grabbed some daylight and was away, sprinting down the field. Behind him, a defender struggled to keep up, arms reaching. I screamed, heart pounding. He was almost there! The defenseman stumbled, and Finn was in the clear, the distance growing between him and the defender. He made it to the endzone, leaping into the air and whooping. As soon as he passed off the football to the referee, he turned serious once more.

I went in for the PAT as a blocker. We made the point, bringing our score up to seven. If Coach had let me kick it, the score could have been eight, maybe. Because kicks are so rare in six man, a kicked PAT is worth two points. But he's the coach, and I'm not. And we hadn't practiced much kicking.

I didn't sit on the bench while I was off the field, but rather, I hovered just over Coach's left shoulder, right there in case he needed me. This turned out to be a good strategy, because late in the second when we were trailing by fourteen, he looked around for someone to replace Tate (who had just run an incorrect route *and* fumbled the ball), and grabbed me by the back of the collar. Yelling the play into my ear, he sent me out to the huddle with a slap on the back.

As I jogged up to the huddle, I jerked a thumb over my shoulder at Tate, who didn't even flinch before heading for the bench. He knew he'd messed up. Finn looked at me through the helmet. "The play?"

I told them, repeating it just as Coach had said it. Finn gave a sharp nod, and we formed up, with me wide on the line, Nathan in my peripheral. Nathan snapped it, Ethan Wilkes caught it, pitched it to Finn, who started scrambling, looking for a receiver. His designated receiver, Alejandro, was covered up, couldn't get free. He scrambled a bit longer, and I thought he was going to run it, even though that wasn't what Coach called. Instead, he passed it to me. It was a short pass, tipped high, and I jogged to get under it. The ball landed in my arms with a sweet *smack*, and I tucked it under my arm to run. I didn't make it very far, but I still made the first down.

When we huddled, Nathan slapped my butt and grinned. "Good catch."

Finn nodded. "You saved my ass."

Then two plays were running, Finn and Ethan Wilkes weaving through. We got the first down, and then Coach pulled me off the line in favor of putting in an experienced junior, which made perfect sense. I was still thrilled I'd gotten to play.

We won our first game of the season to the thunderous cheers of half the town. It was awesome.

Naomi was leaning over the fence, waving at us. Nathan jogged over to give her a knuckle bump.

"Don't you want to give me a hug?" Finn asked, opening his sweaty arms wide.

She made a face. "I think I'm good for now."

"Aw, don't you love me?"

"Not that much." She waved her hand in front of her nose and curled her lip dramatically.

He aimed a squirt from his water bottle in her direction, and she squealed and dodged away. He roared a laugh, then jumped in the air and whooped again, high on victory.

We jogged to the locker rooms, yelling and cheering about winning, and jumping in celebration. Coach calmed us down enough to give us his post-game talk and sent us on our merry way.

My dad hadn't come to the game. I guessed I was skateboarding home, even though it was dark and I was tired. Gathering my things, I arranged them to distribute weight evenly. Board tucked under my arm, I headed out.

As I walked toward the gate, I spotted Nathan by the concession stand, holding a hot dog. There was another boy with him, someone I didn't recognize. He stood in front of him, blocking Nathan's way. I came up behind them, and as I heard their conversation, started walking faster.

"You gonna do it? Or are you too chickenshit?" the other boy asked.

"I'm not doing it," Nathan said quietly, standing with his feet planted firmly, but not meeting his eyes.

"Yeah, you think you're all high and mighty, playing out there on that field, but when it comes down to it, you're just a big ol' coward."

Nathan ducked his head, saying again, "I'm not gonna do it."

The boy snorted and pushed at Nathan's shoulder, knocking the hotdog to the ground.

I jogged to close the distance. "What's going on here?" Casually, I bumped my shoulder against Nathan's in solidarity, standing beside him. The boy eyed me in disgust. He wasn't especially large, but he was mean looking. I wasn't sure what he wanted from Nathan, but it didn't seem good.

"Who the hell are you?"

"Zed. I'm new around here. Who are you?" I returned with snarky politeness.

"Buzz off. This doesn't concern you."

"I'm curious by nature." I let irritation creep into my voice. What folks didn't know is that I'd seen at least one fight per week back home. It was a city school, shit happened. I knew a few things about defending myself and those I cared about.

"You've got a smart mouth."

"And a smart brain. Which appears to be more than you can say." Maybe I shouldn't be egging him on, but I did anyway. At this point, I was ready for a fight.

He growled and went to shove at me.

"*Hey!*" That was Finn, jogging toward us from the lockers. "What are you doing here, asswipe?"

He sneered at Finn, who was so much shorter and thinner than him, but took a step back.

"That's right, get lost." Finn stepped into his space, bowing his chest up, despite his lack of height. "Go on, git."

He backed away. "This isn't over," he said, pointing at Nathan.

I looked to him for an explanation.

He sighed and rubbed the back of his neck. "Thanks. You didn't need to do that."

I shrugged. "S'nothing."

Finn was watching me appraisingly. "Caleb Hanson has had it out for Nathan for forever. Since, what—fifth grade?"

"Sixth. When we moved here."

"Forever," Finn repeated.

Naomi came up from the direction of the parking lots. "Nathan, mom and dad are waiting..." She glanced around at us. "What happened?"

"Caleb Hanson wanted me to hide weed for them. Said I'd never be suspected."

Naomi heaved a sigh, closing her eyes. "Someday, Nathan, you should just punch them. Then they'd leave you alone. You're bigger than them, now."

He shrugged. "Wouldn't be right. Caleb hasn't hit me since I was thirteen. I'm working on that 'turn the other cheek' thing."

"Doesn't make it okay," she said. "Finn, you need a ride?"

"Nah, I've got my truck. You coming to Whataburger?"

She shook her head. "Not tonight. Curfew."

He pulled a face like something smelled nasty. "Lame." He nodded at me, the murderous glint in his eyes replaced with something firmer, but less dangerous. "See you Monday?"

"Monday," I confirmed.

He gave us all a smile, even me. "Later, losers," he said as he left.

Nathan also headed for the parking lot. With a smile, Naomi motioned for me to follow. "Thanks for standing by him."

"It's not a big deal."

"Caleb Hanson has always picked on him. His daddy doesn't like our daddy, so...it feeds on itself."

"Ah."

"One day Nathan will fight back or something, then they'll leave him alone."

"Hm."

"You have a good weekend, okay?" We were in the parking lot, the bright white lights illuminating the cars.

"Yeah."

"Hey, are you skateboarding home?"

"What? Oh, yeah."

She frowned, a little pinched thing. "We'll give you a ride."

"It's okay."

"No, really." Then she turned and yelled, "Nathan! Tell mom and dad we're giving Zed a ride!" Without looking back, he gave a little salute. "You can't say no now, my mom would be so disappointed." I gave her a look. She looked right back at me, brows raised, confident I would give in.

"Naomi—"

"Nope."

"Nao—"

"You're coming."

"Na—"

"Coming with me!"

"Na—"

"Uh-uh."

I sighed. "Fine. I'll ride with you."

"Yes," she whispered, doing a little fist pump.

Mr. and Mrs. Peterson didn't even flinch at my sudden appearance in their van. Nathan climbed into the way back, all elbows and bending legs, and Naomi and I took the two seats in the middle.

"Hi, Zed," Mr. Peterson said. "Naomi tells me you just moved here."

"Yes, this summer."

"Well, welcome to the best town west of Abilene." He grinned and stuck his hand over his shoulder for me to shake.

"Where are we taking you?" Mrs. Peterson asked, and I gave them the address. When I told her, she said, "Oh, I think I have a student who lives over here."

Naomi rolled her eyes. "Of course you do."

Nathan and his father kept up a steady stream of conversation about the game, rehashing good plays and the way the other team played. It was then, in the car, that I realized Nathan saw the game differently than anyone else on the team. He spotted plays before they happened, openings a second before they appeared, understood strategy on a visceral level. He was almost as perceptive as Coach.

Naomi was scrolling on her phone, the light illuminating her face gently in the dark of the car. "Do you like movies, Zed?" she asked in a hushed voice.

"Who doesn't?"

"Superhero films," she clarified.

"Heck yeah."

"Maybe you'd like to come with us next weekend? Finn wants to see the latest Marvel."

"Sure, okay. Text me the details?"

She grinned, opening her palm for my phone. "This was all an elaborate ploy to add you to our groupchat." She punched in her digits swiftly, adding a little sunshine emoticon after her name.

"Thanks." I took my phone and pocketed it. Later, I was still thinking about that tiny yellow sunshine.

***

On Monday I stepped out of my house, skateboard under my arm, to the sight of a battered red four-door idling in my driveway. I squinted, trying to figure out if my father had mysteriously bought a truck without telling me.

Finn rolled down the driver's window. "Well, are you getting in or what?"

"Uh..." I responded intelligently.

The back window rolled down and I was treated to the sight of Naomi's freckly face peering out at me smiling. "Come keep me company!" Like I needed any more convincing than that.

"Yeah, okay." I climbed in the back seat.

Naomi handed me a styrofoam cup of coffee. "It's black right now, but I have creamer." She fished around in her backpack and emerged with those little travel packs that are at hotels.

"Uh, sure." Still baffled at the truck in my driveway, I took one absently.

Nathan, sitting in the passenger seat, still looked sleepy. "You should know, Zed, that Naomi swiped a sleeve of cups from the church just to bring us coffee. My own sister, a criminal." He shook his head mournfully.

Naomi rolled her eyes. "The trustees committee will never know."

Nathan scrolled through the songs on Finn's phone and turned on a country song, all guitars and twang.

"Heck yeah, bro," Finn said, tapping on the steering wheel.

"What are you doing here?" I said finally.

"Driving you to school. What's it look like? Ya numbskull."

I looked to Naomi, not understanding this sudden burst of kindness from Finn. Today she was wearing blue jeans and a light blue top decorated at the hem and cuffs with tassels that may or may not have once been on a lampshade. She offered me a sunny smile, nudging my knee with hers. "Hope you don't mind. I knew you always skateboarded, so I gave Finn your address."

"Welcome aboard the Redneck Rover!" Nathan said.

"We have *got* to get a better name," Finn sighed, turning into the parking lot.

I ate lunch with them, as I had every day for the last two weeks. But this time, maybe for the first time, I didn't feel like an intruder, a burden. Or like I was just their charity case. I felt like maybe…I was their friend.

***

Running laps around the football field, I jogged to catch up with Finn. "Hey," I panted. "Thanks for giving me a ride."

"You're not welcome," he said flatly. "I hate you."

Startled, I looked over at him and found a smile curling at the corners of his mouth, sharp amusement glinting in his eyes. I was learning this harshness, the insults, the prodding—it was all part of his way of showing affection.

I managed a weak chuckle. "I hate you, too?"

He barked a quick laugh and blew out a gust of air. "Whew. No talk. Only run."

I hid my smile and kept pace with him the rest of the way.

***

The next morning, Naomi handed me a styrofoam cup of coffee in the backseat again. "Coffee, little cream?"

"Yeah." I took it with a grin. "Thanks."

4

I'd spent nearly three weeks of lunches listening to them. They talked about teachers, local gossip, and plans for the weekend. "What are you angry about today, Finn?" asked Naomi.

"Ugh, fricking Camilla Johnson. She wore a short skirt today, and should have been dress coded, probably."

I recognized the name vaguely as belonging to one of the six cheerleaders. "Didn't know you were crushing on Camilla Johnson."

"He's asked her out four times," Nathan supplied helpfully. "She's turned him down every time."

Finn threw a balled up napkin at him. "It's unfair, that ass with those legs."

Naomi frowned. "Objectification is unkind."

He glared at her but it lacked any real malice.

"And anyway, you don't really want to date her."

"Who says?"

"I do. I happen to know she's quite nice, but very invested in cheerleading and gymnastics. Wants to be an Olympian. Which, good for her, but it leaves very little room for anything else."

Finn rolled his eyes. "What's she go wearing short skirts for then?"

Naomi rolled her eyes right back. "Maybe because she likes them. They *are* against dress code, though."

"Your face is against dress code," he mumbled.

"Speaking of girls, Zed," Naomi turned her bright eyes on me. "What's your type?"

Startled, I gulped down a large bite of food too soon. "My type?"

"Yeah! We know all the girls in this town, we're sure to find you a good date. So what are you into?"

I stumbled, choking back words like *curly brown hair* and *blue eyes* and *freckles*. "Uh..."

"Do you like athletic girls? Small girls? Girls with red hair?"

"Um...I like...bright girls."

"Bright?" Nathan furrowed his brow. "Not sure what you mean by that one, bro."

I flushed. "Yeah, like. Girls who light up the whole room when they walk in. You can't help but be happy when they're around."

Naomi looked thoughtful, and Nathan still looked confused, but Finn was watching me keenly. "You got someone in mind?" he asked.

I shook my head quickly. "Anyway, I'm not really looking to date right now. Just got here and all." I swallowed, poking at my lunch. "Do you have a type, Naomi?"

Startled, she leaned back in her seat. "Well. I suppose...No, not really. I guess the most I'd want is someone I can have fun with. I know that's not really a *type*, per se, but I'd like dating to be fun. Not that I've ever dated."

"Anyone would be happy to date you," I blurted, and now both Finn *and* Nathan were looking at me speculatively. "I mean...you seem like people like you. You're cute, I guess."

"Awww, Zed is *crushing!*" Finn sing-songed.

"No, I—I'm not!" I panicked.

The twins laughed, and Naomi said, "I'd be honored to be crushed on by you."

"Gross," I muttered, which set off more laughter from all three of them. Face flaming, I ducked my head bashfully.

"Nah, we're just teasing you, bro," Finn said. "No worries."

"Great," I said flatly, and hoped the cafeteria floor would promptly open up into a sinkhole and swallow me on the spot.

***

Our second game did not go as well as the first. We lost that game, and it was the first time I saw Coach get mad. He kept taking his ball cap off, slamming it back down on his head, and finally, late in the third, when the refs made a call he particularly disliked, he yanked it off and threw it to the ground. I moved to stand closer to Coach Carlson.

He patted me on the shoulder pads. "Stay out of his way, you'll be alright." He set off after Coach.

"See, he's the 'gitback coach,'" Nathan said, out the side of his mouth.

"The what?"

"His job is, 'get back, coach.' Watch. Coach C will reel him in."

Sure enough, Coach Carlson walked up behind Coach and talked him down, nearly hooking a finger through his back belt loop to haul him back. Coach was mad, red in the face, and practically growling at Coach Carlson, but at least he wasn't yelling at the ref anymore. That could get us in trouble real quick. They don't do red cards in football, but they do have penalties and a penalty against a coach counts against the whole team.

Anyway, we lost.

We trooped to the locker rooms, sweaty and defeated. Someone mumbled something about next week being better, and Coach snapped, *"It better be."*

The Petersons took me home again, a silent ride through the dark. I could see Nathan taking it all on himself, tallying up where he could have done better, worked harder, spotted a different play. If I'd known how to stop him spiraling, I would have; but as it was, I said nothing.

Naomi, in the middle row of the van, reached around behind her and patted his knee. He tapped his fingers across the back of her knuckles. That was all.

Saturday, Naomi texted me about the movie. Her name popped up with the little sunshine by it, making me smile. I gathered my house key and wallet, preparing to leave, when my dad caught me leaving.

"And where are you heading off to?"

"To see a movie with some friends."

He grunted, already turning back to the TV.

"Is...that okay?" I asked.

He shrugged. "Just don't come home too late, I guess."

I made for the door.

"Don't drink! Or do drugs!"

I tossed him a look over my shoulder, as if to say, *Dad, it's me,* but he wasn't looking at me. When my sister was my age, she'd gotten a curfew and twenty bucks. I got neither, so maybe it evened out.

Finn's truck idled in the driveway. "C'mon, loser, let's go watch weirdos with lasers blow stuff up," he said.

As always, Naomi sat in the back seat. Today she wore jeans that were denim to her knees with a weird flowy lavender fabric attached to the bottom that made them almost reach her ankles, and a light purple top. On anyone else I would have said it looked stupid; on Naomi it looked carefree and cheerful. My sisters would have commented on the oddness of the pants. (My older sister Hailey used to get saddled with me on trips to the mall with her friends when she was in middle school. I accidentally learned a lot about clothing. I could tell Naomi liked to sew her own clothes, simply because I do not think anything like that could be found in stores. Nor did I think it was in style.)

"Zed!" Finn shouted, which wasn't that unusual, really, it was like his default volume. "We have a very important question for you!"

"Okay."

"Would you rather get trapped in space with Iron Man..." He paused for an inordinate amount of time. "Or be trapped in the ocean with Captain America?"

"Uhh...space, I guess."

Nathan crowed, punching at Finn's arm. "See, I told you!"

Finn blew a loud raspberry. "I still think Captain America would get you out of there faster."

"Well, like, Iron Man has the suit, right? Could probably build us an air tank or whatever," I said.

"Exactly! And there's no guarantee Captain America would be able to save you fast enough," Nathan continued.

"You're all lame, and I'm still right, because I'm driving," Finn concluded.

"That makes *no* sense whatsoever," Nathan said.

I asked, "What do you think, Naomi?"

"I am clearly above such uncivilized discussions," she said. "But also, Iron Man in space."

"Perfect." Nathan reached his hand around for a low-five.

"Space is cool," she added. I agreed.

We headed about half an hour over to Big Spring, which, compared to Terrytown, was a bustling metropolis. For example, they had a movie theater. This first trip to the movies with them, I discovered they had a tried-and-true ritual of movie-going. Nathan took our cash and bought four tickets while Finn bought a large popcorn and two large sodas. Naomi disappeared to the ladies' room, reemerging once we had our tickets. The reason became apparent once we had taken our seats (halfway up, middle of the row, legs kicked over into the seats in front of us). I was on the end by Nathan, which was unfortunate because Naomi was on his other side. She opened her blue patterned crossbody bag (which I recognized from it being constantly shoved in her locker) and out of it emerged several boxes of candy, the kind the Dollar General sold for eighty-nine cents.

"I didn't know your favorite, so I guessed." She held up boxes of Mike and Ikes, Milk Duds, and Nerds, the purple kind.

"Anything but the Nerds."

"See? Told you." She tossed the box into Finn's lap amidst his grumbling. "No one wants your gross sugar lumps."

I took the Milk Duds, reaching across Nathan.

"Next time you'll come with us. We were running behind today." She threw a pointed look at her brother.

"I couldn't find my *shoe*," Nathan whined.

"If you'd put them away, for once, you wouldn't have this problem."

He made an exaggerated frown like he was mimicking an overly strict teacher, and tugged on a strand of her hair. She poked his arm. He slapped her hand.

"*Children,*" Finn said. "Do shut up." Then pulled a face at me, as if we were the only adults among a crowd of toddlers.

I chuckled.

Soon, the theater darkened and the previews started rolling. Finn offered his opinion on every single one, loud enough for our little company to hear. "This looks stupid. They're just reaching for money," or, "That looks good. Damn, that actress is hot," or even, "I thought this movie came out last year? Oh, it's a remake. It's probably terrible." It was at this point that someone in the rows ahead of us turned around to angrily shush him, as though previews are something you're meant to be quiet for, and as though Finn wasn't both accurate and hilarious.

But we made it out of the movie with no other major conflicts, and we stumbled into the sunlight with our minds full of explosions and our hearts full of superpowered dreams. Finn kept talking about how cool the fight choreography was and Nathan kept comparing it to the comic books.

"What about you, Zed? What did you think?" Naomi asked as we climbed into the car.

"I'll tell you what I think," Finn said, "That lady was *hot.*" He made a swooning face. "*Hot.*"

"Hey, shut up, Finn, Zed was just about to tell me what he thought," Naomi snapped without real anger.

"Batman will always be the best," I offered.

"Preach," mumbled Nathan.

"But I still think *Rises* is the best. One of the best movies ever, probably."

Naomi nodded like I'd presented a deep thesis. "That's a good point. I think Nathan rewatches it, like, once a month."

I shrugged. "As he should."

Naomi chewed on her cuticle for a moment before saying, "I think it was nice Catwoman got to be, y'know, there. Instead of dead."

Finn scoffed, "Please, she's just there for the boobs."

Naomi rolled her eyes.

They took me home. I spent the next hour drawing a stylized version of one of the scenes, explosions and all. I even pulled out one of my Greg Capullo comic books as reference.

I stuck my sketchbook in my backpack and promised myself I'd show them at school on Monday.

***

Most days now, Finn picked me up in his truck. A couple of times he texted to say he couldn't, so I still rode my skateboard occasionally. And while he sometimes took me home after practice, there were other days when he had to pick up his sisters, so Nathan and Naomi's parents would drive me, or I would walk. Or skateboard.

It was a Wednesday, after practice, when Finn said, "Hey man, I can take you home, but I have to pick up my sisters first. Is that okay?"

"Yeah, absolutely."

"Cool."

We slumped on the bleachers, sweaty and thirsty after a long practice. Nathan's parents had already picked him up. I didn't know how Naomi got home every day, since she was never around for practice, but I imagined it was either her parents or one of her many, many friends. Sometimes she was in rehearsal, her own kind of practice, and one of her costars would take her home.

Finn squirted water into his mouth, swished it around. "Okay. Let's go get the brats."

I got to ride shotgun, which was rare. That was Nathan's place.

We pulled up to the Baptist church, where the girls' afterschool program was run out of the children's wing. Finn opened the back door for them like they were high-born ladies climbing into a carriage. The girls flooded the back seat with a sea of sparkles and pink, all of them talking over the other to be heard by their big brother.

He grinned as he got back in the driver's seat. "Alright, Zed, this is Phoebe, Ashley, and Mary-Kate. In fourth, third, and first grade, respectively. Girls, this is Zed. Please don't traumatize him too much." They looked at me, big-eyed. Mary-Kate, the littlest, touched the back of my head curiously.

I let it slide at first, and then her small hand crept to the top of my head, where my curls were longer and prone to frizziness. "Please stop," I said, turning around to look at her.

She snatched her hand away. "Your hair is pretty."

"Thank you."

"I've never seen hair like that." Her hand crept forward again.

"Congratulations?" I said, ever awkward.

She grinned, revealing a missing tooth, and put her hands back in her lap.

"Who wants a shake?" Finn called.

They cheered, and he headed toward Whataburger. "Hope you don't mind," he said in my direction.

I shook my head, still entertained by the commotion in the back seat. I had sisters, too. I hadn't seen them since I moved. They were older than these girls, Hailey being older than me and Stella aged only twelve. I was used to being around girls. I wasn't used to them finding me so strange. Human curiosity was alive and well in the backseat.

"Where are you from?" "How old are you?" "Do you play football?" "Why are you wearing all black? Are you sad, is that why you're wearing black?" "Are you going back to where you're from?" "Do you miss home?" "Do you like my shirt?" All of them spoke over each other, making it hard to tell who asked what.

I fielded the questions as best I could all the way to Whataburger. There, Finn ordered them all small shakes. "And what do you want?" he asked me.

"Chocolate," I decided quickly, and dug around for cash.

"Hey, no need," he said, pushing it away.

"Whatever, bro," I said, and folded it neatly to hide in his cup holder. With any luck, by the time he found it, he wouldn't remember what it was for.

Dairy and sugar worked like a pacifier for the girls. Suddenly all their chatter was replaced by quiet slurping sounds. Finn exhaled. "I'll take you home now," he grinned. "Thanks for keeping me sane."

I shrugged, unsure what my presence had added to the situation, but he seemed happy enough.

I flipped through radio stations, trying to find something that wasn't country or in Spanish. Finn batted my hand away. "Quit it or plug in your phone, whatever, just quit distracting me." He always said things like that like he was upset or grumpy, but really he was just straightforward. I liked that about him.

I left it on the country station, and one of the girls opened her ice cream-sticky mouth to sing along.

***

"I met Finn' sisters yesterday," I told Naomi at lunch the next day.

Her brows went up. "Excellent!"

"They're cool. Kinda reminds me of my sisters. Except tiny. And blonde."

She gave a nod. "They're so sweet. I haven't seen them in awhile."

"Well, obviously it's because he likes me better than you."

"You wish," she said, scrunching her nose and sticking out her tongue.

I mimicked her, realizing the partial truth of what I'd said. Finn had finally accepted me, finally decided he liked me, that he could put up with me. I had a feeling he only introduced his sisters to people he *really* liked.

And that, for some reason, was it. I was in. It took me so long to realize it, to accept it, despite their near-constant badgering and insistence that I be their friend; but as soon as I knew for sure, and accepted it as certain, I knew I'd be okay. I'd had friends before, certainly. Friends I missed, friends I thought of fondly. But none of them had so much as reached out to me since I'd moved, not even my teammates from soccer. But Nathan, Naomi, and Finn were different. I'd certainly never had friends that *wanted* me, that made certain I'd be their friend, that insisted I not leave them or shrink away or fade into the background. They made friendship an action, something to be done, something to be grasped and held onto. It made me want to grab back and hold on. I couldn't let it pass me by. I couldn't let *them* pass me by.

5

Our third game of the year was an away game, so we loaded up on the bus to drive two hours to play. This was by no means a luxury transport bus. This was simply a school bus: sticky seats, grimy floors, and no air conditioning. It was not, to say the least, the most pleasant of experiences. I was sweating before the bus even pulled out of the parking lot. Opening my window to relieve the heat only served to blow dust in my face.

Nathan slumped next to me, doodling on his homework. I piddled around on my phone, snapchatting with Hailey. The heat and noise of the bus were making it hard to focus on what she was telling me, but I put on a good show, keeping my gaze fixed on the screen and ignoring the rowdy boys around me.

Nathan nudged me. "You any good with geometry?"

I snorted. "I'm not good at math, like, at all. But I can try."

He moved his notebook closer, sliding it partially into my lap. We bent over it, looking at the request. He was supposed to prove that a rectangle was a rectangle, which is one of the stupidest things I'd ever heard.

"It just *is*," he said in frustration, "I know it by looking at it."

"Are there, like, rules about shapes?" I vaguely remembered this from some intro stuff I'd seen back in Houston. "Like things that apply?"

He twisted his lips and cocked a brow. "Two sides are longer than the other sides?"

"Sure. Write that down. Maybe that'll help."

Finn popped up behind us, leaning over the seat so his head was right between ours. "Ugh. Math." He began trying to shove his finger up Nathan's nose. Nathan batted him away, as though he were an errant fly. Finn switched tactics and started rubbing at the soft shaved ends of Nathan's hair. Nathan ducked his head out of range. Finn looked over at me. "Who's that you're snapping? A girl?"

"My sister."

He mashed a finger into my cheek and began moving it around. "Nerd."

I let him. "Is Camilla Johnson going to be there tonight?"

He pouted. "Yes, but she's not going to notice me. We always take cheerleaders to away games. We also, tragically, take the band." His head lolled as he looked over at me.

"Mm. So I'll prepare myself, then."

"They're not *that* bad. It's just the beginning of the season, that's all."

"They're just kind of...sad sounding. Small." I didn't know how to explain what it was like to go from a full marching band to our little group.

"Oi, I resent that remark. Being small." He puffed himself up as though to demonstrate how very cool it is to be small. His hair was rumpled, poking out in interesting directions, though at one point it had been all swept neatly forward. "The best things come in small packages."

"What, like your dick?" I said, and braced for the barrage of slaps he rained upon me.

***

Most fields we played at didn't have actual turf, so I wasn't expecting much, but this one looked especially worse for wear, all pockmarked and bumpy. It was going to be a rough night.

There was only one set of bleachers and no locker room for us. We changed on the bus, wriggling into padded pants and uniform t-shirts.

The Petersons sat up in the bleachers, wearing their orange t-shirts with *Comets* lettered in black. Naomi was there, too, and my heart swelled at the sight of her. I didn't think she'd come to an away game. My dad certainly showed no interest in attending. He still hadn't been to my home games, either.

I had the honor of joining the kickoff team, starting the whole game. I ran down the sideline as Eathan Wilkes kicked. We weren't a kicking team, so he kicked it low to the ground, and we converged on it, trying to drop on it as soon as it made the required yardage. Our opponents got the ball first, so we were on defense. Which meant I was out and Nathan was in, mostly because he's one of the bigger guys on our team.

Their first drive, they ran the ball, and their running back broke through our line, and raced down the paint, right along the edge. Though our boys put in good effort, he was too far gone, and ended up scoring. That's the way it goes in six man sometimes. The guy is just too fast and he gets away from you.

Our first drive was a slow crawl, and we didn't even make the first down.

It was going to be a long night.

Finn took the field for every offensive drive, and Nathan just about never left the field, either snapping as center or tussling on defense. Pretty normal for six man, but I don't know how he did it. I ran on offense sometimes as a route runner, and only a few plays on defense, chasing their running backs. Their team was relentless, making us fight for every inch of field. Them boys were big, and I dug my feet in the pock-marked ground, sweating and panting.

We only scored twice the whole game, but I got to assist one of them. I was mostly hitting their defensive back, shoving at him, when I heard Finn screaming my name. Being in a helmet is a little disorienting, but I tried to spot him. He zipped past me, feet pistoning the ground, ball tucked close to his side. A defender was hot on his tail.

I shook off the player, sprinting to catch up. I hit the man in pursuit at full steam, plowing into him and knocking him clean out of bounds. When I popped back up, Finn was in the clear, a perfect path to the end zone. I watched him score and threw my arms up in celebration. He jogged to me, grinning, having spit out his mouth guard. He slapped fives with me, threw his shoulder against mine.

"Awesome block, bro!"

"Way to score!"

Elated, we jogged to the sidelines so the freshmen could make the PAT.

Even though we lost that game, I still remember how it felt to help him score that first time. There's nothing like it. No other sweet elation or joy ever compares.

At the same time, there's no pain quite like losing a game you fought hard for. When you put your heart and sweat and blood out there, and walk away with bruises and cuts and no victory to show for it. We jogged through the "good game" line, slapping fives and shaking hands, feeling hollow, tired.

Coach rounded us up after the game, face lined with irritation. "Boys. We gotta work on our defense. They were ripping through us."

We nodded and mumbled, "Yes, coach."

He gave us a few other critiques, voice sharp. Like we didn't already know what we'd done wrong.

When he was done, Coach Carlson said, "You played hard. That's nothing to be ashamed of. There's one thing I can't teach you. What's that?"

"Hustle," we mumbled.

"That's right. And you certainly had that. Keep your heads up. You can carry this and mope about it until we get to the bus. But once we get on the bus, put it behind you. Start thinking about next week and what we can do better. Let's break this out. Ready? 1, 2, 3—"

"Comets," we chorused, too exhausted to offer much more.

The bus ride home was quiet. It was too dark to read now, but Naomi kept texting us as a group, lighthearted things meant to cheer us up, like how it was the weekend and we were going to hang out. She was trying to distract us, I think. It wasn't working very well, but I gave her credit for trying.

I opened a separate text conversation to her. I debated for a long time before sending the message. *Thanks for coming to the game.* The blue bubble floated to the top of my screen, the first message we'd exchanged. My phone pinged not three seconds later.

Naomi [sunshine]: You're welcome.

6

Practice after a loss isn't much different than after a win. We work on our weak points, run the plays for the next game. If we'd won, we'd maybe have gotten acknowledgement of our strong points, too. Our passing game could have been better, so we did several drills involving passes. Single file, we quick-stepped to the line and threw directly to Coach Carlson. I, for one, cannot throw a football especially well, because till now I'd never needed to. Obviously, now that I played a sport where you had to touch the ball with your hands, I needed to work on it just a bit. My pass went wide, but Coach Carlson still caught it, stepping to the side and reaching an arm out to snag the ball. Finn, however, with all the energy and anger only a teenage boy can muster, threw the ball so hard it sailed clean and true and high. Coach Carlson, squinting into the sun, lost track of the ball. He raised a hand to shield his eyes, but it was too late. When it hit him in the nuts, he grunted and took a knee.

A chorus of stupid chuckles rose from us.

"A moment of silence for Coach Carlson," Coach said, hiding a smile.

"Heh, sorry, Coach," Finn said, openly grinning.

Alejandro's little brother, a fifth grader and our main water boy, jogged out to him with an ice pack, which made the giggles start afresh.

"Alright, get after it," said Coach, signaling for us to start the drill again, albeit without Coach Carlson's involvement.

Finn and Nathan partnered up for some snapping, receiving, and passing drills, snagging me as their third. We ran each scenario until it flowed smoothly, the ball sliding from hand to hand with clean precision. They slapped my shoulders and back when we were done, dripping sweat and smelling rank.

As practice ended, Finn called over his shoulder, "Hey, see you tomorrow!" with a rare, toothy smile. I responded in turn, grinning and throwing up a casual wave.

Heading home, I thought about how none of my friends back in Houston had made any effort to keep in touch with me, and how I hadn't felt a particular need to keep up with them, either. But with these boys—and Naomi—I didn't think they'd let that happen. Like, if I moved back to Houston tomorrow, they'd force me to stay in touch. Thinking of home made me realize I hadn't talked to my mom in a while. So I video called my sisters. I hadn't seen them since we moved, and I missed them. Wondered what they were up to. I hadn't had time to call them since the start of school.

Stella answered, grinning at me already. "I'll go get Hailey," she said by way of greeting. The video jiggled and blurred as she sprinted through the house. Soon both of them were bent over the screen in Hailey's bedroom. I could see the similarities between them so well—the thick dark hair we all shared, the defined cheekbones and brown eyes. Hailey's face was rounder, while Stella's came to more of a point. My own face, miniaturized in the corner of the screen, parallelled theirs. Curly hair, freckles, smooth tan skin. Everyone always knew we were siblings when they saw us together. Our mixed race heritage made for a distinct look between the three of us. Were we black? Were we Hispanic? Were we Pacific Islander? We were biracial, mixed kids, and that was that.

"How are you?" I asked.

"Great! School's going great. I have my best friend in my classes, it's awesome." This was from Stella, who was starting middle school this fall.

"I'm so busy," Hailey said. She was a senior, likely to be Valedictorian, and president of several clubs. She had always been way more popular than me, the quiet broody brother.

"You'll survive," I said. "You always do."

"Oh yeah. Besides, I'm going to see if I can get in with the Key Club and be president. That would look great on college applications. And scholarship applications."

"True." My sister's ambitions were always big; to be the best, do the most.

"I started running cross country," Stella said. "I kind of hate it."

"Ugh, so much running, right? Apparently track is mandatory for football players here, so I'll be miserable with you."

"Yeah. But there's lots of cool people, so it's okay." Stella grinned. She was all glitter pens and braces and converse shoes, freckles and cheery smiles. She didn't care about big ambitions, she just cared about her friends. She kept chatting, catching me up on all the latest family gossip.

I missed them so much it ached. When we first moved, I was so angry at having to leave them, I didn't talk to my dad for nearly a week. To be fair, he wasn't talking much to me either, but it helped to at least feel like I was giving him the silent treatment.

My mother appeared in frame, smiling. "Hello, baby," she said. "How are you?" She perched on the edge of the bed by Hailey. She had on her red lipstick and hoop earrings, so familiar and constant. I hadn't realized how much I'd missed the sight of her until it crashed over me in that moment.

"Hi Mom. I'm—I'm okay."

"Just ok?"

"Being away is...it's hard."

"I know, baby." She smiled, tinged with sadness. "How is it way out there? Are you getting good grades?"

"So far."

She bit her lower lip briefly. "And not getting into trouble, right?" she asked cautiously. Like I was a wild animal she didn't want to spook.

"Nope."

"Good. I'm proud of you. Have you made friends?"

I thought of my little group, of how last year at school I hadn't had hardly any friends at all. I was too quiet, too weird, too artsy. Too prone to getting in trouble. "Yeah, Mom, I am making friends. You don't need to worry about me."

She pulled a face. "I always worry." Her gaze dropped away for a minute, and I knew she was wondering, as she had so many times before since the first talks of divorce, if they had made the right decision. I wondered again if their decision to separate us was really the best option.

"I'm—I'm playing sports and everything. I'm doing better." I pressed my lips tightly together. I didn't like talking about last year much, even in vague allusions. I spent a large part of that year in detention, remedial tutoring, trouble. I passed, but barely. One of the reasons I moved with dad was for a "fresh start;" the hope that a new environment would help me.

It was like my parents couldn't put two and two together—that telling your kid they're splitting up, that dad was going to look for jobs somewhere else, that siblings would split up, that their life was imminently changing, might be a little stressful and traumatic. My mom probably put it together privately, but refused to speak it aloud. I don't know about my dad. He didn't seem very observant at the best of times. For example, Hailey was supposed to be named "Halley," after the comet, but he misspelled it on the birth certificate, and she was Hailey forevermore. Imagine being so out of it that you misname your own firstborn. But I digress.

"What are your friends like?" Mom asked.

"They're—" I thought about Naomi's weird clothes, Finn's sharp words, Nathan's easy smile. "I've never met people like them."

She nodded. "Are they kind? Staying out of trouble?"

I laughed. "Yeah. A couple of them—the twins—I don't think they've ever been in trouble."

"Good. You need nice friends." Her face softened, eyes getting a little damp. "Oh, Zed—" her voice went watery "—I really miss you. I worry, and it's good to know you're okay."

"Yeah. Yeah, I'm okay." My own voice grew pinched at the sight of her tears. I looked away and blinked hard. I wish I'd called home sooner. I wish she'd called me. Perhaps she was guilty about the whole thing. The divorce, the move, the pain.

She heaved a shaky breath. Hailey patted her shoulder, gently, and Stella leaned across both of their laps. She raised her brows, trying to look silly. "Guess what I can do?"

"What?" I asked, knowing she was trying to break the tension and make us laugh.

"I turned a whole cartwheel yesterday! And I didn't even break anything." She made jazz hands.

I chuckled. "Good for you." Across the internet waves, she smiled back.

We were a bit like mirrors of each other, the same face from different angles. We share brown eyes, tan skin, dark hair. Hailey looked the most like mom, her jawline and smile a perfect replica. When she was at her happiest, her walnut brown eyes glowed warm, just like Mom's. Her hair though, she got more from dad, like me. Our hair is thick and wavy, curly on good days, but Stella stood alone with the curliest hair, tight coils all over her head. She's a bit lighter than the rest of us, with more golden undertones to her skin. Dad never knew what to do with her hair, possessing fine hair he kept cropped close to his head, like a soldier. And my mom—she had brown skin, brown eyes, brown hair, big smile, red lipstick. In all of our family photos, she smiles the biggest. Dad kept his face more contained, more controlled. Since he and mom split, I hadn't seen him smile at all.

I'd done a family portrait a long time ago, when I wasn't nearly as skilled as I was now. I'd spent hours mixing paint to try and match the exact shade of everyone's eyes, hair, and skin. I'm sure Mom still has it somewhere, because moms are sentimental like that. I wondered how I'd complete a family portrait now. Would there be two groups? Perhaps I'd just do my siblings. Or perhaps I'd better not think about it at all, and instead imagine drawing my friends instead.

***

"So," I said, situating my lunch tray at the table, "How did y'all become friends? Because you," I pointed at Nathan, who grinned, "are much too nice for you," then pointed at Finn, who sneered playfully, "and you," before finally pointing at Naomi, "are like, in a separate class from these two yahoos."

She laughed. "It's been so long now, I forget we're so different."

"Yeah. It's, like, jocks don't hang out with drama kids, and siblings don't hang out period, so." I waved a baby carrot around to indicate the three of them: Finn, wearing a ratty t-shirt, Nathan, in a polo, and Naomi, in a dress made from a men's button-down and creatively decorated with ribbon.

"We moved here in sixth grade, right?" Nathan said.

"Summer before," Naomi agreed.

"Yeah. It was awful."

"Well, not awful, not really. Just—moving is the worst, and we were starting middle school, and we're the preacher's kids, so people already knew us."

"She made friends right away, she always does—"

"No surprise, everyone loves you," Finn cut in. "Don't know why." He aimed a smirk her way.

Nathan resumed, "I don't, not easily, but I joined the football team, and Finn was there."

Finn nodded sagely. "Big ol' seventh grader. Very wise in the ways of the world."

"And—that was it really."

Naomi rolled her eyes. "You're leaving out so much. The team was terrible that year, truly atrocious. And you can only lose so many times before it starts making friends out of you. Not to mention Caleb Hanson."

Nathan groaned. "Finn made him leave me alone. Still is making 'em."

"I'm very protective of what's mine," Finn said, giving me a dangerous smile.

I remembered how he'd looked at me in the beginning, how he'd always wanted to place himself between me and the twins. *Protective.*

"And anyway, Nathan didn't care how mean I was to him, he just kept coming back. Like a puppy or something. Couldn't make him leave." Finn jostled Nathan's shoulder.

"I liked you," Nathan said.

"And he's like my older brother now. And I hang out with them because I like them, believe it or not," Naomi finished.

"We really need to get you better company, babe," Finn said.

She shrugged, and smiled, wrinkling her nose like something was funny.

"Huh," I said, wondering at the ways in which the world throws people together and lets them emerge as friends. I thought briefly of my own stumble into companionship with them. It was a fragile, beautiful thing, this friendship. I was grateful for it.

7

The week before Homecoming, signs started appearing in store windows. *We support our Comets. Proud to be a Comet. Go Big Orange!* Yard signs popped up in the patches of grass along the highway. *Homecoming game, Friday, 7:30. Support your local Comets! Homecoming bonfire, Wednesday, 6:30.*

On said Wednesday, Naomi and Nathan brought me to their house. It was the first time I'd been over to their house, and the only time thus far I'd ridden the bus from school. Finn had gone to pick up his sisters from school, get them home and situated, before returning to school for the bonfire.

Their house was an older ranch-style home with a small concrete porch overflowing with potted plants. The garage door was closed, so they waded through the mess to unlock the front door and let us in. Inside, the living room shelves overflowed with board games and books. The couches looked old and saggy, but in a comfortable, lived-in way. There was a wall of decorative crosses on one side, and a wall of photographs of the twins on the other. I was struck, suddenly, that this was a *home*, a space where people lived and loved and shared time together.

There wasn't a single framed photo in my house. Nothing at all, really, but a T.V., and a sectional couch and a chair.

Nathan dumped his backpack in an armchair, while Naomi hung hers from a hook by the doorway. She rolled her eyes at Nathan's backpack, then hung up his, too. I set mine on the floor beneath theirs.

She followed him to the kitchen, rummaging for snacks. He was staring into the pantry, and she stood on tiptoe to look over his shoulder.

"This is really nice," I said, to make conversation.

"Thanks," Naomi said, "We've made it our own. We *can't* give him that," this was directed to Nathan, who put a box of what looked like bargain-brand granola bars back in the pantry.

"This is a parsonage. Like, the church owns it for the preacher to live in," Nathan said, by way of explanation, "But it's still, like, *ours*, y'know?" He shut the pantry door.

"Yeah, of course."

"We have to get permission from a committee to change anything. Plus it's expensive. So we painted and then left it alone," Naomi said.

I sat down at the table as they pulled out fruit and cheese for snacks. They didn't seem to need to talk much as they did so, passing each other small knives and plates. There was a bulletin from Sunday sitting on the table, with the prayer concerns highlighted. "You guys must do a lot of stuff at church, huh?"

"Only if we want to," Naomi said. "But like, we usually want to. And people like it when we do." She set down a plate of cheddar cheese slices, followed by a plate of apple slices and grapes.

"Our dad's a preacher and our mom's a teacher, so everyone always knows who we are, wants to know our business," Nathan said ruefully.

"Like living in a fishbowl," Naomi agreed, opening the fridge. "Ah-ha! I knew we had some!" She pulled out a package of cookie dough and punched buttons on the oven. "But it's not terrible. Like, Dad never makes us do church stuff if we don't want to.

Like tonight. We're going to the bonfire and youth is canceled. And that's okay with him."

"And contrary to popular belief, I actually *like* going to church." This from Nathan, and honestly, I never expected any different from him. He was always so genuine, it was hard to imagine him doing something he disliked.

"People always think we're either perfect and holier-than-thou or we're going to rebel and be bad, but it's not like that," Naomi said. "I'm just like anybody else; sometimes I want to go to church, and sometimes I don't. Two or three cookies, Zed?"

"Uh, three. Do you want to be a pastor, too?"

The twins shared an exasperated look. "Why does everyone always ask that? Do I ask you if you want to work in the oil field?" Naomi complained. I ducked my head in embarrassment. "Plus," she continued, "Dad also works in the county water department, and it's not like people ask me if I want to monitor droughts and regulate lawn watering."

"Sorry. I just—yeah."

"I don't want to be a preacher," Nathan said. "I used to think I did, but not anymore." He shrugged, before heading down the hall to his room.

"Yeah, no," Naomi said. "Plus there's a ton of complicated stuff about women preaching—I won't get into it now—but it's just not for me. Might be a worship leader though."

"Are you in church every Sunday? Is that why you never want to hang out on Saturday nights?"

"Usually. Yes, sort of. I help lead worship, so I like to get to bed early on Saturdays."

"I didn't know that! Are you a singer?"

"Sometimes. It's usually guitar, though."

"Cool." She'd just gotten way cooler right before my eyes. Why did she even bother to talk to me? "You should play for me sometime. If you—if you want."

She smiled, that soft, private tilt of her mouth reserved for moments of quiet affection. "I will." The oven beeped. She slid a tray in. "You should come to church sometime. Then you can hear me play there."

I hesitated. We'd never been a church family, going occasionally on Easter or Christmas when my mother insisted. I knew about Jesus, and I knew about sin, and I knew I was doomed if I didn't repent, yadda yadda. "Maybe," I said finally.

She smiled again, and seemed just about to say something more when Nathan returned.

"Prepare to be beaten, bro!" He slapped a deck of cards down on the table, followed by a box.

"What's this?"

"It's a Batman card game, dude! It doesn't get much cooler than this! It's a deck builder, ever played one?"

"You're such a nerd," Naomi said affectionately, and rumpled his already messy hair.

"Can't say I have, but I'll learn. Hit me with it," I said, and prepared myself for an immersive Batman experience, already examining the art on the cards.

***

The bonfire was crowded, humidity amplified by the hundreds of people packing the school grounds. The whole school and half the town congregated behind the school, where dry limbs and scrap wood were gathered in preparation of the bonfire. Old folks from the Baptist church were passing out hotdogs and lemonade. Across the way, the Methodists were giving out chocolate chip cookies. The school had set up a number of fairground games, ring toss and cornhole. I gathered with the rest of the football team, waiting for our cue to run in front of the gooseneck trailer that served as a little stage to be cheered for and introduced, as though half the town didn't know us already. We all had on our orange jerseys and blue jeans, though I noted I was one of the few wearing converse in lieu of boots.

Finn sprinted up, fifteen minutes late. "Sorry. Had to get my sisters here, and Phoebe lost a shoe, and Mary-Kate was crying—it was a whole ordeal."

"Sounds like."

"Where are they now?" asked Nathan.

"With my mom. They'll want to tell you hi, later." He turned to me. "Ashley still has a massive crush on him, ever since he told her he liked her pigtails when she was in third grade."

Nathan cringed. "Still kinda regret that."

Finn pinched his side. "Sure you don't want to marry her? We could be brothers for real." He went in for another pinching attack, this time aiming at his chest.

Nathan leapt away, covering his nipples reflexively. "No thanks. She's a little young for me."

Finn settled for pinching Nathan's bicep instead. "Well, you're the only person I'd be okay with any of them marrying. Except maybe Zed, here. I like you, Zed."

"Thanks?" I said, unsure if I wanted in on this or not.

The cheerleaders went onstage, chanting about how proud they were, West Texas accents flattened and amplified by their efforts. Then we all trotted up front to be cheered for, like we were hometown heroes or something. In a small town, there's not much else to do, except worry about your oil field job getting cut and talk about the weather (or economy, or whatever else old men talk about). We, the football team, gave them something to cheer for. Something to be proud of. Something to dream about, maybe, even if it was a small dream.

In the grand scheme of things, high school football, especially six man, is nothing. But it meant something to these people. It meant something to me.

The seniors carried a torch to the pile of old pallet wood and logs, touching it to the wood and watching it catch. A cheer went up, though for what I wasn't sure. Naomi suddenly appeared beside us, holding hotdogs for all of us. Finn scarfed his in three bites, and tackled Nathan into the grass to playfully tussle for his hotdog. Naomi giggled beside me, firelight reflecting off her face. In the orange glow she looked ethereal, lovely, a heavenly creature, descended from the stars above. She smiled, and my heart pounded so hard I thought I'd regurgitate the bite I'd just swallowed.

How was I so lucky to be friends with her?

***

And then Friday actually came.

You ever heard of a homecoming mum? I hadn't. Guess that was something folks in the big city didn't care about. We rolled up to school on Friday to see girls wearing the largest ribbon-flower creations on God's green earth. They were hanging from necks, covering whole torsos, garish in color and style. Ribbon, tulle, polka-dot, school colors, they had it all. To be fair, some girls had little ones, or none at all. But other girls, like Camilla Johnson, had mums almost as large as themselves. One girl had a whole wooden sign reading *Seniors!*

I stopped dead in the doorway.

Finn crashed into my back. "Oi, some of us are trying to walk here! What's got you—oh." He heaved a sigh. "Welcome to the south."

"I'm from the south," I murmured back.

"Not this part of it."

"What *is* this?"

"The part of the show where girls compete to have the biggest mum based on money and time. I think boys are supposed to give their girl one, but really, girls make them themselves, or their moms do it."

Naomi sighed. "The goal of a mum is to have the biggest and most beautiful. It gets turned into a popularity contest. It's terrible."

"Do you have one of those?"

She raised her brows and pointed to herself. "Do you really think I have one of those?" She pointed to a girl walking past, supporting a mum that hung from her neck with both hands. It had three little orange stuffed animals, a tiger, a clownfish, and a fox.

"Never mind," I backtracked. "How could I be so foolish?"

I didn't go home after school. Coach wanted us to run warm-ups and drills, get our jitters out and excitement down.

The game was slated to start at 7:30, and by 7:00, the stands were already filled up. A sea of orange rolled and moved, everyone and their cousin bringing bleacher seats and blankets to sit on, holding noisemakers and the little orange flags sold at the concession stand. The concession money went to the band, and the flag and t-shirt money went to the athletics department. Small schools, man.

The sun hung low on the horizon, big and orange. The stadium lights beamed down, bright and white and blinding. Concessions was busy, selling hot dogs and nachos and sodas. It seemed the whole town was here, primed and excited. Maybe they were. I'd even seen a sign on the local Mexican joint that they were "closed for big game."

Coach sent three seniors to do the coin toss. We won, and elected to receive.

In our pre-game huddle, Ethan Wilkes, a senior, gave our hype speech. It ended with all of us putting our hands in the middle.

"Ready?" he called. "Break! Comets!"

"Comets!" we all repeated, throwing our hands in the air. A few of us jumped in the air, slapping helmets and shoulder pads and backs.

Finn fidgeted in the starting lineup, only stilling at the last moment before Nathan snapped. Ethan caught it, pitched it to Finn. We were on our way.

We fought hard for every yard, our boys running and weaving through defenders. I stood over Coach's left shoulder, waiting to be of use. He kept up a stream of grumbling under his breath, and kept switching his clipboard from hand to hand, squinting at the field. Finn scored our first point, a pretty little scramble route that ended with him diving into the end zone and knocking over the pylon. I went in for the PAT, hunched over the line. Pushed hard after the snap, cleats digging into the turf. From the corner of my eye, I saw Alejandro fall over the line for a point.

It's hard to hear anything on the field, least of all calls from the stands. But I could hear the cheering. It was beautiful. I cast a glance at the billowing sea of orange and black in the stands as I walked to the sidelines. Glorious.

The next play, our defenders lined up for the first drive. Our opponents snapped. I tracked the ball as the player tried to push through, but was brought down. The next play, they snapped, tossed, fumbled, and Finn recovered. I threw my hands up, yelling as he raced for our goal. Sprinting, legs pumping, ball tucked, he ran, juking one defender and twisting away from a second. A third finally grabbed a fistful of jersey and pulled them together, bodies crashing to the ground at the ten yard line. I screamed along with everyone else, until Coach grabbed my jersey and yanked my ear to his mouth.

He hollered the play into my ear, and I ran it to the huddle, replacing Corey. I called the play, and Finn yelled, "Ready, break!" We clapped. We set up in diamond formation, me about seven yards behind the O line, close to Tate. Nathan snapped. Tate received, tossed it off to me. The ball landed in my hands. Suddenly everything snapped into over-saturation, colors brighter and sounds muted. The orange of Nathan's jersey. The white stitching and the brown pebbled leather under my hands. My own breathing echoed loud in my ears, my tongue pressing against the smooth mouth guard. I tucked the ball into my arm, each step a mile as I pistoned my legs, feeling my cleats dig into the dirt and release, spurring me on.

Like a distant siren, I could hear someone behind me screaming my name, but I could see the endzone, and I was too caught in the rush of the play. Arms grabbed me from behind. Letting out a guttural yell, I pushed forward two more steps and landed, face-down, with my ball-carrying hand in the endzone.

The ref's arms went up. Whistles blew. I handed the ball to the ref, then leaped into the air, whooping. Through his helmet, I could see Nathan grinning. Finn slapped my butt and the top of my helmet, yelling unintelligibly. More hands slapped my helmet, and I laughed for no discernable reason.

I'd done it! I'd actually scored! Not just assisted, but scored! I let out a whoop of my own, pumping my fist in the air. I pivoted, like a reflex, to the stands.

It took me a moment to realize this wasn't a soccer game, I wasn't in Houston. My mom was not in the stands.

And neither was my dad.

I looked away from the roiling waves of orange, swallowing.

Finn grabbed my elbow and yanked me off the field so the PAT could get set up. Coach Carlson gave me a high five and Doc tossed me a water bottle. I pulled off my helmet to squirt water directly into my mouth, cool breeze tickling my ears after being in the sweaty helmet.

"Good job, son, that was awesome! You stuck with it, didn't give up even when he was grabbing you!" He slapped my shoulder pads, smiling big. I smiled back at him, at how much he looked like a young boy even with his graying hair and crow's feet. I guess football makes young men of us all.

Thanks to me, we were up by fourteen, and it was still the first quarter.

I've always wondered what "hometown advantage" was. It seems mostly superstition, silliness. Even when I played soccer I didn't truly get it, didn't truly feel like I had the same pride as my teammates. But that day, that first homecoming, I got it. There's nothing like having your friends cheer for you, as you drive and drive to win. There's nothing like watching your new best friend score. Or your other best friend bend down for the snap, confident, even though he's just a sophomore. Or your other *other* best friend, cheering in the stands, her hair bouncing around her as she screams and claps. She's surrounded by hundreds of people you don't know, and a few you do, and they are all cheering, too. And they're cheering for *you*, for your team, and maybe you want to prove to them that it's worth it. That they're right to trust in you. That you can do anything you put your mind to, you and your team.

We won homecoming.

By nearly forty points.

***

Saturday night was the homecoming dance. I had no intention of going. When I voiced this to the others, they agreed. We ended up at the twin's house, watching movies and eating copious amounts of popcorn. The Petersons went to bed, Mr. Peterson saying, "Children, I'll see you in the morning. Zed, Finn, get home safe or let me know to thaw out some bacon."

Naomi rolled her eyes.

"This is way better than any lame dance," Finn said.

"For real," I agreed. "What's the point of them anyway?"

"Right? I don't have a date, so like, eh," Naomi said. "Y'know?"

"Hm." I refrained from saying I would've been her date.

"Who cares about homecoming anyway? Screw 'em," Finn said, upside down on the couch.

"Dunno, winning the game was pretty awesome," Nathan said thoughtfully.

"Don't be sentimental. Gross." Finn threw popcorn at him.

Nathan shrugged and fished the popcorn from between the couch cushions to eat it.

8

Getting a ride home from Finn had become a routine. After practice, we'd clamber into his battered old truck and he'd take me home, sometimes after picking up his sisters, before heading off to his shift stocking shelves at the grocery store in Big Spring about thirty minutes away. His mom worked full-time, and his dad was—gone, somewhere, out of the picture—and the father of the three little girls lived a town over, only getting them on weekends. So it became his job to get his siblings home from school, make sure they had an after-school snack, and get settled in with their homework.

Coach held us late at practice one evening in mid-October, and it was the sort of day where the sun turned orange and cast long shadows across the field. We had recently lost (again), and since we had an away game coming up, he wanted us to get our asses in gear. By the time he let us go, Finn sprinted to tear off his gear and threw himself into his truck. I jogged after him, wondering if I should throw in my lot with Nathan and the bus, or just skateboard home. But it was just this side of chilly, and I didn't have my leather jacket, so I wanted a ride. Besides, I liked

Finn. I wanted to hang out with him. I didn't mind running errands if it meant I could do so.

Finn glanced at me as I climbed in the passenger side. He looked at the clock and swore under his breath. "We've gotta go." The truck roared to life and skidded out of the lot. Finn chewed on his lip as he went. "We'll get the girls first, then—we don't have much time. I think I'm going to have to run by the house." He looked at me, looked away. "You okay with that? You got somewhere to be?"

"No, it's whatever. I'm good." If Finn didn't mind the reek of my sticky body, it'd be fine. I had a sketchpad.

We picked up the girls, and the three of them climbed in the back seat, already chattering about their days and the things they did and how excited they were for the weekend. I had a very serious discussion with Ashley about whether or not Unicorns had wings, or if that was a separate creature entirely.

And that was about the time I realized we were going a direction I'd never been. Finn had this focused, determined look on his face.

"You okay, bro?"

"Yeah. Just. Was already late once this week. Can't do it again."

"Let me know how I can help, yeah? I've been told I'm an expert PB and marshmallow sandwich maker."

This brought a short laugh from Finn. "Yeah, whatever, you've got nothing on my chocolate cookie skills."

"What, the from-scratch kind?"

"Nah, break and bake. Who do you think I am, Gordan Ramsay? Paula Deen?" In a southern drawl, he said, "We only settle for the best around here. The finest Nestle Tollhouse money can buy."

The girls giggled.

Finn turned down a road with an arched sign over it: *Welcome to Southlake estates*. We passed a dilapidated trailer house with trash out front. And another. And another. Outside one, a shirtless fat man sat in a lawn chair, cigarette in one hand

and canned beer in the other. A woman, wearing a mumu and with rollers in her hair, yelled at a dog chained to a tree.

I glanced at Finn. He steadfastly avoided my gaze.

We passed a house with three cars clustered out front, rusted, rotting, and overgrown.

It wasn't until the back of the park that Finn pulled into the gravel patch by the rickety front steps, and parked. This house was cleaner than the others, no trash in the front grass. Yard could use a trim but it was no jungle.

Finn climbed out, opening the rear passenger door. "Alright ladies, this is your stop. Please take all trash with you when you exit, and remember to give your driver a five-star review."

They raced inside, high voices squealing, glittery backpacks bouncing.

Finn slammed the door behind them. He gave me a hard look, daring me to say something. It's moments like that I remembered he could be dangerous. He could be sharp. He'd throw blows over someone he loved.

I put my hands in my pockets and followed him inside. It was cramped with the couch pressed against the back wall, the recliner shoved in the corner, and table squeezed in the miniscule kitchen. Dirty dishes stacked up by the sink and mail lay piled on the counter. To one side I could make out the master bedroom, scattered with women's clothes. To the other, I assumed there were rooms for the girls and Finn, but they were blocked off by a curtain and the TV.

Mary-Kate stood in the middle of the kitchen, big-eyed. "Do you *really* make peanut butter marshmallow sandwiches?"

"Uh," I said, glancing at Finn.

"Don't look at me, bro, you got yourself into that one."

"Well. Let's see." I poked around the kitchen, taking a gamble that they'd actually have marshmallow fluff. It was true luck that they did, half empty and probably stale, but it was there. I slapped together three sandwiches, the other two girls appearing as if by magic as the sandwiches were finished. "This is what I like to call 'Zed's special high-brow magical unicorn fart fluffernutter.'" The girls giggled, taking bites that left trails of peanut butter and marshmallow on their cheeks. I had a flash of Stella, back when she was close in age to these girls, giggling as I monkeyed up the shelves in the pantry to reach the forbidden marshmallow fluff to make our own special high-brow magical unicorn fart fluffernutters.

Finn reemerged from his room, turning on the TV and tossing the remote to Phoebe. "Watch cartoons, get your homework done, don't get in trouble, mom should be home soon."

"We know," the girls chorused, rolling their eyes.

Finn headed for the door. Mary-Kate crashed into his legs, wrapping her skinny arms around his knees. "Love you," she said, and let him go.

We got back in Finn's truck, quiet as we pulled onto the highway. He got up to speed, then pushed over the limit.

"So," he said, stiff and quiet.

"So?"

"So you've seen my house."

I remained quiet, unsure of what he was getting at.

His fingers tightened on the wheel, his next words harsh and prickly. "Don't say a word to *anyone*. Savvy?"

"What would I say, Finn?"

"Trailer trash," he spat. "Meth house. *White trash.*"

"Finn," I gentled. "I'd never."

"Better not," he growled again, but this time with less heat. "I'll end you if you do, I swear I will."

"There's nothing to tell," I said. "Your house is your house. Doesn't matter what it looks like. And you're my friend. Why would I say anything at all?"

Finn exhaled sharply through his nose. "Sometimes people say shit just 'cause."

"You can trust me," I said, looking out the window.

For a moment, Finn said nothing, then, "Geez, I'm already late. My boss is going to kill me."

"Canned corn won't stock itself. Obviously you're the only guy to do it."

"That's me, canned corn organizer extraordinaire."

I went back to being silent, and remained so for the rest of the ride to my house. Finn, so protective of what he loved, carrying a pride the size of a football field. Finn, my friend. Finn, my brother.

He dropped me off at my house, and nodded goodbye before speeding away.

***

We lost a lot of games that fall. Despite our best effort, we just weren't that good. We lacked strong seniors, the class small, and Finn's talent could only cover so much. There were no playoffs in the future for us, no hope of the championship. But sometimes, that's the way it goes. Better luck next year.

After one of the practices before our last game of the season, Coach kept us in the locker room a bit later than normal. We slumped on the seats, sweaty and exhausted. "Gentlemen, there's someone I'd like to reintroduce. This is Luis."

The boy in question raised a hand in a small, cheerful wave. I'd seen him around before, a freshman with loose shaggy hair around his ears, on crutches and a boot on one leg. The boot was gone now, as were the crutches. But the hair remained, thick black waves curling at the ends of dark, shiny hair. Skin somewhere between olive and golden, he looked tan and well-rested. He looked like he'd spent his semester lounging around, instead of running himself ragged on a football field.

"Luis will be joining us again next fall, and I know you have all missed him."

There were a few laughs from some of the middle schoolers, raspberries blown by freshmen. The older kids jostled each other, low hum of conversation picking up.

I turned to Nathan, because he'll know who the kid is and why he's important, even if only by extension because Naomi knows everyone. "So who is he?"

"He's really good, that's who he is," Nathan supplied. "Played middle school last year and scored, like, all of their points. His spiral is so pretty, it'll make you cry. And can juke like nobody's business."

I looked over at Finn, sitting a short distance away. He fixated on Luis, eyes sharp and predatory.

"Bet he and Finn will make a good team."

"Sure hope so. He broke his ankle right before the season started. Coach was pissed."

"Was he at practice at all?"

"The first few, maybe, just before he broke it."

"Hey Luis!" Finn crowed, finally making his play. "How'd you break your ankle?"

A few scattered chuckles came from the peanut gallery.

Luis shrugged, unconcerned. "Stepping off a curb."

"You stepped off a curb." Finn's voice crackled with mockery.

"Yep." His voice was deep and slow, the rhythms of his words unhurried. "I'm just clumsy, tripping over my own feet all the time. My limbs are like—too long for the rest of me, that's what my mom says." He paused, scratching his jaw. "She told me that I have to grow into my own body, which like, what a weird sentiment, y'know? It's my body growing at it's own pace, so like, my limbs should be the perfect size for my body."

At this point I wondered if we'd hear the story of his broken ankle before Christmas. Apparently Coach did, too, because he slapped his shoulder and said, "Your ankle?"

"Oh, right! I stepped off a curb and my ankle gave out and bent sideways and snapped. I have screws in there, now, like I'm a robot or something." He stuck out his foot and rotated it in a slow circle, holding out his arms for balance. When he started to wobble, he set his foot down with a thump and grinned at us.

I traded glances with Nathan, who shrugged. "Don't look at me, man, I don't know him. Ask Naomi about him."

Naomi. Of course. Truly, how did she know *everyone*? One person shouldn't be able to hold that much information in their mind. It makes them too powerful.

I caught up with her after school, before one of our last practices. "Hey, do you know Luis? Martinez?"

"Luis? Yeah. He's in the musical with me."

Right. The play scheduled for the first weekend of December. "Is he good?"

"Oh yeah. Super good. Especially for a freshman."

"You're only a sophomore," I pointed out.

"I know. But a lot of the freshman are...meh. I was. Had to learn some stuff."

"Sure."

"But no, he's a solid kid. Why?"

"Joined the football team today. Was wondering who he was."

"He's had a broken ankle."

"I know. He told us. Very slowly."

She giggled prettily, her nose scrunching. "Yeah, he's a rambler. Takes *forever* to get to a point," she added conspiratorially. "But a good kid. Wicked talented with football, I hear."

"I guess I'll find out about that."

"You're coming to the show, right?"

"Uh, sure." High school theatre was one of the most cringe-worthy activities, in my opinion, but I kept that to myself. I'd go for her sake.

She flashed me a grin. "Great!"

At our last practice before the last game, Luis joined in for drills, just for fun. He wasn't going to play, because he hadn't been with us all season. He took the furthest point of our diamond spread, with Nathan snapping, naturally. Finn was on the left, and I was on the right. Nathan snapped, I caught it, and I pitched it to Luis, a pretty little arc right into his waiting gloves. I scrambled downfield, shaking off Tate with some of my sweet soccer footwork, keeping an eye out for the ball. When Luis passed, it soared beautifully over everyone's heads, right toward where Finn was running. Finn slowed up just a hair, and the ball dropped into the cradle of his arms. And of course, once Finn was gone, he was *gone*. Racing ahead of everyone, spreading his arms in victory, even though it wasn't a real game.

"That's what I'm talking about!" Coach Carlson said, pumping his fist. He offered me a high five as we jogged back to the sidelines.

Coach nodded and grunted, which was about as high praise as we could ever expect to get from him.

***

We won the last game of the season. Not that it mattered much, because we weren't going to playoffs or anything, but it was still nice to end on a high note.

This time, Coach put me in for the kickoff. I didn't get many chances to kick, so I vowed to do my best. The six of us ran forward, and I kicked the ball low to the ground. Heart in my throat, I kept my eyes on the ball as we shifted positions, praying I'd made it go fifteen yards. I counted seconds in my head as the ball slowed, and our boys raced the opponents to the ball.

Tate dropped on the ball.

We had possession. I sprinted to our huddle, knuckle bumping and shoulder slapping.

"Just call me Mr. Hands," Tate said, flexing his hands.

"No one calls you that, bro," Ethan Wilkes replied.

"Nah, everybody calls me that. You know it!"

"What, you gonna get some Beckham gloves? Have sticky hands?"

"Man, I'll get my hands all sticky. Just for you."

"That's disgusting."

Alejandro joined the huddle, squeezing in with his broad shoulders. "Spread, 10-split, drag, flare left, post."

Finn nodded at the call. "Ready? Break."

We traded off scoring for the first quarter, like kindergarteners forced to share, reaching fourteen points each. But in the second, it was like something clicked for our defense, and suddenly the other team wasn't scoring anymore. By halftime, we were up thirty-six–fourteen.

At halftime, Coach reminded us what would happen if we got up by forty-five points: the slaughter rule. If at any point after halftime, one team gains forty-five points over the other team, it's sudden death. It happened to us once this season, which was deeply humiliating. Maybe we'd get a chance to try it out for ourselves.

Through the third quarter, their defense fought hard, picking it off once and stopping us twice on the drives. But in the fourth quarter, we scored twice more. If we'd had more time, I'm certain we would have used the slaughter rule.

But at the end of the game, it was certain we would win, and out of courtesy for the other time, we used our last plays to run down the clock rather than rub their nose further into defeat.

Coach put me in for the last run. Nathan snapped it to Finn, who passed it lazily to me, and the buzzer sounded. I ran, and they tackled me swiftly. I popped up, grinning. We lined up to shake hands, breath puffing in the chilly air. As we headed for the locker rooms, I caught the flash of Finn's grin, coupled with a back slap from Nathan. In a knot of players after the game, we shouted and whooped, jumping up and down in sync, feeling good about closing our season this way. I knew I'd stay on the team for next year, for sure.

Coach, smiling more than I'd ever seen, talked to us in the locker room after. "It was a good season, boys. But we'll keep pushing, and get even better next year. We have some things to work on, but that's okay. You played hard this year, and that's all I can really ask for."

Coach Carlson added, "We're proud of you, and you should be proud of yourselves. Remember, I can teach you to block, pass, run, punt, tackle, and throw. But what's the one thing I can't teach you?"

"Hustle," we chorused.

"That's right. And you had that. You had that for sure."

"Indeed. Pray us out?" Coach looked at his assistant.

"Yessir."

We shuffled into a circle, bowing heads and putting hands in the middle. Coach Carlson prayed for us, and even if I didn't really go for all that stuff, I stayed quiet, eyeing Nathan from the corner of my eye, at his furrowed brow and earnest nodding head. Doc and Coach looked serious, too, but I noticed Finn with open eyes across the circle. He made a double chin at me, and I smothered a laugh.

"Amen," Coach Carlson said, and everyone echoed him, a rumbling chorus.

"Wilkes," Coach said, nodding to the senior to send us off one last time.

"Right, Coach. Who are we?"

"Comets!"

"Who are we?"

"Comets!"

"I said, *who are we?*"

"COMETS!"

"One, two, three, *COMETS!*"

We pulsed our hands and broke apart. I cast a look at Ethan Wilkes, who didn't seem any the worse for wear for it being his last game, his last chant, his last time with the team. Neither of the other seniors seemed too upset, either.

As I cleaned up to leave that night and headed for the Peterson's car, I caught sight of Coach Carlson walking with a woman in an orange polo shirt. He had his head turned toward her, listening intently to what she was saying, nodding occasionally. Under a parking light, he opened her car door for her and walked it shut behind her, before walking around to the drivers' side and getting in himself.

I looked away, jogging to catch up with Nathan and Naomi. I'd never seen my father do that for my mother, not once, not ever.

9

When Thanksgiving break rolled around, I got up early to catch my dad before he left for work. "Uh, Dad?"

He grunted, pouring coffee into a thermos.

"I...have a question."

"What?"

"Am I going home for break, or...?"

He paused, barely tearing his gaze away from his phone. "Figured we could watch some football here."

"Uh. Okay."

"C'mon man, getting you home would be a hassle." He sounded almost whiny.

"Sure," I said softly.

"Kay. See ya." He headed out the door.

Well, there went that hope. On Thursday, we watched the Macy's Thanksgiving Day parade and ate a store-bought rotisserie chicken with a pre-made pumpkin pie. We sat on the couch, plates balanced on our knees, drowning in our separate pools of sadness.

Maybe I should have tried to make conversation, or at least be more civil, but I let myself be mopey. I wanted to go home. He could deal with it.

About three in the afternoon, Dad motioned at a good play and said, "You ever do anything like that?"

"No, Dad. I play six man, it's different. Which you'd know if you ever bothered to come to one of my games." I punctuated this statement with a glare.

"Don't you take that tone with me." He looked at me hard.

I clenched my jaw.

"Yessir," he motioned for me to speak.

"Yessir," I mumbled. We never brought it up again.

***

Naomi's play opened on the first Friday of December, so I put on a black button-down with the sleeves rolled up to my elbows and waited for Finn to pick me up. When he arrived, I felt that initial jolt of strangeness that there was no one else in the car—Nathan was with his family, and Naomi was in the play. I sprinted through snow flurries and climbed into the passenger seat, blowing furiously on my hands to warm them.

"Pfft," Finn rolled his eyes, "it's not even cold."

"For you, maybe," I grumbled. "I'm from Houston. It doesn't snow there."

"Wimp," he said, and grinned.

"Says the man wearing a coat."

"This," he said snootily, "is a windbreaker."

We took seats in the middle section of the auditorium, closer to the right aisle. The Petersons sat a few rows up, almost right to the stage. Nathan came over to kneel on the seat in front of us, facing backwards.

"That seat's going to fold and break your legs," Finn said. "Just—" He clapped his hands in imitation of the seat closing. "And you'll be trapped there forever."

Nathan shrugged, his easygoing smile in place. "I'm surprised you have enough weight to keep it open," he said to Finn, who sputtered in mock offense.

"I could bench you," he said.

"Uh, I don't know about that," Nathan shrugged, looking down at himself. "I'm heavier than I look."

"No, I can," he insisted, and climbed over me to the aisle. "Come on, let's try it!"

"I don't think that's a good idea." Nathan scratched at the back of his head.

Finn yanked on his wrist. "Come on!" He promptly laid down on the carpeted aisle, feet higher than his head on the slanted floor. He grabbed at Nathan, untucking his shirt and tugging on his hands. Nathan stood over him, sheepishly giggling as Finn tried to wrangle him into a bench-able position.

Mrs. Murray, the English teacher, hissed at us. "*Boys!* Stop it!" She aimed a red painted fingernail at us, pointing at each of us in turn.

"What did I do?" I said, spreading my hands.

She narrowed her eyes. "You're there," she said, as though my simple presence was enough to implicate me in the crime.

Finn scrambled up and back over me, grumbling. "We'll settle this later."

"Sure. Fine. Cheer hard for Naomi, ok?"

"As if we would have done anything else," Finn grumbled. He made a show of crinkling and rustling his program, casting glares at Mrs. Murray until the lights dimmed.

You're a Good Man, Charlie Brown was a show I'd never seen before—but then, I hadn't watched a play since I was a little kid and my parents took us to see an outdoor show at an amphitheater. I guess they picked it because the cast was small and the costumes were easy—all things that could be pulled off on a shoestring budget. Luis played Schroder, which mostly involved him crouching in front of a toy piano and looking unimpressed. There were more girls than boys, which shouldn't have been surprising, so Linus was played by a girl. Naomi played Snoopy.

She was amazing. Even in a baggy white onesie with face paint, she was beautiful. And she was clearly having the time of her life. She kept the audience laughing, all while wearing the biggest grin. She had a whole number involving dancing with her dinner bowl, and her doghouse was center stage the whole time. I don't think she left the stage much, just hid in the doghouse. There was no question–at least in my mind–that she completely and wholly stole the show.

I sat in the audience, heart pounding as though I was the one onstage. Holy smokes, I was gone for her. I felt sure I didn't blink the whole time, I was so enamored with the performance. It didn't matter that Charlie Brown's acting was subpar, or that the costumes were largely just people's clothes from home. It was a beautiful show, worthy of any Broadway stage, and it was all because of Naomi.

After, the cast flooded the auditorium, posing for pictures with each other and with their families, holding flowers their parents had bought them, all while telling everyone how nervous they were. It took Naomi a long time to say hello to everyone she knew (because she knew everyone) but eventually she made her way to me.

"Hi," I said, like an idiot.

"Hey! Did you like it?"

"Oh yeah. You were..." *Showstopping. Amazing. Brilliant. Gorgeous. The best up there.* "...great."

"Thanks! I'm so glad you came!"

"Yeah." *Say something nice, you idiot! Tell her how awesome it was!*

"Where's my favorite comic character?" Finn popped up over my shoulder, grinning and opening his arms to her.

She squealed and hugged him, kicking up a foot behind her.

I shoved my hands in my pockets.

"Come on, let's take a picture," she insisted, motioning us closer and flagging down Nathan. We huddled together, Nathan holding his phone in his long arm, pressing our faces together and smiling wide. Just as Nathan snapped the photo, Luis sprinted behind us, opening his mouth in a wide smile, throwing up a hand with splayed fingers to photobomb.

Naomi took her phone back and laughed. "Luis!" she shouted, and moved away to tease him.

That's the first photo in existence of the five of us. It didn't seem important at the time, because it wasn't. But it is now. In fact, a lot of things didn't seem important at first, and they wouldn't be until later. Like going to that play. And maybe it wouldn't have been, if Naomi hadn't invited us all to Whataburger with the rest of the cast for a post-show snack.

If I hadn't ended up wedged in a booth between Nathan and Luis, Finn across from me, with Naomi on one side and Annabella Gutierrez on the other (she played Sally Brown). If we hadn't ended up mostly squashed by theatre kids, still in weird stage makeup, all talking loudly and rehashing moment after moment from the show and rehearsals. If I hadn't ended up dragging my fries through my milkshake, silently observing the way Naomi's curls slowly fell from her bun to frame her face in dancing beauty. If Luis hadn't requested to try my shake and then ended up sharing it with me. If Nathan hadn't ordered twenty chicken biscuits with honey butter and threatening to eat them all before sharing them with everyone at our table. If Finn hadn't started throwing fries into Luis' wide mouth. If Naomi hadn't ended up taking fifty four-second videos of us being silly, if Luis hadn't started talking in a British accent to make everyone laugh, if Finn hadn't lobbed a ketchup packet at Nathan and spilled it all down his shirt...

But we did. So it was important. And I'm glad that it was.

10

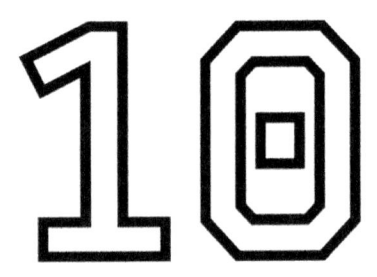

For Christmas break, I went home with Mom. My parents drove three hours apiece to meet in the middle and do a hand-off. For me, it was three hours of near-silence with Dad and three hours of nonstop chatter from my sisters with Mom. I'll let you guess which ride I liked better.

My sisters had stopped sharing a room in my absence, so I slept on the couch, which wasn't too bad. I sleep like a rock most of the time, and it was break, so everyone slept late. They had already decorated a tree, but there were plenty of other traditions to complete. We baked cookies and decorated a gingerbread house from a kit. Two days before Christmas, Hailey banged her way out of her room, yanking on an army green jacket, and pausing in the living room to zip up knee-high boots. Sprawled on the couch, I raised an eyebrow at her.

"Put on your shoes," she commanded.

"What, why?" I griped.

"Do you have a Christmas gift for Mom?"

"No, but—"

"Then put on your fricking shoes, jackass." She directed a peeved look at me.

"Fine, fine, I'm going!" I whined, rousing myself from the couch and grabbing my tennis shoes.

Stella bounced into the living room, wearing loud pink leggings and glittery shoes. "Let's go!" she shouted, grinning and showing off pink and glittery braces. She'd get along so well with Finn's sisters.

Hailey jingled her keys. "Let's go!"

Yanking a black beanie over my ears, I followed her to the car, scuffled with Stella for the front seat, and claimed it jubilantly while she pouted into the back seat.

"It's so gross back here!" she whined, shoving aside random articles of clothing, trash, and other detritus found in a teenage girl's car. Her dash had three different air fresheners clipped to the air vents, all of them empty.

"I don't see you offering to clean it," Hailey retorted. "Right, we're going to the mall to get Mom's Christmas gift. One of the those smell-good candles from Bath and Body works, and some of that aroma therapy lotion she's always going on about—"

"Lavender and cedarwood or eucalyptus and mint," Stella recited.

"A bag of starbucks coffee grounds, and we're going to get that photo printed."

"What photo?" I asked.

"The three of us had a girls day and took some really cute photos." Hailey at least had the good grace to look embarrassed.

"Oh, well, if that's all," I said grouchily, hurt at being left out. I'd been on far too many trips to the mall with my sisters before to be excited about this. I knew we'd get sidetracked four times in girly clothing and makeup stores, I'd get exactly thirty seconds to glance over the fancy alcohol brush pens I definitely couldn't afford, and we'd have to stop and smell candles that gave me a headache. The fact that this house seemed to have fully shifted into a girl's zone didn't make me more enthusiastic about it either.

We drove to the mall, and Hailey blasted R&B while Stella complained and begged for pop music. I am not what I would consider a "music person," though Naomi would probably hope otherwise. The most I ever cared to turn on was lo-fi while doing art or some hype rap music before games. By the time we rolled up, I was ready to escape the noisy and confined space. Hailey took the lead, her heeled boots clacking on the linoleum floor. She practically marched directly to Bath and Body Works, where all progress stopped as she and Stella traded off huffing candles and shoving them in my face. I trailed them in a slouch.

Look, it's not that I don't love my mom and don't want to get her something nice for Christmas, but it's always been this way: Hailey is in charge of the gift giving, Stella gets excited and cute, and I sort of get lost in the background. I wished Nathan was there to help me make fun of the silly candle names like "moonlight forest kiss" or whatever. "Moonlight forest kiss" isn't a smell, it's a teenage vampire fantasy or something. Nathan would have thought that was funny.

We'd moved on to a makeup store by the time I quit being broody. I'd been handed the Bath and Body Works bag to carry, which I knew for a fact had more than just Mom's gift inside.

"Wait, Zed, c'mere," Stella said by the eye makeup. "We're basically the same color, let me try this." She nearly stabbed me in the eye with a brush.

"Hey! Point that thing someplace else!"

"But I want to see how it looks," she pouted. "And I don't want to use the tester on me, gross!"

"So you're going to use it on me?" I raised a brow at her.

"Please?" She gave me puppy eyes.

"Just do it on your hand," said Hailey, swatching a lipstick on her own hand. "Zed, what do you think?"

"It's pink," I said noncommittally, again dodging Stella's brush. "Would you quit?"

Hailey whacked Stella in the shoulder. "Stop it, I need his artist opinion." She held her hand up to her face.

"Um..." I looked from the lipstick to her face. "Maybe try a more berry tone? You've got a lot of warm tones in your face."

"Huh, you're right. Good call." She went back to picking through the lipsticks.

"I think I want this palette," Stella said, holding up a huge palette from a brand that definitely wasn't a drug store brand, and not in the same price range either.

"I'm not paying for that," Hailey said.

"Okay," Stella shrugged. "I have money. Hey, Zed, can I do your makeup at home?"

I groaned. "Stella, really?"

She gave me puppy eyes again. "Pleeeeease."

I waffled, knowing I didn't really have a choice. She'd get her way eventually. Baby sisters have a way of doing that.

"I'll pay you twenty dollars," she said.

"Wow, you must be really rolling in the dough."

"I started babysitting," she said, striking a cutesy pose and flashing her braces smile.

"I'm not doing anything until I see that cash," I said, crossing my arms.

Stella handed me her makeup pallet and dug through her little purse that was shaped like a slice of cake, coming up with a twenty. "Deal."

I took the cash. "Deal," I acquiesced.

She did a happy dance. "You're the best brother ever!" she grinned, and squeezed me around the middle.

I was right about getting sidetracked—we trailed through three stores stocked only with girls' clothes—though I did get a conciliatory trip through the shoe store to look at fancy cleats I could not afford, and I did get to drool over those alcohol pens.

We passed a nail salon and Stella really wanted a manicure, but Hailey denied her, so then she turned to me. "I'll give you another twenty to paint my nails."

I made the mistake of saying, "I'd do that for free."

She got a sly look on her face. "Perfect. Then the twenty is so I can paint *your* nails."

"Oh boy."

She waved the bill under my nose.

In front of us, Hailey snorted. "Maybe I'll straighten your hair while we're at it."

Resigned to my fate, I took the money and trailed them around the mall, but with the added bonus of being forty dollars richer. So I forcibly dragged them into stores I wanted to visit, and grabbed a few things of my own.

When we got home, I hauled a kitchen chair into the bathroom we all shared—which, let's be honest, it was the girls' bathroom and I just got a hook for my towel and a corner of the counter for my toiletry bag. They painted my nails and contoured my face and gave me winged eyeliner, but I drew the line at lipstick. Hailey took a straightener to my curly head, relaxing all my curls to smooth fine dark brown hair that flopped over my eyes and ears.

At the end of it all, they snapped photos and giggled and told me what a pretty boy I was. I took a single selfie, unsmiling, and after some deliberation, sent it to Finn. *Sisters,* I said.

A moment later, he replied with a photo of his own—his spiky hair littered with barrettes and clips, haphazard costume makeup smeared on his face. *The worst,* he said. *I hope you know I'm keeping this for blackmail.*

As am I, I replied.

On Christmas Eve, we all got in our pajamas to watch Home Alone. It's not the greatest Christmas movie the world has to offer, but it's important to us.

Mom cast her arms around us, reaching to tug Hailey in. "I love you," she said. "Merry Christmas."

"Merry Christmas," we parroted.

"I know things are...different, now. I wish they didn't have to be."

"It's okay, Mom," Stella said softly.

"Sweet girl," she murmured and stroked her hair.

Mom was the first one up on Christmas, and her puttering around in the kitchen woke me up. I shuffled into the kitchen, rubbing my eyes and reaching for a mug.

"Merry Christmas," she said with amusement at my groggy state.

I saluted with two fingers, pouring coffee.

"Hey, what are you doing? You're too young for that!"

I poured it anyway, splashed some milk in, and took a sip.

She sighed, resigned. "I suppose you *are* getting older." Leaning against me, she said, "You're almost as tall as your father, now."

I grunted.

"Zed...how's he doing?"

I shrugged. "Don't know. Don't see him much." She frowned at that, so I continued, "But there's always food in the fridge and if I need anything he's there."

"Parenting is about more than just...feeding and clothing you."

"It works for him, I guess." I moved away, clutching my coffee cup. "Did Hailey sort the gifts under the tree into piles by recipient again?"

She peeked around me, laughing. "So it seems."

I received those coveted alcohol markers. I was quite touched.

It was good to be home, even just for a couple weeks. I returned back to Terrytown the weekend before classes started again. Cold, frozen, barren West Texas.

I exited the car onto the damp driveway, wondering if we would get a snow day this semester. In my room, a soccer ball gathered dust in the corner, a reminder of the soccer season going on right now.

Did I miss it? Not really. Not with more than a passing thought for all the time I'd spent devoting myself to it. But now, there was West Texas, Terrytown, and the Comets. And though it was cold and barren, it was where I was now.

At least Terrytown had Naomi, Finn, and Nathan. At least that.

***

On the first day of classes after the break, Finn picked me up with the others like usual, all of our breath steaming in the cold air. "My heater doesn't work," Finn greeted me. "There's like three blankets back there."

Naomi handed me a little green bag with tissue paper sticking out. "Merry Christmas. Late."

"Thanks." I plucked the paper out and cast it aside. Inside was a little black thermos. It was the perfect size for my hand and small enough to tuck into the side pocket of my backpack. The outside had a little cloth sleeve, dark gray, embroidered with my name.

"It's so I can keep bringing coffee." She held up a large camping thermos, unscrewed the cap, and poured into my waiting cup. She passed me a creamer packet.

"You mean it's so you don't go to *jail.* For *theft,*" Nathan said.

"Hey, I bought these creamers with my own money."

"Thank you," I said. She shrugged like it was no big deal.

"Don't think you're too special," Finn said. "We all got one." He and Nathan toasted each other with their own thermoses.

"Oh please," said Naomi, "if anyone is *special,* it's you, Finn."

I almost snorted coffee out my nose. I coughed to clear my throat. "I have stuff for you, too." I handed out my (unwrapped, because I'm not fancy) gifts. For Nathan, a mug that said *World's Best Dad.* For Finn, a car air freshener.

"Ha ha, very funny," he said. He hung it on the rearview mirror anyway.

And for Naomi, a CD of the broadway soundtrack of *Wicked.* (Do I know anything about musicals? No. But Stella assured me it was popular). I was proud of myself, and my little presents.

Naomi seemed happy, too, which felt like the most important part.

***

"Well," Coach Carlson said, standing at the front of the class, "Mrs. Laurence had her baby a month early, so I'm afraid you're stuck with me. Welcome back."

I leaned over to Nathan across the aisle. "I didn't know Coach knew history."

"Yeah. He subs for all the levels."

"What?"

"Gentlemen, is there something you'd like to share with the class?"

"Uh, no, Coach," I mumbled.

"That's alright then, let's begin."

Having Coach C teach was a little bizarre; I was familiar with his tactics on the football field, but to have him give us facts and homework rather than plays and techniques struck me as odd. He wore his glasses in class, too, down on the end of his nose, so he could tip his head back to look through the lenses at the board or the book, and sometimes he would tip his chin down to look at us over the rims. History was my first class, so if I was late, I was on the receiving end of Coach C's disappointed face, which was somehow worse than any punishment my parents had ever given me.

But aside from having Coach C as a history teacher, I coasted through sophomore spring easily. Finn picked me up every morning. We ate lunch together, now with the added presence of Luis, who came when Naomi invited him and brought his lunch from home. He wormed his way into our company, but no one save Finn minded his added presence. Finn was grouchy because he was Finn, and he took every opportunity to tease Luis, like a big brother. It wasn't long before Luis was a permanent fixture of our lunch table.

We passed Valentine's day with no more acknowledgement than it deserved: mildly disgusted facial expressions at all the sappy high school couples who probably wouldn't last beyond graduation, and a batch of red velvet cupcakes from a box. Actually, the cupcakes were all Naomi, which she brought to share, and they were quite tasty.

It remained cold and frosty up here for much longer than I was used to, the wind whipping across flat planes to nip at hands and ankles and ears. It made the mandatory track practices even more miserable than they needed to be, all of us shivering between runs. By spring break, the sun had returned, making it officially "wear a sweater in the morning and regret it by noon" weather.

"Are you going back to Houston for break?" Naomi asked me.

I picked at my cafeteria meal. Before I answered, Luis drizzled sriracha sauce on his meal, something that seemed mostly grain with some veggies thrown in, and Finn pounced on the opportunity to tease.

"What even is that?" Finn pestered, getting in his space.

"It's a quinoa bowl," he said slowly, folding the sauce in. "It's quite healthy. Lots of protein."

"Ew. That's some rich white people crap right there. Why aren't you eating, like, tacos or something normal?"

Luis looked aggrieved. "Do I ask you why you aren't eating plain butter noodles? Unsalted white rice?" A cocked eyebrow in Finn's direction. "Mayonnaise flavored potato salad?"

"Potato salad is good though," I said.

Luis gave me a *look* that spoke volumes. "I'm sure it is, for you. For him?" He made an expressive gesture in Finn's direction.

"I don't understand why you don't just eat pizza like the rest of us," Finn said.

"I'm reducing personal food waste and maintaining a balanced diet. I found this recipe on the internet, and it's very good," Luis said primly, and took a big bite.

"Hey, Houston?" Naomi repeated.

"I don't think so."

"Oh, good. We can do something fun."

For a second, I thought she meant just the two of us, and my brain flatlined, before stuttering back to life as I realized she'd meant we *all* could do something fun, together.

"It looks like garbage." Finn prodded the grains with his pointer. "Like, literal garbage. The stuff that's leftover after you cook a meal."

"It's not garbage," Luis protested, stabbing at Finn's finger with his fork. "There's nuts, cucumber, sweet potato…"

"See. Garbage."

"Literally none of that is garbage, Finn," Nathan butted in. "Lay off."

"What do you think about going for a movie?" Naomi asked. "Is anything good showing?" She raised her voice to get the others' attention. "Hey, ding-dongs, movie over spring break?"

The other three whipped their heads to focus on her.

"That sounds like fun," Nathan said.

"What are we seeing?" Luis asked.

"Probably nothing you're interested in, what with your fascination with crappy romance films. And anyway—" Finn continued over Luis' grumblings that *they aren't crappy, thank you,* "I'll probably be working a lot. Or at least have to take care of my sisters. Besides, movies are expensive."

"You know, I have a pool." Like a turtle, Luis meandered to his point, taking us along for the journey with him. "It's currently winterized, but it only takes a couple days to get ready. And if I ask my mom soon we could have it done in time. Chlorine and everything...course, she'd probably have to order the tablets, like, tomorrow, to make sure they got here in time, but...It might be cold, but I have a game room, too." He stirred his lunch, and that absorbed all his focus for a few seconds. Then he continued, "And an old swing set. And probably some craft supplies. And all of that is free."

Finn blinked at him. "You *do* like to ramble on a bit."

"We could hang out there, if you wanted. You could bring your sisters along."

"Wait, that sounds great!" Naomi said, clapping lightly.

"What kind of game room?" Nathan asked.

"There's a pool table, a regular table for games, I've got my Xbox One set up in there...I disconnected the Wii, but it's around somewhere. Wouldn't be too hard. Got these big comfy couches, all fluffy."

"And your mom wouldn't mind all of us being there?" I asked.

"Nah, she'd probably be thrilled."

"Sick, bro," I said, reaching across to knuckle bump him.

And so it was on the Monday of spring break, Finn drove us out to Luis' house, sans sisters this time, turning into a long driveway through a wrought iron gate. He whistled through his teeth. "Looks like Luis ain't doing too shabby."

"I think when his parents divorced she got a big settlement or something," Naomi said, proving once again she knew everyone and everything. "And I think his mom has some fancy job out of Dallas. Something fashion or interior design related, unless I'm mistaken."

"What're they doing in the boonies?" Nathan asked.

"I guess they like it here."

"What's not to like?" I said softly and caught Naomi's eye to share a grin with her.

Luis let us into a house—more like a mansion—with shining hardwood floors that made me conscious of the dirt on my converse, fancy textured throw pillows on all the sitting furniture, and bedrooms set up like they were for a showing. He led us through the kitchen, which had a huge stove with like six burners.

"You guys want a snack?" he asked, reclining against the spotless kitchen island, which held no trash or cooking utensils, only an artistic bowl of mangoes.

Still in awe of our surroundings, we mumbled the affirmative.

Inhaling a deep breath, Luis yelled across the house in rapid Spanish.

Floating from a further room came the voice of a woman responding in Spanish.

Luis grinned, and threw open the pantry. "Behold!"

The pantry was stocked full of a teenager's dream: chips, candy, snack cakes, soda—you name it, it was there. There were also several glass bottles of virgin margarita mix, which Luis assured us we could use the blender for if we wished.

Luis' mom stepped into the kitchen to briefly wave hello. She was dressed in pressed gray slacks and a blazer indoors on a Moday afternoon, as well as having a hefty diamond necklace. When Luis wasn't looking, I cast a glance to Naomi, and mouthed, *loaded*. To which she responded, *lucky*, pointing at Luis. Whatever her job was, Luis said it kept her in front of a laptop in her office, required lots of phone calls, and frequent trips to metropolises across the country. She promised to make us mangonadas next time, to which Luis said, "Those will change your *life!*"

Arms full of Gansitos, Takis, Marquesitas, and potato chips, we charged to the back door. Stepping outside we confirmed it was, indeed, too cold to swim, so we crossed the tiled patio to the separate game room on the other side of the pool. The couches were big and cushy, and Luis draped himself over the back of one and grinned at us. "Welcome! To my favorite place in the world. Well, actually, that might be the theatre stage...but this comes in a close second."

We took in the sight of the room, which was practically a dream. We descended on the game cabinet and couches. Finn kicked Luis' butt at Madden repeatedly, who took it with his perpetual good humor. Nathan and I played several decent games of pool, and then Naomi schooled us at Monopoly, which can be played very quickly if one of you is a money-grubbing board game tycoon. Y'all, money may not be able to buy happiness, but it can buy a game room and lots of snack food, and if that's not happiness, I don't know what is.

Finn did end up bringing his sisters on another day. They immediately attached themselves to Luis like barnacles and forced him to play tea party with them, fluffy pink boa and all. He didn't seem to mind. In fact, he seemed to enjoy the sparkly sunglasses and spoke in a silly accent the whole time.

His mother seemed to enjoy having us every time we came—she stocked the game room fridge (and seriously, who has a separate fridge in their game room? Who has a separate game room, period?) with plenty of sodas, Topo Chicos, and even more snacks. She always told us she was so glad we came.

***

Over spring break Naomi invited me to church. The first Sunday of April, she said, would be a good time. Easter fell late, and she mentioned she'd be leading worship that day but it wouldn't be anything fancy.

I biked to church, wearing my nicest pair of jeans and the same button-down I'd worn to her play. I'd even combed my hair into a semblance of neatness, used mousse and gel and everything. I slipped in right before service started, sliding into the back row.

The church was small, two sections of wooden pews in a building lined with stained glass windows and an altar at the front. Mr. Peterson (Pastor Peterson? Reverend Peterson? I don't know) wore a suit, but not the fancy robes I'd sometimes seen. Naomi was already on the stage, wielding an acoustic guitar, standing beside the pianist. I didn't get a chance to tell her hello before the service. We all stood to sing a hymn, and then a song that reminded me of the acoustic pop music on the radio, except it was about Jesus and not romance. Mr. Peterson preached about how we were all terrible people and how lucky we were that Jesus had died for us, hooray; though I'm not sure he would have characterized it that way.

But he stood in front of the congregation and lifted a loaf of bread, tearing it in two. "The night that Jesus died he took the bread, gave thanks, and broke it, saying, 'This is my body, broken for you for the forgiveness of sins. Take and eat. Do this in remembrance of me." He lifted a cup, like a goblet from a medieval film, and repeated the words, except this time, he talked about blood.

And then he invited any of us who accepted Jesus as savior to come forward and partake in Holy Communion.

I tensed, sitting in the way back, debated whether or not to move. Would people judge me if I didn't? Would I get weird looks moving to the front?

All thoughts fled my head as Naomi stepped forward to the microphone. She was dressed probably the most normal I had ever seen her. Long skirt, blue and patterned with little white flowers, with a heavy amount of swoosh as she swayed to the music of her own making. She also wore a close-fitting tank top and a loose sleeveless macrame over-shirt thing—I wasn't sure what to call that. It fell past her waist, just knotted string to form a shapeless, flowing garment, but you could see right through it, like it wasn't even there in the first place. I'm not sure what the point of it was, to be honest with you. Her hair tumbled over her shoulders, brunette curls falling everywhere.

She stood in front of the microphone, fingers plucking at her guitar, eyes on her hands. The microphone caught her quick intake of breath as she began to sing.

I'd never heard most of the songs we sang that day, but this one in particular struck me as important. She sang it so carefully, the microphone catching her shaking breaths. Here, I'll include the lyrics for you:

It starts with the bread.
It starts with the wine.
It starts with the precious body of Christ.
So take this bread,
and take this wine,
remember your sins gone by sacrifice.
Come to the table.

Her verse complete, she stepped back, looking down to focus on her fingers plucking out the melody on the guitar.

What a sweet invitation. *Come to the table.*

So enamored was I in the dance of her fingers on the strings and neck, in the fall of her eyelashes against her cheek, in the play of the light on her shoulders and tendrils of hair, that I missed the chance to take communion even if I'd been sure I wanted to. But it was alright. Watching her was holy enough for me.

Mr. Peterson closed the service, and before I could escape, Nathan rushed to me, weaving through the crowd to snag me by the elbow in the narthex.

"Zed! I'm so glad you're here!"

"Thanks."

"Should'a let me know, you could've sat with me."

"Ah, that's okay. Wouldn't want to disturb your family."

"You could never." He pretended to rest his elbow on my head, but I ducked away from him.

Naomi hurried to us, her guitar case in one hand. "Hey! I'm so glad you made it."

"Hey. You—you sounded amazing."

She beamed, lit up like the sun glowed inside her. "Thanks."

"I really liked the last song you sang. About the table?"

"Thank you," she said sincerely, pressing a hand to her heart.

"What's she's not telling you is she wrote it," Nathan interjected.

"*What?*"

"Yeah, uh. Did you know I write songs sometimes?"

"Uh, *no*. I think I would've remembered that."

"Most of them are no good, anyway, but this one's okay."

"She'll be a star one day," Nathan said, puffing up with pride.

"For sure," I agreed.

"Please." She waved a hand as if dismissing our comments. "Do you know how hard it is to make it in the music industry? I'd be lucky to even make an album."

"If anyone can do it, it's you," I said firmly.

She smiled. "Thanks. It means a lot to me that you came today. Do you want to come to lunch?"

"Crock pot roast with potatoes and carrots," Nathan said.

"Your parents won't mind?"

"Zed, they never mind when we bring home friends, and they certainly don't mind you. They like you," Naomi said.

"Okay. Thanks."

"Anytime," she said, and smiled.

11

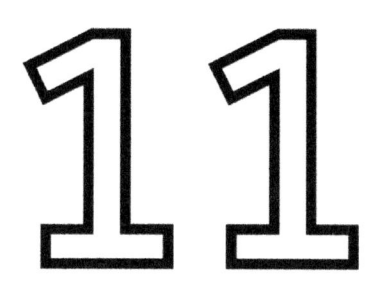

School lasted for two more months, which dragged by with frequent interruptions by tornado warnings, and then it was summer. On the last day of classes, Coach Carlson stopped me before I left his classroom.

"Have a good summer, son," he said. "And if you need anything, give me a holler."

"Okay. Sure, Coach," I said, wondering why I would call him if I needed something.

"I'll see you at training?"

"Yes, sir."

"I'm looking forward to it. Take care of yourself."

"Okay."

At home that night, having pizza for dinner (again), Dad grumbled, "What am I going to do with you all summer?"

"Don't worry, I'll stay out of trouble."

"You and those friends of yours. You stay busy?"

"Yes?"

"Well, just don't eat me out of house and home and don't get arrested." He glared at me over his pizza. "And stay out of my hair."

"Don't worry." I rolled my eyes. "I do need to get some driver's ed done, though," I added timidly.

He swore under his breath. "Can't have you wrecking my car."

"I promise I'll be careful."

"And I don't have time to teach you. Isn't there a class you can sign up for?"

"I...guess but I know it has an entrance fee."

Dad grumbled to himself, tossed the crust of his pizza into the trashcan. "I guess we'll have to figure something out. But you won't be sixteen for another year, anyway."

I hesitated, unsure if he'd actually forgotten my birthday. "No, I-I turn sixteen in a month."

He stared at me blankly for a moment. Then, "Shit. I guess you do."

"Did you forget my birthday?" I asked, incredulous.

"No, of course not. Just lost track of time."

"Do you know I need new shoes, too? This one's got duct tape holding it together." I waggled my old battered converse.

"Didn't I just get you some of those?"

"Like, two years ago! I grew, Dad! That's what teenagers do!"

"Oh, so now I'm the bad guy because you didn't bother to tell me you needed new shoes."

"How is it my fault you're barely home?"

"I am breaking my back for this family—" he stopped, and I heard an echo of things he'd said to mom. "I'll order the shoes tomorrow," he grumbled, and headed off to his bedroom, closing the door behind him. A minute later came the muted sounds of WWE.

I sighed, clearing away paper plates and the empty pizza box. Hello, summer.

∗∗∗

Texas summers are hot. You've probably guessed this, and I already knew this (thank you, Houston), but every year I am reminded with new intensity how much I hate the heat. Which was why I was so thankful for Luis' pool. We spent a significant portion of our days there, attempting to drown each other with vicious water fights, throwing ourselves into the water immediately upon arrival while Nathan fruitlessly waved a bottle of sunscreen at us. Naomi spent equal time swimming or tanning while floating on an inflatable. I never thought one-pieces could be flattering until I saw one on her. She had two, I think, one blue and sort of sporty, designed mostly for actual swimming. The other was yellow, tied behind her neck, exposing the smooth expanse of her back, the sloping ridge of her spine. She wore that one on days when she relaxed and floated, or sat on the edge with her feet in the water until Finn and Nathan saw fit to throw her in. She'd emerge, sputtering and laughing, stray hair clinging wetly to her forehead and cheeks. One afternoon, she saw fit to take her revenge by bringing Luis and I slices of cold watermelon, and none for the other two. A trail of juice ran from the corner of her angelic, innocent smile. As they whined and cajoled, she slowly situated herself on the edge of the pool again, twirling her toe in the water.

When it got too hot, or when the pool reached the temperature of bathwater, we made good use of the game room and the fifty-five inch flatscreen. One time we binged the entire Lord of the Rings movie series, a feat that left us stumbling across the driveway as the sun punched us directly in the eye sockets.

I intended to pass my birthday quietly. I was going to see my mom and sisters the week after, but the actual day of my birthday I thought would slide by with ease.

I woke up to the honking of a horn outside.

My father and I stumbled out of our bedrooms, equally disoriented by a car horn at six A.M. on a summer morning. I made it out the door first, to see Finn's truck in my driveway.

He leaned out the driver window. "Get dressed, you delinquent! We're celebrating!"

"Uh..."

Naomi poked her head out the back window. "And make it snappy! We have big plans!"

Blearily, I turned around to get dressed.

Inside, my father glared at me. "Get those hooligans out of my driveway."

I hustled to throw on clothes, grabbing my phone, wallet, and keys.

I slammed the truck door behind me.

"*Happy Birthday!*" Naomi yelled.

"Yes, happiest wishes on the most glorious occasion of your birth," Luis said, slowly. He patted my knee, slowly. Pat, pat.

There was a pause.

"Happy day of womb emancipation," Finn and Nathan chorused, and laughed, barely holding it together long enough to get the words out.

"Thanks, guys. But how did you even know when my birthday was?"

"I'm a ninja," Naomi whispered, narrowing her eyes and making a karate-chop motion. "Also, I stalked you on Facebook."

"But I—haven't used facebook in ages."

"Still has your birthday."

"You're kind of creepy."

"I know everything."

Nathan twisted around to nod at me with big eyes. "She used to blackmail me all the time."

"Shut up, I only did that as a kid!"

"You're still a baby!" Finn said. "You're like, so young! Zed is older than you now!"

"You're only one year older."

"Which means you're ancient," Luis said.

"Oh, right, you're like, an actual child," I said. It was easy for me to forget he was only fourteen. An old soul, I guess.

"So, birthday boy, here's the plan," Finn said. "Pancake breakfast. Then over to Big Spring for a movie. Then cake for lunch. And then swimming!"

"So basically what we do every day," I said.

"But today, I don't have to work, so you are blessed with my glorious presence. And, there's cake."

Luis said reverently, "Cake is always special."

"Absolutely correct," I said. "Onward!"

"Do you get to take your driver's test?" Nathan asked.

I looked down at my lap, mumbling, "I haven't learned to drive yet."

"*What?*" Finn squawked.

"Yeah, I just haven't."

"Well, shit, bro, we can fix that. I'll teach you."

"That's illegal," Naomi swiftly interjected. "You have to have like, an actual adult do it. I think."

"I'm not comfortable breaking any laws," Nathan said, "even on a birthday."

"That's unfortunate," Finn said.

"What's a little law breaking between friends?" Luis asked.

"Um, still illegal," Naomi said. "Is your dad going to teach you?"

"Uhhh—I don't know."

"What about your mom?"

"Maybe."

"We're doing an online thing," Nathan said. "And dad's doing the car stuff because it would stress Mom too much."

"Yeah, I don't know, guys. But I'm really excited for pancakes! Who likes whipped cream?"

"I do!" Luis said, raising his hand.

This sufficiently switched their attention, but I caught Naomi looking at me shrewdly. She was way too hard to fool.

***

When I went to see my mom, I hung out with them for two weeks straight. It was nice, fun. She did end up taking me to drive around in parking lots, which was fine, if a bit boring. And then she made me drive on the loop and on the beltway and various roads, sitting in traffic or zooming eighty on the freeway with Mom's panicked but silent gripping of the door handle in my peripheral. Unfortunately, I didn't get to take the test before I went back west.

"I don't know what you're going to do, sweetie. We can't finish it today, and the DMV wait is ages long."

"It's okay, mom," I said, "I'll figure it out."

She looked at me, features soft. "Do you have someone you can ask to help?"

"Um. I don't know about that."

"I'll talk to your father," she said, "I'll see if I can figure it out."

Please don't do that, I thought, imagining him snapping at me from the passenger seat. Or scrolling on his phone the whole time. I said nothing.

***

I stared at the call button a long time before tapping it. I canceled immediately, taking a deep breath to quell the shaking in my stomach. I tapped call again and lifted the phone to my ear.

"Hello, this is Ray."

"Um—hi, Coach Carlson. This is Zed."

"Hello, son, how're you?"

"Um, I'm good, Coach, but I think I need a little help."

"Okay, son, what can I help you with?"

I screwed my eyes shut. "I need a ride. To my driver's test."

Silence, on the other end of the line. I counted heartbeats. One, two, ten.

"Okay, I think I can help you with that. Do you need help with the class, or...?"

"No, I finished that in Houston."

"Have you driven out here yet?"

"No."

"We should do that first. Driving out here is different from in Houston, for sure."

"Uh...I don't really have a...can you...teach me?"

Another pause, shorter this time. When he did speak, his voice was softer. "Sure. I can. Let me think about some things, and then we'll figure it out."

I exhaled in relief. Coach C wouldn't yell at me. Everything was fine.

***

Everything was not fine. Sitting in the driver's seat of Coach's car, I stared down the narrow county road lined by cow pastures. The blinker clicked expectantly. "I don't know about this, Coach."

"It'll be fine. My kids learned on this road, so can you. There's not a lot of traffic, but you do need to stay up to speed. Unless you're behind a tractor. Then you'll be going very slow."

I shot him a glance, his words less than comforting. Still, he looked unworried, his crow's feet deepened by a smile, his gray hair bare of the orange ball cap I usually saw him in. "Okay." I pulled onto the highway.

"Now get up to speed," he urged.

I pushed down on the pedal. The speedometer ticked upward. This was fine.

A car appeared in my rear view.

"Now actually get up to speed, son."

I pushed downward.

The car pulled up behind me, lingered there for a mile or so, and sped around me.

I gripped the wheel tight. "I am going the speed limit, what more do they want?"

"Son, out here, the speed limit is five to ten over."

"But what about curves?"

"Even around curves. Aren't you from Houston? Did your parents ever go eighty on the freeway, weaving through cars?"

"Uh…" I checked my mirrors, clear; speedometer, a little scary. I didn't mention about the yelling matches they'd gotten into about reckless driving and running late.

"You're doing, fine, son. We'll get you fixed up in no time. Here comes a car, give 'em a hello."

"A hello."

"Yeah, raise a finger or two off the wheel. Just being polite. Maybe three fingers if you know them. Four fingers–eh, that's too many."

I shot a quick glance at him and could see the laughter at the corners of his eyes. I smiled too, raising two fingers at the next passing car.

It didn't occur to me then that he was taking an enormous risk to teach me. I wasn't on his insurance, nor was I related to him. He barely knew me. I could have wrecked his car, gotten him in trouble, and racked up huge fines. He never mentioned any of this to me.

So I learned to drive in my coach's car. I passed my test at the end of the summer. My friends celebrated by making me drive them in Finn's truck, never mind how I wasn't supposed to have more than one person unrelated to me riding as passengers.

***

Summer was a blur of driving, drawing, and goofing off with my friends. Naomi and Nathan went away for a week to church camp. Finn worked a lot, sometimes for ten or twelve hour shifts. I spent large swaths of time avoiding my father. I ate literal pounds of take-out or frozen pizza.

Conditioning began in early July, in the mornings or evenings when it wasn't so hot. Coach made us run, commanded endless pushups, squats, and jumping jacks, and reminded us of how if we were well-conditioned, we'd do much better on the first games than other teams because we could stand the late-game heat and exhaustion. Coach C held pads for us to tackle him, and Doc threw water bottles and Gatorade at us. We ran passing plays, usually with Finn as quarterback and Luis as his receiver, Nathan in the center. During running plays, I was a switch, offense or defense. I attempted to memorize the playbook, though I'd never be at Nathan's level of knowledge. I'd settled into a "mostly receiver" or "kind of a tight end" or "sometimes a defensive end" type of role—utilizing speed and footwork. I had the realization that now I was one of the orange-clad boys doing planks on the football field. I wasn't the new kid on the block anymore. I'd fully enmeshed myself with this team. We functioned much smoother than we had last year. When we closed out practices with our hands in the middle, shouting *ready, break, Comets!* I looked across the way and saw the fire in Finn's eyes, driven by his senior year.

School started in August. I'd never been so happy to return.

Katie Gage

JUNIOR YEAR

12

We moved through Junior year as a quintet. Nathan, Luis, Naomi, Finn, and me. Slotting into each other's spaces like pieces of a puzzle. It is so rare to find a friend that understands you well, rarer still to find a best friend who loves you as deeply as you love them. I was lucky enough to find four.

    I loved seeing them be their unfiltered selves. I loved being an essential part of our unit. Mostly, I loved seeing their true selves, the ways they morphed and changed for one another. Perhaps it is the artist in me, to catalog moments and facial expressions and snapshots, remember little details. I always noticed the little things happening, and I saw how we influenced one another. Other people bring out sides of your friends that you never see. Finn was the only one to make Nathan do stupid things, like try to fit an entire bag of gummy worms in his mouth at one time. Luis was the one who brought out Finn's big brother side, the side of him that rumpled hair instead of grinding his knuckles into your scalp. Nathan could make Naomi laugh harder and louder than anyone else.

Naomi brought out everyone's gentler side, I think. Everyone softened themselves for Naomi. I think we were more conscious of the fact that she was a girl, sometimes. It was why we needed her so much. Without her, we were just unkempt and scraggly boys. And with her, we were pushed to be better. Or at least, I was.

I think she was our center. She pulled us together, kept us grounded, made sure we stayed with each other. Without her we probably would have hung out a lot less, been less likely to seek each other out outside of football. Maybe it's a guy thing, to not need to see each other without external reasons. Maybe it's a modern world thing, where we're so caught up in the digital world we forget the real one beside us. Either way, Naomi kept us together and kept us strong. I know I, at least, would have followed her anywhere, and I'm betting the other boys would say the same. And those boys—those boys were my brothers, no doubt about it. But Naomi was special to me. We were a bit like planets, I think, all suspended together in the same solar system; and she was the sun around which we orbited.

***

Our first game of the season was a home game, thank goodness, and it promised to be an easy game. We were in peak condition, and our practices had shown a real growth in our team, a gelling and understanding we'd lacked last year. I was ready for the game, energy zipping through me all day. Focusing in class became impossible. The true purpose of school, to me, was the game. Not class, not grades. Only football.

As always, the crowd packed our tiny bleachers, spilling into the space around the field. The lights burned bright as the sun went down. We sang the anthem, lost the coin toss, and set up for kickoff. I had the honor of kicking it; Luis, Finn, Alejandro, Tate, and Matteo lining up in an unbalanced formation. Four men behind me, one in front. I teed the ball and backed up. I took a deep breath as the sounds of the crowd faded away and my vision narrowed to the ball in front of me. I held up my hand to signal, *wait*. My arm dropped and I sprinted forward. My toe connected with the ball. Heart in my throat, I watched the ball tumble across the ground, clearing the required yardage. They scooped it up, tucked it in, and Alejandro tackled the runner. I breathed a sigh of relief and jogged to the huddle for the play call.

I set up on the outside of the line prepared to chase any runner that got away from the blitz. Fortunately, they tried a passing play, which Finn neatly intercepted and sprinted for a touchdown, spurred on by the wild cheering of the crowd.

I was removed for the PAT, because Coach liked to keep PATs for freshmen and sophomores without much experience.

Our pick-six was an omen for the rest of the game. We racked up points so quickly, the other team didn't even have a chance. It was almost like they were caught off-guard by this new, smooth, gelled team. We'd grown as players and as teammates, and our unity guided our game play. I did not feel constantly two steps behind, still struggling to learn the game. I was part of this team now, part of the dream. I slapped fives with the boys, chest bumped with Finn after a score, and playfully chased Nathan to squirt him with a water bottle at half time. Three minutes into the third quarter we raised our score to 52, enacting the slaughter rule and ending the game. Elated and sweaty, we celebrated in the locker rooms, laughter and cheers echoing off the cinder block walls.

Coach, with an expression on his face that was as close as he ever got to smiling, said, "Good job, boys, let's keep it up for next week," and proceeded to remind us of the mistakes we did make and the things we'd work on in practice come Monday.

Coach Carlson, ever the calm to Coach's storm, said, "You played a great game with good hustle, and we couldn't ask for more." He smiled at us, and we returned it gratefully.

We celebrated a bit more, smacking shoulders and backs good-naturedly. Finn pulled Luis into a headlock to ruffle and mess up the freshly washed hair, laughing all the while.

Finn drove me home, riding high. "Did you see their faces?" he asked. "They didn't know what hit 'em."

"Sure." I agreed, watching his fingers excitedly drumming on the steering wheel.

"I tell ya, between you, me, Luis, and Nathan, this team's going all the way. We've got this in the bag."

"I hope so."

"Gonna be the best team in Texas. For sure."

"Yeah," I said, and a big grin spread across my face.

He jostled my shoulder with one hand, keeping the other wrist draped over the wheel. "Senior year, and I'm going to be the best." He rolled down the window, leaning his head out to holler. "Did you hear that Terrytown? The *best!*" He whooped, probably scaring a few cows. The truck swerved as he waved his arm out the window.

All I could do was laugh.

***

"What're we doing this weekend?" Naomi asked, setting down her lunch tray.

"We're doing something?" Nathan looked bewildered.

"Well, we should do *something*, at least. School's back, your second game is Friday, so we should hang out on Saturday."

"But...homework," I mumbled.

Naomi waved this away like an annoying fly. "Oh, forget homework."

"Gladly. Homework is forgotten," Finn said.

Luis, just now having joined the table, said, "You really should make an effort to do your homework."

"Homework's stupid though," Finn said, smiling at the boy.

"Perhaps a movie?" Naomi asked.

"Homework is important," Luis said, slowly.

"I don't think anything good's showing," Nathan said. "Nothing will until November. Unless you want a scary movie." He made a face.

"Homework is *boring*," Finn rolled his eyes dramatically. "And anyway, after this year, I won't have homework anymore."

"Yeah, yeah, rub it in," Nathan said.

"Yes, you will," Luis said.

"What? Why?" snapped Finn.

Naomi tried to interject again, clearly spotting the impending doom. "Guys, I just want to know—"

"You're going to college, aren't you?" Luis asked, oblivious to the storm brewing in Finn's eyes.

I took a big bite, filling my mouth, so that I would be an innocent bystander for the murder, and not an unwilling accomplice.

"No, Luis, I'm not," Finn said, deathly quiet. "I ain't got the money for that."

Luis shifted his gaze away, letting it trail around the room. "Oh."

"Yeah, *oh*, and I'd appreciate you not rubbing it in." Finn bit into his fries as though they had personally wronged him, but at least he hadn't jumped down Luis' throat.

"Right."

"Actually," Finn said sharply, and I realized I'd been prematurely relieved. "Where do you think you get off? You have all that money, the big house, the fancy car, the work from home mom—you think you're hot shit, don't you?"

Luis, bewildered, started, "I didn't mean—"

"Some of us don't have that! Some of us have a part time job and a mom that works double shifts and it's still not enough! Do you ever think of that? God, rich people make me sick."

"Jesus, Finn, I'm sorry."

Finn stabbed his fry into his ketchup. "Whatever. It's not like it matters anyway."

Silence fell. I shifted on my tailbone. Naomi looked like she might cry, and she swallowed and blinked hard. I looked away.

Nathan cleared his throat. "And anyway, I'm not going either. Me do not have the smarts."

"Shut up, you're plenty smart," Naomi whacked him gently in the bicep.

Luis jumped on the subject change. "You could be a football coach, easy."

"Nah, I think I'd rather go to trade school. But I haven't got to decide now."

"So," I wiped ketchup off the corner of my mouth, trying to redirect, "what are we doing this weekend?"

"We're winning a football game," Finn said, a little sharply. "That's what's important." He swept up his tray, stalking out of the cafeteria and out of sight.

The rest of us finished lunch tense and awkward. I brooded over what Finn had said. Was there any way to help him? Would he even accept help?

Nathan directed his full attention to shoveling fries into his mouth, but Naomi kept up a stream of stiff chatter. "I'm so nervous about auditions. Are you nervous? I'm always worried I'm going to, like, pee my pants or something in the middle even though that would never happen. Or maybe I'm going to puke all down my front."

Luis, biting a homemade empañada nearly in half, spoke with his mouth full. "Don't worry about it. Obviously that won't happen." His voice, in stark contrast in Naomi, remained slow and measured.

Naomi stirred her ketchup with a fry and painted red streaks across her plate. "Totally. It's never going to happen. I don't know why I get so worried. I'm just really stressed. "

"Yeah, you need to relax. Just take a deep breath, go to your happy place, you know?" He tapped his temple and smiled, revealing cilantro caught between his front teeth.

"Right. Totally. It's all in my head. Auditions are no big deal. I don't know why I'm so stressed." She bit her cuticle, examined the damage, and bit it again.

I looked away. My own chest felt tight, and I wondered how Luis didn't notice the tension. I hated seeing Naomi hurt like this. She was so sunny, seeing this anxiety in her made me uncomfortable. I cleared my throat. "Hey, Nathan, over under on the score for Friday?"

Nathan looked up from his meal. "Oh, let me think." He seemed to do some calculations in his head, then started spouting stats. Luis listened, occasionally offering a comment. For a second, things felt normal, and then I looked over at Naomi again, who was pressing the pad of one finger to stop the trickle of blood from the cuticle of the other—apparently she'd bit it too hard.

When the meal was done, we cleared the table. I leaned towards Naomi. "Are you ok?"

"Yes. I mean, not really."

"You're not really that nervous about auditions, are you? You always do great."

She flicked a guilty glance at me. "Caught me. I hate it when Finn is like this. It's about weathering the storm, but...it still hurts, you know?"

"Yeah. Sorry."

"It's not your fault."

I shrugged. "Sorry?"

She laughed, but it was half-hearted. Still, as we threw our trash away she bumped her hip against mine, and wrinkled her nose at me.

***

Even with the sun still hovering over the horizon, casting golden hour glow over the field, the stadium lights blinded me as we left the locker room. The crowd cheered as we took our place, hometown orange blazing strong. I spotted a grandmotherly figure with a bowl in her lap, shelling peas. A little girl with pigtails imitated the waving of the cheerleaders: hip out, wrist fluid, making sassy faces. The Petersons stood together, Naomi's hands cupped around her mouth as she yelled. Home game season opener? The pressure was on to put on a good show and have a good win.

We stood for the anthem and the coin toss, which we won. We started on offense, and Coach sent in what is his—in my humble opinion—best lineup. Diamond formation: Nathan as the center, Luis on the left, me on the right on the line with Finn as the point of the diamond, flanked by Alejandro—a big boy, constantly on the verge of knocking his opponent over in blocking drills—and Tate, a junior with speedy cuts.

We did not disappoint. I watched the snap sail through the air, caught by Tate, who pitched to Finn. I ran, looking back, dodging the grasping hands in front of me.

"I'm open, I'm open!" He didn't see me. Tate was covered up.

Finn scrambled in the pocket, scanning the field. He danced a minute longer, then tucked and ran.

He gained five yards. Ten.

First down.

Lining up again, Tate swapped out with Matteo.

Again, Finn danced away from the defender, winding up for the throw.

The football sailed across the perfect blue September sky. Sunk into Luis' waiting hands.

Another first down.

"Keep it up, boys," Coach Carlson called to the huddle.

We were on the twenty now, in the red zone. Tate ran back in with the play. We broke the huddle as one.

"Break!" *Clap.*

My blood thrummed within me. We were so close to a touchdown I could taste it. Could imagine the cheers of the crowd, see Naomi's smile. I vibrated, coiled like a spring.

The play started, a flag flew, blown dead. Alejandro smacked himself on the forehead of his helmet, his false start backing us up.

"Shake it off," I muttered, slapping him on the back.

He gave a nod.

We lined up again. *This time*, I thought, *I can feel it.*

The ball snapped.

We moved, grunting as our cleats dug in.

I was open—I looked back—I saw the ball—

Smack. Right into my arms.

I tucked it to me and *ran,* ran for my life, for my team. Dodged one man. Hands were on my shoulder, but my feet were almost there. I *reached, stretched,* fell over the goal line.

The whistles blew, and the play was over.

I leapt to my feet, yelling. I tossed the ball to the ref just as Finn threw himself at me in a clatter of pads. Nathan slapped the top of my helmet and Luis slapped my butt, even as we jogged for the sidelines. The rest of the boys offered me high-fives and knuckle-bumps. Alejandro's little brother handed me a squeezable water bottle, which I took and emptied into my mouth.

The PAT started on the field and I watched long enough to be certain we made the point before chugging more water. Coach Carlson held his hand out to me. "Good play, son."

I slapped it. "Thanks, Coach."

I looked to the stands, wishing briefly that my own father could have seen it. But Naomi saw, and the Petersons saw, and my teammates saw, and my Coach saw. Perhaps that's all that matters.

We won the game, with Luis scoring twice and Finn once, on top of my own touchdown. The other team put up a fight, but it was not meant to be. We were simply the superior team, and it showed. And I know, I know, I'm arrogant, I'm a teenage boy with too much testosterone, but sometimes the facts are facts. And the facts were: we were better and the rest of the world could effing suck it.

After the game I saw Coach Carlson and his wife again, saw how he gave her a hug. A quick one, just a wrapping of arms around her middle, her squeezing around his back as response, and then they parted.

I froze in the parking lot halfway to Finn's truck, skateboard tucked under my arm, a voyeur to their sweet, casual moment. He opened the door for her as she stepped in, and he closed it with a quiet thump. It wasn't a thing of significance. It was a quiet moment, and I stole it for myself.

"Zed!" Finn yelled, irritated, spreading his arms as if to say, *what's the hold up?*

I shook the cobwebs from my brain and jogged over.

"Hurry up and get in, will ya?" He cranked the engine, throwing an arm behind my seat to back out. "Geez, did you see Camilla tonight? That *ass,* bro. I bet I could have some fun with that."

I hummed noncommittally in response. He cast a glance at me from the corner of his eye, then snapped his focus back to the asphalt. For a moment, I wondered if I saw shame in his gaze, and the way he didn't meet my eyes. I'd never say something like that about Naomi. Then again, I could hardly say anything about Naomi at all.

***

"Did you see there's a coffee shop opening?" Naomi asked me.

"Where?"

Naomi slammed her locker shut, holding a book to her chest. "Across from the Dollar General. In that old brick building; used to be a diner."

"Bro, I totally thought that place was haunted."

"Well, apparently not. Supposed to open in a couple weeks."

"Huh. Do you think it'll last?" I swept aside crumpled papers to grab a notebook.

"If it's any good. You know how many high schoolers pass through there on the way to class? If they make a good latte, they could make *bank*."

"Hm." I shut my own locker, tapping my nails on the green metal. "You doing anything this evening? Wanna hang out?"

"Youth group. I gotta run, I have rehearsal." Halfway down the hallway, she called back, "You're always welcome to come!"

I waved at her retreating form, with no intention of ever going to youth group ever. I was, however, thinking about the new coffee shop.

I'd thought about trying to get a job in passing, mildly enticed by the thought of having my own money. The problem was I didn't have my own car and I knew my father would never allow me to use his. The additional problem was most of the high-school appropriate jobs in this town were already taken: somebody always had a sibling or cousin or best friend's brother's second cousin twice removed who could really use the job, so they were filled almost before the position opened. The remaining kids got jobs in Big Spring (again, the car problem), or didn't get jobs at all.

I skated home after practice, waving off Finn's offer to drive me, telling him to worry about his sisters and I'd take care of myself. Not quite fully autumn, the air hovered between comfortably warm and the first threat of chilly. I skated through town, past the Dollar General and the hardware store, to the old brick building. The brick was darker where the "Mama D's" sign used to be.

I skidded to a stop, kicking my board up to hold one end.

Above the door, a cheap banner read "Coming Soon!" Taped to the double glass door was a piece of printer paper. On it was written in blue sharpie: CUP OF JOE'S GRAND OPENNING IN OCTOBER. I grimaced at the misspelling. Cupping my hands around my eyes, I peered into the dark ex-diner, spotting drop cloths, paint trays, piles of remodeling dust, and a single folding chair. An old man walked in from the back, wiping his hands on a rag. Ah. He'd made the sign, and must have misspelled it. It seemed like my grandparents, or old people on social media, always had some sort of typo or something going on.

I backed away, considering. It'd be best to leave. There's no way he'd want me, an inexperienced kid who was more likely to be a drain on his resources rather than a help.

The glass door swung open before I could make a decision. "Can I help you?" he asked. He peered at me through his thick glasses, his eyes distorted by their lens. A farmer's cap with a mesh back sat high on his head, and he wore navy blue coveralls spattered with white paint.

"Uh—are you hiring?" I blurted. I still wasn't sure this was a good idea, and this guy looked so old. I didn't think he'd see much value in hiring me, especially with the disparity in our ages. Was it even worth taking this chance?

"Nope, but that shouldn't stop someone with good, old-fashioned grit and determination! Come on in!" He stepped aside to let me pass.

I followed him in, and he set up another folding chair, motioning for me to sit. "Good to see the youngsters of today still see the value in hitting the streets and knocking on doors!"

I resisted the urge to roll my eyes.

He took a seat, bracing his hands on his knees and lowering himself slowly, letting out a grunt. He asked for my name, and then asked, "So, you want a job?"

"I'm thinking about it." Truthfully, I wasn't sure, and the absolute boomer vibes this man was giving off made me rethink it.

"Oh, no, there's no thinking about it, boy, you have to know what you want, and reach out and take it! Let's try that again. Do you want a job?"

"Ah. Um. Yes?"

"Hmm. Do you have a resume?"

"Uh, no. I've never had a job."

He looked at me a little closer, squinting through his glasses. "How old are you, boy?"

"Sixteen."

"The perfect age for getting your first job, then. Why do you want this job?"

"It's close to my house and school, and I don't need a car to get here."

He shook his head. "You're absolutely botching this interview. If you were at corporate, they'd kick you out." He heaved a sigh. "Do you want to make coffee?"

"I guess." I could hear my dad grousing, *speak to me with respect!*, but this guy didn't say anything.

"Do you want to make money?"

"Yes." This for sure, I knew.

"What hours can you work?"

"After practice, and on weekends. I can even work Sundays."

"That's the Lord's day, we won't be open anyway." He shook his head. "But that's what this country's come to, lost all respect for our roots and our Lord." Still shaking his head again, he gazed into the middle distance for a moment.

I cleared my throat, wondering if perhaps he'd forgotten I was there. "I do have football on Fridays."

"Ah, a Terrytown Comet, are you?" A smile grew on his face.

"Yes, sir."

"I used to be one myself, back when I was young and strapping." He leaned back, slapping himself on the chest.

I forced a chuckle.

"I'll have to think about it, but I'll let you know. We could use some youngsters on the staff."

"Are you doing this all by yourself?" I snuck a look at the renovation detritus.

"No, no, my granddaughter, she's helping me, but she can't be here all the time. Got kids, y'know."

"Oh."

"Yep. She's the real hero here." He seemed about to stare into the distance again, so I stood hastily.

"Thank you for your time, Mr..."

He grinned, his face dissolving into a thousand wrinkles behind his glasses. "Joe. Like the sign says? Cup of Joe's! Like a cup of Joe! See, old people can still be funny!" He frowned at my silence. "Joe? Like coffee, like the name?"

"Oh. Haha."

"Hmmm. Well, there's no accounting for no sense of humor. I'll see you around...Zed." He felt his way around my name like it was foreign. Perhaps to him it was.

I saw myself out, retrieving my board from where I'd stashed it against the wall. Old people are so weird.

13

We played our first away game three hours away, which is not unusual for six man teams. There's not that many schools that play it, so we're pretty spread out by the nature of the schools that participate. Anyway, the football team skipped half of their Friday classes to go to the game. I'll tell you, being a student athlete is no joke. We'd have makeup work, not to mention our regular homework. But, we suffered through our noisy, bumpy bus ride, and got to a field in poor condition, with no locker rooms. So we shuffled into the bathroom, changing in there, modesty be damned.

Our opponents were King's Hill, their mascot a cartoon knight with a flag flying behind him. And across the field, I could see that they had twice as many players and at least a hundred pounds on each of us.

"High knees boys, let's go!" Coach called as we started our warm-ups.

Just before the game began, I cast a look to the stands, but couldn't find Naomi among the sea of faces. A bit downhearted, I turned my focus to the game.

Right from the get-go we were at a disadvantage; we fought like hell but were unable to compensate our manpower for their size. The one area we had them was speed. Between Finn and Luis, we had the two fastest players on the field, which was sometimes enough to make or break a game. I wasn't exactly slow myself.

At the end of the first quarter, they had scored twenty-one; we sat at a big, fat goose egg. In six man though, three touchdowns is nothing. Three touchdowns is five minutes and seventeen seconds. Heck, I've seen it happen in a minute and a half.

Nathan looked a bit drained as we set up for the second quarter, pulling off his helmet to rub his neck and roll his shoulders.

Hoping to lift his spirits, I patted him on the shoulder.

He gave me a tired nod and drained his water bottle.

I was benched for our next offensive drive, standing just over Coach's elbow. Beside him, Coach Carlson stood with hands on hips, watching King's Hill's players. Trying to guess their strategy, I'd assume.

I watched Nathan snap, then immediately crumple to the ground, driven down by the force of their defense back putting a hand in his back and shoving, then sitting on him.

"Nathan," I breathed.

Coach yanked me down to ear level by the horsecollar of my pads, giving me the play. I sprinted for the huddle.

"V-spread, thirty cross."

Standing in the backfield, I had a good view of what happened next. Though I started running as soon as the ball snapped, I saw the defense back reach over, grab the back of Nathan's shoulder pads, and drive him face-first into the ground. I missed what happened next because a defender slammed into me, knocking me back with enough force to drain the air from my lungs.

In the huddle, Nathan rotated and popped his jaw, adjusting his mouthguard.

"You good?" I wheezed.

"Yeah, just getting slammed."

"They didn't give you enough time to get up."

He shook his head.

"Damn," I mumbled. There'd been no call on the play, or any play previous. By rules, Nathan should get at least one full second—longer than you think in a football game—to get up from the snap and defend himself. But these guys were jumping down his throat right after the snap, nearly in the middle of it.

By halftime, we were down by two touchdowns, a gap that began to feel insurmountable, especially with the special treatment Nathan was getting. They kept sitting on him, or belly flopping on top of him. Or just shoving his face in the dirt and leaning their weight on him for a minute, watching the play, and using his back to shove off and run, leaving Nathan to flounder face-down in the dirt.

Coach gave us a new strategy, one that relied heavily on Finn's ability to scramble and our general speed.

Nathan lay back on the grass, eyes closed.

I gave him a worried look, but returned focus to Coach. He bit off his words, grumping through the talk. He gave us very little encouragement.

Coach Carlson, too, had a crease between his eyes and kept casting worried looks at Nathan.

We stood for the breakdown, putting hands in the middle.

"This game isn't over yet," Finn said. "Keep your heads up. Who are we?"

"Comets!"

"Who are we?"

"COMETS!"

"Who are we?"

"Comets!"

"Ready? Break!"

"Comets!"

We filed to the sidelines once again. Nathan moved through the team, patting shoulders and offering encouragement.

Then we were back at it again.

As soon as the ball left his fingers, the player slammed Nathan's face into the field, over and over. A hand on his back, or just straight up plowing him down like a train. As Coach called a timeout, I jogged to the sidelines where Coach Carlson was storming toward an official.

"Mr. Official," he said, angrier than I'd heard him. "Mr. Official, how do I make sure those boys give my center one second? One second from the snap! Just a moment to stand up, *please!*" He punctuated this statement by slapping his palm with the back of his hand.

The referee frowned, turning his back to the crowd and forcing Coach Carlson to turn. "Well, I don't know Coach, but I know you need to let me do my job and I'll let you do yours."

Coach Carlson frowned, irritated eyebrows furrowing behind his glasses. He stepped away, chin held high.

Coach gave the play, punctuating his statements with jerky arm movements.

We broke the timeout huddle with, "Ready? Break. Comets!" and I saw Coach Carlson grab Alejandro by the shoulder, bending to whisper in his ear. Alejandro nodded, once, sharp. And then we were on the line again.

Thanks to my diamond position, I got a front-row seat to the way Nathan was once again pushed to the ground.

Alejandro stormed in, grabbed the player by the shoulder pads and knocked him clean to the ground, cleats kicking up clumps of grass. Alejandro laid him out and stood over him for a moment.

The message was received loud and clear. *You mess with one of us, you mess with all of us.*

After the game, Nathan never mentioned it, unless we prompted him to tell the story, which he'd then explain, beleaguered, how he'd spent half the game with his nose in the dirt. He shakes off any animosity toward them, explaining they'd simply played to win.

We lost that game, in part because of the referees, who missed several other calls like Nathan's, but also because the sheer size of their team dwarfed us. I may be biased but, despite the strength differences, if the refs had been better, I think we might have won.

We circled up, tired bodies drooping.

Finn stood by me, tension rolling off him. "Damn refs," he muttered. "Screwed us over, that's for sure and certain."

Luis shrugged, squirting some water in his mouth from a squeeze bottle. "Happens sometimes. Losing is part of the game."

Finn gave him the stink-eye, then snatched the water bottle and squeezed quickly so it sprayed all over Luis' face and neck. Luis coughed, making to snack the bottle back while Finn laughed.

"*Gentlemen,*" Coach C said in warning, and the boys stilled. He launched into the post-game speech.

Coach remained mostly silent, though he tossed out a few grumpy remarks. He refrained from throwing his hat to the ground, though he fingered the brim several times.

"Gentlemen," Coach Carlson said, "We win some, we lose some. And that's the way it goes."

We nodded, mumbling in agreement.

"I am proud of your tenacity. I am proud of your perseverance. And I hope to be proud of you for losing with grace."

Finn made a quiet sound in his throat, rolling his eyes. I punched him in the shoulder.

"Keep your chins up," Coach finished. "Let's pray."

The team bowed their heads, but I kept my eyes open, taking in our bruised arms, our tired muscles, our dirty uniforms. We'd done our best, I knew. And the refs had messed us up, probably. I tamped down on that flare of anger. Coach C said to lose with grace. And Coach C, even in his anger, has still spoken to the ref like a person. We were all just doing our jobs.

As we cleaned up, I asked Coach Carlson, "Hey, Coach, why didn't the ref's call the no-wait thing?"

"Probably didn't know about it. We're scraping the bottom of the barrel." He sounded tired and resigned.

I emptied a water bottle over my head, shaking the drops free like a dog. "You don't have a problem with the calls most days."

"It's like this." He stacked his fingers like a bulleted list, holding his hand on its side. "Pro refs. College refs. 6A UIL refs. All the high school games—and then six man. At the bottom. They don't know the rules, they don't want to be here, and we can't pay them enough. So we take what we can get."

I nodded. "You get what you get and you don't throw a fit," I said, quoting what my mother used to say to me as a child.

"Absolutely." He patted me on the shoulder. "You played a good game, Zed."

"Thanks, Coach."

"Hey, anytime you want to come to dinner, you're always welcome."

I nodded, touched. "Thanks, Coach."

On the bus, Finn kicked at the seat in front of him, grumbling to himself.

"Better luck next week," I said.

He scoffed. "Right. Maybe next week nobody will've paid the refs off. And maybe Nathan won't get his face ground in the sand."

"Hey," I said, "don't be like that."

He growled, "We lost."

I retreated from his angry gaze. "Whatever."

He continued kicking at the seat and floor, swearing to himself.

***

Football and homework, that was my life. With the occasional spatterings of hanging out with friends, admiring Naomi privately, and passing my dad in the house every day with stilted acknowledgment. We were nearing fall, though the days still peaked warm and nearly sweltering. It all felt the same beneath my hot, heavy, football pads.

At our next home game, when I scored, I looked to the stands to spot Naomi, cheering and waving her arms. Beside her, her parents whooped and clapped, but it was her I looked for and beamed my affection at, pretending I was telepathic. She pumped her fist in the air, bouncing up and down. And then Finn tackled me, and all I could see were the blinding lights and goalposts above me.

We won, of course, another notch in our belts.

As I trudged from the locker room afterward, still a bit damp from the shower, someone flagged me down.

"Hey, Zed! Young man!"

I turned, spotting an old man coming my way. It took me a moment to place him, since he wasn't in coveralls anymore, but then I remembered the awkward conversation in the half-finished coffee shop. "Howdy." The word, country in nature, came out of my own mouth and threw me off guard. It wasn't something I'd said in Houston. Guess this little town had already started to rub off on me.

"You still want to work for me?"

"Yes, sir."

"Good. You start next weekend."

I blurted, "What? I mean, sir?"

"Well, you want to work, don't you?"

"Yes, but I don't understand—"

"I've hired you!" He spread his arms, grinning like he'd told me I won the lottery.

"Oh. Thank you!" Much like signing up for football, I wasn't sure I'd meant to get into this mess, but I was in it now. I pasted a grin on my face.

He scoffed. "I'll see you a week from tomorrow, then?"

"Uh, yes, sir."

He turned away, muttered something that sounded like, "Kids these days."

So. I had a job. My world got a little bit bigger, and I got a little bit richer.

***

Our next week was a bye week, so no game, but that didn't mean we could stop practicing. In fact, we earned extra practice as a reward. We ran plays, did drills, conditioned until our muscles quivered.

Coach Carlson told us we were playing the "Bye Week Lazies," and laughed about it with Coach and Doc. Such a dad joke.

So Friday night we all went out and had dinner together, except it was just Whataburger, because that's the only restaurant in town. And our parents—and by our parents I mean specifically the Petersons—didn't want us driving too far for dinner. So we got Whataburger.

Luis beelined for the corner circle booth, and I followed close on Naomi's heels to squeeze in beside her. Our knees bumped under the table, jolting electricity through me. Naomi was focused on Luis' story, laughing as he meandered his way to the point. The other boys slid in on the other side, completing our little circle that huddled over the table.

Nathan and Finn kept up a debate about Batman, something about villains and actors. Meanwhile, Naomi and Luis were talking about some Broadway show I'd never seen. I kept one ear on the Batman stuff–Christian Bale was totally the best Batman–and one ear attuned to Naomi–I was certain Naomi was correct and *Natasha, Pierre, and the Great Comet of 1812* was a totally underrated musical, even though I'd never heard of it. Food arrived, to a chorus of "Yessss!" and "Duuude, this is the best!"

Finn unwrapped his burger and took a bite, sticky sauce dripping from the corner of his mouth. "Dude, you ever had a honey butter chicken biscuit?"

"Uh, no?" I responded.

"Bro, it's the best. We *have* to get one. It'll change your life."

"Doesn't that only come available after, like, midnight?" Nathan asked.

"Eleven. We *have* to get one."

"We have curfew," Naomi said reluctantly.

"Pfft." Finn waved it off. "Curfew Shmerfew. Ask forgiveness, not permission."

"Um, not if you ever want us to come out with you again," Nathan said.

"Ughhhh, rules are the worst. Why's your family so boring?"

"Um, excuse me, you're hanging out with half my family right now," Naomi said, gesturing between herself and Nathan.

Finn ignored her in favor of lavishing attention on his burger instead. "Families are annoying," he garbled.

"But also, like, I feel like we're kind of a family," she went on. "Like, friends that became family."

"Awwww," Luis crooned, spitting a little bit of lettuce onto the table. "That's like, so sweet. I love that."

Nathan made a face and tossed a napkin over the chewed-up lettuce.

"Nuh-uh, case in point, families are annoying," Finn repeated.

I nudged her knee with my own, causing her to look at me with a smile. "I like it. We're a little family."

Her brilliant, sunshine grin flashed at me.

"Getting all gross and sappy over here," Finn said loudly.

"I feel like we could all go on an adventure and take over the world," said Nathan.

"Like Lord of the Rings or something," I said.

"Yeah, exactly. Go fight some dragons, kiss a pretty girl."

Unbidden, the thought of kissing Naomi ran circles in my mind. I imagined looking in her eyes just before, the way our lips would meet. Would she want to kiss me, too? I shifted in my seat, attempting to beat back the invasive thoughts.

"Hell yeah to that," Finn said, raising his Styrofoam cup in salute before slurping loudly.

"Look guys," Luis burst out. He had two French fries dangling from under his upper lip. "I'm a walrus!"

We all laughed even though it really wasn't *that* funny. It was always like that with us, silly and carefree, full of good feelings and love.

I caught Naomi typing something on her phone and smiling before tucking it back into her pocket.

I bumped her with my elbow and raised my brows at her.

"Lyrics," she answered.

"Can I see them?"

"No, they're not fit for human consumption yet! But maybe someday. Sometime you can come over and I'll play for you, okay?"

"Yeah, okay," I agreed, gathering up that little invitation and tucking it away somewhere safe. Sometimes I wanted to tell her how much she meant to me. But always, I didn't, for fear of losing what we had.

***

My phone alarm jolted me from sleep. We'd stayed out late to get a honey butter chicken biscuit, and it had been good, though not life changing (like mangonadas were; Luis had been right about that). For a minute I thought it was time for school, then remembered it was Saturday, then remembered again that I was supposed to have my first day of work. I flopped back on my pillow, groaning and rubbing my eyes.

The birds chirped as I left the house, locking the front door behind me and skating down the street. I hunched in my hoodie. Who knew how today would go? If I would even like the job and put up with Joe, or if he'd decide I was too inept at coffee to even consider having me back.

The front door of the shop was locked, so I peered in and knocked on the glass. When Joe opened the door the smell of new paint wafted out to me.

"Come on in!" Joe said, his face all wrinkles with his smile.

He showed me around, pointing out the different machines to me. "The drip coffee will sell with us old fellers like me. We're simple, just like the machine. Water, coffee, power." He indicated each item on the machine as he said it. "Your lattes, that'll work well for the younger folks and the youths like yourself. My granddaughter likes lattes." He showed me the espresso machine and tapped the steamer spout. "Espresso's in a bunch of stuff." He pointed to an index card taped to the counter with different drinks and their ratios written out, like "americano 2/3 hot water 1/3 milk." Joe tapped what he called a chemex, which looked like a large hourglass with an open top. "This is for pour overs, and once I get the rest of this figured out, we'll do some cold brew." I only knew two things he'd mentioned—the regular coffee pot and a latte. But I'm a fast learner, I knew I could grasp it.

The snack counter was simple—muffins, brownies, and bagels. "I'm hoping to get some breakfast tacos figured out, too, but we're not there yet. And maybe some scones. Oh—the tea." He pointed to a row of mason jars labeled with little chalk signs: chamomile, earl gray, and English black. "Tea's here and the steep times are listed. I'm not sure why we need it—I think there's a reason we dumped it all in the harbor—but my granddaughter says we need it."

I spotted the index card with the steep times. "Do you really like coffee? Like, different brew methods and stuff?"

"Me? No, just black. But I like people. I wanted a place where people could get together, spend time together. And a coffee shop seemed just the way!" His face spread into that wrinkly smile again. "We can host board game nights, family events, and a place for us to go to read the morning paper. Shoot, by the time me and my buddies get through jawing in the mornings, we can solve half the world's problems before lunch." He gave me a grin. "What about you, boy, you like coffee?"

I nodded. "I don't know much about making it, though."

"Well, I've learned a whole bunch. Got my food handler's certification and everything. You'll need that, too." He slapped me on the shoulder. "For now, let's start with some basics."

We spent time making different types of espresso drinks, boiling water in the fancy teapot with the thermometer in the handle, and setting up loose leaf tea to steep and strain without leaves leaking into the brew. I learned how to grind the beans, pack the espresso, steam the milk, and where to dispose of the coffee puck after brewing. But my favorite by far was making lattes. I was already attempting latte art after the first cup. The first attempt came out sort of lumpy and weird, so naturally I sent a picture to the group and captioned it: *Me after getting tackled*.

I promised myself I'd get better. It was art, but a new medium. And making art at work couldn't be the worst first job to have.

Joe sampled my drinks and gave his stamp of approval. When his granddaughter stopped by that afternoon, she told me there was a "perfectly balanced blend of flavor" in my latte, and I was proud of it.

Maybe this job would be a good thing after all.

14

As always with away games, we rode the smelly, bumpy, grimy bus, and spent three hours pestering each other over seat backs to thwart attempts at homework.

The team we were playing was a Fort Worth private school, and as we rolled up, our players whistled through their teeth as they observed the buildings of the private school. Our entire school consisted of maybe two buildings plus the gym and the football field. This school had multiple buildings, sports fields, and a whole locker room just for us. After weeks of bathrooms and bus-as-a-changing-room protocol, this was practically heaven. Gray concrete floors, sleek blue lockers, bathroom stalls and showers with proper water pressure.

We jogged onto the field to see the biggest team I'd ever laid eyes on in the six man arena. There were at least twenty-five of them, more than enough for an eleven-man team.

"Bro, why do they have so many players?" I asked Nathan. "Seems a little disproportionate."

Finn, eavesdropping, whistled. "Whew, that's a four-dollar word."

"Shut up," I countered easily.

Nathan shrugged. "Could be they've recently expanded." He glanced over at Coach Carlson and lowered his voice. "Word is, most of these kids have been expelled from other schools, so now they're here."

"Damn," Finn muttered. "Wish I got that treatment instead of just sitting in the principal's office."

Nathan shot him a worried glance, adjusting his gloves. "You good, bro?"

"Grades," Finn said in disgust in his tone.

"What about them?" Luis sauntered up to join us.

"None of your beeswax," Finn snapped. "None of y'all's."

"I didn't say anything," I protested.

"Boys!" Coach snapped. "Warm-ups, let's go!"

Despite the nice facilities, there were no bleachers, so our families and friends sat in yard chairs and on blankets while the and band had to cluster on the sidelines. Fortunately it was still early enough in the season (for Texas anyway) that the weather was still warm, but the setting sun would send cool shadows over the field and spectators.

"Alright boys," Coach Carlson said in the huddle. "Them boys is big and them boys is plenty, but you've got determination and you've got hustle. Don't throw away the game before it's even begun, y'hear?"

"Yes, Coach," we chorused.

Coach laid out the game plan, which included me on the starting line. We won the coin toss, elected to receive. I stood, my heart in my throat, as the kickoff went. I watched the burnished brown ball roll down the field, crossing white lines and trailing through the grass, until Finn's hands scooped it up, and I then exhaled, my heartbeat quieting. I jogged onto the field, my world narrowing to the ball, the play, my team. My boys.

Coach Carlson was right: them boys *was* big and them boys *was* plenty. Seemed like every time I turned around they were subbing in a new player, keeping them fresh. They hit hard, continually leaving us gasping for air and rubbing newly sore muscles. They pulled ahead by the end of the first half, leaving us trailing by three scores. But we weren't done yet. By halftime we were worn pretty thin, but we retreated to the beautiful locker room to listen to Coach talk new strategies, trick plays, and new formations.

I looked around. Nathan's hair was plastered to his forehead with sweat, and Finn's head hung between his shoulders, elbows propped on his knees. He flicked his eyes over to me, and I saw the hard glint of determination, and that anger that fueled him through every game. Luis looked a little more relaxed, but I'd hardly ever seen him anything less than completely suave, cool as a watermelon on a Texas afternoon.

After the half, we lined up for the offensive drive. That's when everything went to shit.

As we lined up, a particularly big kid set up directly in front of Nathan, grinning through his mouth guard, sporting a crooked nose.

Nathan snapped. I started running, but as I took off, I saw Nathan take air and fly backwards, his feet fully off the ground before he landed full force on his back. I cast a look over my shoulder and spotted him stirring for just a second, leaning forward, then collapse back to the earth.

I did not know how many yards we gained. I did not care. The minute the play ended I sprinted back toward him. Coach knelt over Nathan along with a ref, squatting with his hands on his knees. Matteo took a knee nearby, and I immediately followed, halting my sprint about three yards away.

The rest of our team dropped to the ground also, just like the pros. In the crowd, Naomi leaned halfway out of her seat, hands over her mouth, and I spotted her parents were already standing on the out of bounds line. His mother's hands pressed to her lips, face drained of blood.

The big kid who started the whole thing leaned into his buddy, jostling shoulders. The sound of their laughter, low and stupid, drifted to me. The bully pulled off his helmet, grinning like the cat that got the canary. I gritted my jaw and squeezed my eyes shut to block out their smug faces.

Beside me, Tate grumbled, "I saw him. Stuck his hand under the facemask and grabbed him to throw him back. Dirty cheater."

Should we even be surprised?

And out of everyone, why did it have to be *him*? A concussion–every footballer's worst fear–can knock you out of play for several games, possibly leave you with life-long problems with memory or vision or processing. And this, this is the worst it could be—

Because it's Nathan, it's *Nathan*—

"Mother*fucker!*" and that was Finn charging from wherever he'd ended up after the play, slamming his helmet down as he went.

"Finn—*Finn!*" I shouted, jumping up and sprinting after him, trying to intercept him before he did something stupid.

He got in one good punch to the jaw on the kid before I grabbed at his horse collar, yanking him back. The other kid grabbed a fistful of Finn's jersey, landing a solid gut punch. Finn grunted, pained, kicking and snarling as I dragged him back.

A ref waved his arms frantically, blowing incessantly on the whistle.

Coach Carlson appeared suddenly, wrapping up Finn's arms and throwing him off of me the same time the other team's coach was grabbing at his player.

"Stop it!" Coach Carlson shouted. "You should be ashamed of yourself! I am ashamed of you!"

Finn ducked his head like a kicked dog, lips still curled, but his expression was slipping from anger into frustration, or maybe shame. I walked with him back to the sidelines, and time slowed down again.

Finn knelt behind the rest of us and I stayed by him, my hand on his shoulder pads. He got ejected from the game, of course. So did the other guy.

Moments passed as I chewed nervously on my mouthguard, gaze glued to Nathan's still form on the ground, Doc gently talking to him. Finally, *finally* Nathan slowly rose, supported by Doc and Coach. He walked to the sidelines, slowly, and applause sounded from the team and crowd. He sat on the bench, head between his shoulders, elbows on knees, and I could tell he was done for the game.

Shit.

Finn jerked in his direction, but aborted the move, shooting a questioning glance at me. I shook my head. Better wait.

Coach Carlson strode over, speaking quietly to Finn. "You wait back here, son, I don't want Coach to see you right now."

Finn nodded. "Is he going to be okay, Coach?"

"Minor concussion. He'll be fine." He looked directly into Finn' eyes, serious now. "Finn. I can't have you doing that. I need you, son. I need you this season. When the going gets rough, I need to know I can count on you, and not have you losing your head every time someone makes you mad."

"Coach, it was Nathan, I—"

Coach Carlson held up a hand, stopping him. "I can't have you getting thrown out cause you can't keep your head on straight, at all, period. *I need you.*"

It was at this moment that I chose to back away, knowing what was happening was a private moment. This man, so kind, stood towering over my friend, who was bowing his chest out like he was actually going to fight Coach C. There were things at play here that I could sense but couldn't name. Things about manliness, and right behavior, and fatherhood. Things I wouldn't understand for a long time.

We lost the game eventually, not that it mattered to me in the grand scheme of things. I only cared about Nathan and Finn. Nathan got examined by the EMTs on-site and was let go after being told to go on concussion protocol. Finn paced the sidelines the whole game, keeping his hang-dog look and drooping shoulders.

Afterward, our battered and beaten crew trudged through the motions of cleaning up, rinsing away the grime from falling, trying to wash off the sting of losing. An ugly purple bruise had begun to form on my bicep. I didn't remember how I got it.

Our little caravan of cars and the bus headed home. Nathan chose to ride in his family's quieter, less bumpy car. Naomi texted our group chat with updates. *Head hurts, but not nauseous or dizzy. Just wants to take a nap.*

The rest of us, sitting near each other on the bus, texted back things like, *tell him to feel better.*

Other boys on the team hollered out messages to send as well. *Tell him he flew at least four feet! Tell him to rest up. Tell him to stay away from the light at the end of the tunnel.*

Yo, you better get better or else. We ain't got another snapper. (That was Finn.)

The dude that hit you was so ugly, his momma don't even like his face.

You know who likes my face? Your momma.

And so on.

Back in Terrytown, Finn drove me home, still grumbling about the reffing and the hard hits and everything.

"Just ain't fair. We're scraping the bottom of the barrel for refs, and they hang us out to dry. If they'd jumped on that kind of holding and roughness—"

"Finn," I finally broke in, "Shut up." I hoped he'd switch his mind over to more positive topics, or get out of his own head.

Instead, he sighed, deflating, tapping his fingers on the wheel.

"You gotta work tomorrow?"

"Yeah." He grunted. "You know, I can't imagine something like that happening to me."

"Oh?"

"Yeah. Be out for a few games? That'd kill me."

"Why?"

He looked at me, eyes sharp, hair falling over his forehead. He said, heavy and intense, "Because football is everything to me. *Everything.*" We drove a little longer before he glanced over at me. "Want to take a drive?"

"A drive?"

"Yeah. A drive." He passed right by the turn to my neighborhood and kept going. "Buckle up, city boy, I'm going to show you some real country entertainment."

We sped into the darkness, the headlights illuminating the white lines and yellow dashes, fences lining the road, cows lingering in the fields. We drove into the wilderness, turned, drove past more cows and barns and oil derricks, and back again. We took a big loop around Terrytown before Finn finally turned off the road and drove into a field, through an open gate.

"Are we trespassing?"

"Nah. He knows my mom. We'll be fine."

In the middle of the field, Finn turned off the truck and killed the lights, scrambling out of the truck and into the bed. Tipping back to look at the sky, he threw his arms wide and shouted, "Hello world! It's Finn! And someday, you'll all know my name!"

Laughing, I climbed into the bed after him. "You think they heard you?"

"Heard me? How could they miss me?" He climbed onto the roof of the truck, laughing all the while. "You hear me? One day you'll know me, and you'll think I'm the greatest man who ever lived!"

In the distance, a solitary cow mooed.

"Sure made your point to the cows," I commented drily.

Finn scoffed. "Cows? I'm just getting started! Wait until I talk to the chickens."

I laughed along with him.

Still atop the roof, he looked down at me, a manic gleam in his eye. "Someday, Zed, I'll get out of this dead-end town. I'll get out of here, and make it big somewhere else, and I'll say, *hey, I'm so much better than where I came from, and I can only go up from here.*" Growing louder, he directed his words to the pasture at large. "And everyone who ever said my father was a loser, and that I ain't gonna amount to shit, is gonna eat their words, and beg for my forgiveness! But I won't forget what they said, oh no, I ain't never gonna forget or forgive or give them *nothing*." He flipped the bird in the general direction of Terrytown, and completed his show with an angry flailing of his wiry arms. He spit on the ground. "C'mon, Zed. Let's get out of here." He jumped straight to the grass, landing lightly on his toes.

Not understanding his sudden change of mood, I climbed silently into the truck, and remained silent all the way home, even as he rambled about Camilla Johnson and her short skirts, Mrs. Murray and her unfair grades, and his boss and coworkers who never did their jobs. How the whole world was against him. How he'd prove himself. When we pulled into my driveway, I got out slowly, still thinking of him in the field, his arms flung wide, the manic look in his eye. Desperate, almost.

I felt his pain. My own father was a loser. My own life didn't amount to much. I didn't even know what I'd do after school. Finn and I–we were the same, tethered by the bonds of our families and our pain. Both of us dropped here in this dead-end town, with only our friends beside us and a game to sustain us.

If I'd had the right words to say, perhaps I would have said them, but I simply got out of the truck, and shut the door quietly behind me.

Finn rolled down his window to yell after me, "That was some fight today, huh? I whooped his ass real good."

"Sure," I said, half-hearted.

"Please. I was great! Fantastic, even. Should have seen the look on that idiot's face."

"You shouldn't have done it, Finn." I turned back to look at him, thumbing my house key in the pocket. Though I felt his pain, felt his anger, I didn't think violence was the way to handle it, like Coach said.

"What? That asshole hurt Nathan!"

"I know. You still shouldn't have done it."

"And why the hell not?"

"It wasn't—" I paused, losing my nerve. I didn't want him to be angry with me, too. "Nevermind," I said quietly, wondering what I wasn't saying for the sake of keeping the peace.

"Whatever, Zed," he spit.

I repressed the frustration in me, tamping down on it for the sake of love, for the sake of friendship. "Goodnight, Finn."

He rolled up his window without response.

That was the first time he took me on a drive. After that, it became a bit of a ritual. We drove around the town, through town, in and out and around, sometimes stopping for junk food or a shake, usually ending up in some pasture to end the night.

I was trying to be there for my friend. I was trying to do something no one had ever given me the tools to do, never explained how it worked. And I don't think anyone ever can. When your friend hurts, you love them. You love them, and you support them, even when it hurts. Even when they're hurting themselves. Even when you're watching them tear themselves apart, you love them.

That's all you can do.

.

15

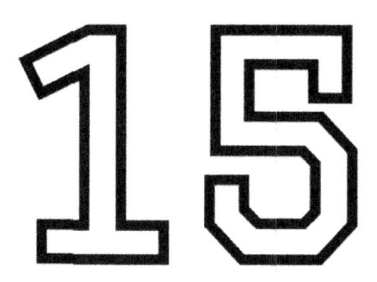

Homecoming descended upon us in a flurry of posters and gossip. In a town this size, every grade was invited to the dance and nearly every student went. Homecoming mums, of course, never ceased to amaze me in their size and ugliness. What did surprise me was that Nathan showed up to school wearing a little corsage of a mum, around his upper arm.

"What on earth's that for?" Finn asked.

Nathan flushed a furious red. "Shut up," he muttered, and ignored every other line of inquiry.

"He's got a secret girl," Naomi whispered to me. "He won't tell me who it is, but I have my suspicions."

"Who?"

"I'll never tell," she grinned mischievously. "I can't betray him in that way."

"What if I said I have a secret girl?"

Her mouth dropped open. "*Zed!* You wouldn't."

"Maybe I would!"

"I don't think so. Not without telling me!"

Unable to maintain the ruse, I shrugged. "You're right. I wouldn't."

Just like last year, the homecoming bonfire happened the week before the game. Finn, as a senior, got to help light it this year. Nathan, Luis, and I were required to be there as part of the football team in our "dress" uniforms (which was just our jerseys sans pads and jeans "with no holes" as Coach C had specified). Most of the guys wore boots again, including Nathan, but I had to stick with my converse.

Again, they had that gooseneck trailer as a stage, and the cheerleaders were supposed to lead the crowd in chants, and the band would struggle through a couple fight songs. Naomi was singing something from the fall play, some group number. So we all hung around an hour early, clustering to talk and stave off boredom until the actual bonfire.

And just like last year, half the town–maybe even the whole town–showed up to support us.

As I stood amongst the footballers, staring vacantly into space, a hand jostled my shoulder and I turned to see Joe, grinning at me.

"Oh, hi, sir, how're you?"

"Good! Just came to wish you luck before Friday."

"Thanks."

"When I used to play, I used to always say watch the knees. A man can fake you with his head, and his torso, but the knees don't lie."

I blinked at him, suddenly realizing that most of the men in the crowd had probably been six man players at one time. What did this mean to them, to watch us play the same sport they'd played at our age? What did it mean to attend the games weekly, vicariously reliving the glory days? (No wonder they yelled at the ref and Coach so much).

I looked at Joe with new eyes. "Thanks for the advice," I said. "I'll be sure and remember that."

He grinned, revealing his crooked, yellowed teeth, and slapped me on the shoulder. "Nathan," he said.

"Oh, hi Mr. Joe," said Nathan, and shook his hand.

Joe waved to the rest of the team, and their reactions varied from polite waves back (most of the guys) to a weirded out face (Finn) to an oblivious and belated smile (Luis). Then he left, vanishing into the crowd.

We let ourselves be applauded and introduced, watched the cheerleaders lead the crowd in a couple chants. And then Finn headed to the dry wood pile, holding a long torch. He cast us a manic grin, fire flickering sharply across his features. All the seniors had torches, and the moment the flames touched the wood, it burst into orange excitement, releasing sparks up, up, up, and above until they winked out.

Once the football team was free to mill about, I found Naomi, watching the blaze with a soft smile.

She said, "It's beautiful."

"Bit pyromaniac of you, but sure."

"Just—the colors and the sparks. Beautiful."

"Sure. It is beautiful." But she was looking at the fire, and I was looking at her.

***

In high school football, you invite an opponent you're pretty sure you'll beat for your homecoming game. Can't be losing in front of all the alumni who made the trek home. In six man, you do the same, except in six man, there's not always a reliable way to tell who will win a game. Still, we met the game with enthusiasm and confidence.

Nathan, still concussed, had to sit out, but he dressed in jeans and his jersey, hovering behind Coach's shoulder and occasionally calling the opposition's play before they even fully formed at the line of scrimmage. Without him to snap, Corey was in, half as accurate and twice as slow. Well, that's a little ungenerous. He snapped fine. (But Nathan was still better.)

Donning my helmet, my vision tunneled to the field in front of me and the ball in play. We made slow progress down the field, and every time I looked up into the stands I saw people making noise, but I barely heard the cheers. Out here, it was just grass, leather, sweat, and speed. We traded scores back and forth, keeping us neck and neck. No one's defense was at their best tonight, but the reffing was good. Right near the end of the fourth quarter, it was third and seventeen, and we were trailing by six points. Coach called a timeout, and we huddled close.

"You," he pointed at Luis. "I want you to throw it as hard as you can. And you," he pointed to Finn. "Run as fast as you can. As *fast* as you can, no half-assing, y'hear?"

Finn nodded, blinking away sweat dripping in his eye.

"The rest of you clear a path."

"Yes, Coach."

Coach elaborated a couple more things before signaling Finn.

Finn said, "Ready? Break!"

"*Comets!*"

As we jogged back to the field, I heard Coach mumble to Coach C, "There's a chance of snow in Brownsboro that this'll work."

Corey snapped. I caught it, though it was high. I pitched it to Luis and took off running, looking to block.

Ahead of me, I heard Finn yelling back over his shoulder, "*Go, go!*"

The ball sailed high, drifting toward him.

Finn slowed up by half a step.

The ball sank into his arms with a gorgeous *smack*. He put on a burst of speed to cross the goal line. Once he stepped over it he leapt into the air, whooping.

Cheers erupted from everywhere–the crowd, the coaches, our guys. Luis and Finn sprinted for each other, slamming their shoulders together and slapping each other on the pads, knocking helmets. I joined them, jumping up and down and shouting indistinctly.

We won the game handily after that, coasting on the wave of that catch through the PAT, winning by a single, precious point. We congregated right after, bouncing on the sidelines.

"Did you see how sweet that was? It was right there, I caught it so smooth—"

"When I threw it, I was thinking, what if this doesn't work? What if I'm intercepted? What if I throw it too far?"

"I wish I could've snapped for it," Nathan said. "That was amazing."

"Incredible, showstopping," I added.

As they continued to clamor, I turned to the stands, where Naomi was standing, pulling on a black knitted sweater, zipping it up the front.

She waved at me, smiling, her hair tumbling in the breeze. I waved back, remembering the bonfire, and her wide eyes, and her ethereal look, and I ached.

***

We all decided to attend the homecoming dance that year. The gym was decorated simply–a few tables with orange plastic coverings, dimmed lighting, and neon spotlights splashing the dancers. The D.J. was our principal, trying to look hip and cool with sunglasses and a backwards cap, but he ended up looking cringey. The music he selected was mostly country or poppy dance beats.

I spent most of my time leaning against the wall, nursing a cup of punch and watching Naomi flit around the room, making conversation with everyone. And also spying on Nathan as he danced with several girls, most of them Naomi's friends. Unfortunately, I couldn't figure out which girl he was rumored to have a thing for. It was hard to gauge since I couldn't tell which lady he favored with his time. Nathan had that easy-going, relaxed quality that made him a safe, brotherly figure to a lot of girls, and since he's no slouch when it comes to two-stepping, they all wanted to dance with him.

Finn came wearing jeans that were a tad too short, his hair gelled into artful spikes (as opposed to his regular, messy spikes). Luis showed up in a full suit, hair slicked back, 50s style, with spray and gel. He even wore a tie. We ragged on him for trying to impress someone and generally showing us all up, and his wide grin and easy laugh filled the space After we had had enough shenanigans for the evening, we all went out for Whataburger, as did half of the rest of the school, just barely getting the Petersons home before their curfew. I can only imagine what those poor Whataburger employees thought, half the school descending upon them in a cloud of formal wear, glitter, and makeup. I've always enjoyed a good patty melt, but there's something about leaning over the table so you don't spill greasy onions onto your good pants that makes it taste better. Or maybe it was the satisfaction of chowing down on a hamburger after a hard game with my hair still drying from helmet sweat that makes the junk food taste all the better. Or maybe I just was content with the laughter from the circle of idiots I called my own.

***

I started taking regular evening shifts at Joe's, along with weekend shifts on Saturdays. Our regulars consisted of old people, because most of this town was old people, but a few high schoolers came around, too, thirsting for a taste of big city life where coffee shops sat on every corner and you could live across the hall from your best friends in an apartment. I never disillusioned them that city life is *not* like that, but I digress.

One Saturday, Naomi came in alone, wearing a sweater with sleeves attached with a thick string tied through metal eyelets. Personally, I wondered why one would want to wear a sweater where the sleeves could come off since warm sleeves seemed to be the whole point of sweaters. It was late October, close to Halloween, the first bits of chill creeping into the air that swept in with Naomi.

She slid onto a bar stool, a worn leather notebook in her hand, and smiled her hello.

As I fixed her a latte—slowly, because I was still terrified of messing up and my latte "art" was still mostly just efforts at "not phallic looking"—we chatted about school and football. Playoffs were quickly approaching and everyone in town was sure we were going to make it.

Drink in hand, she turned pages in the notebook, reading something over and making notations here and there. I cleaned the workspace, shuffled some supplies, wiped down the espresso machine, stealing glances at her every three seconds or so. Her hair swept forward to cover one eye, and she twirled a curl around her finger mindlessly, humming under her breath.

When I could resist no longer, I leaned on the counter to sneak a peek. "Whatcha working on?"

"Lyrics." Her hand half-covered the page.

"I won't look if you'd rather I not."

"Um. Thanks."

"But I would love to hear you play some of them, sometime."

She looked up, blue eyes drilling into me, considering for a moment. "Are you free this evening?"

"Uh. I can be." I had homework, but who cares about homework?

"Why don't you come for dinner? My family won't mind."

"Yeah," I said, almost as soon as the words were out of her mouth.

Something for dinner other than frozen pizza, takeout, or yet another Stoffer's lasagna? Yes, please. Dinner with Naomi? Sign me the heck up. And Nathan too, I guess. Whatever.

She laughed and whipped out her phone to text her parents. I caught a glimpse of the message: *bringing home a stray [smiley face emoji]*

I puttered around the rest of my shift, serving a couple people in the drive-through. I wasn't sure how Joe planned to keep the shop open with how slow business was, but that wasn't my problem. Apparently their busiest shifts were first thing in the morning before school, though I saw glimpses of it on the weekends when Joe had me come in earlier. I suppose the tips were always a little better on those mornings.

Naomi scribbled for a bit, then leaned her chin on her palms to watch me. "Is it going ok?"

"Huh?"

"The job–is it okay?"

"Yeah. I like it."

"We'll have to get everybody here to pester you. All of us ordering complicated drinks and harassing you."

I smiled. "I'd have Joe throw you out."

"Please, Mr. Joe has been attending my dad's church since before I was born."

I raised an eyebrow. "So you're saying he likes you better?"

She shrugged, grinning. "Maybe."

After I cleaned up and clocked out, Naomi drove us to her house. We made it exactly in time for dinner. Mrs. Peterson had made shepherd's pie, something I'd never had. Mr. Peterson thanked her for cooking the meal, and blessed the food before we ate. It was delicious.

Sitting at the table, among her family, I watched how they interacted. Mr. Peterson led most of the conversation, making sure to draw me in. There was never a point where I felt like an intruder, an outsider, or awkward. I was simply another friend at the table, another part of a family. I couldn't remember the last time my own family had eaten dinner all together. It seemed the older we got the more dinner became pots of food on the stove that we all grabbed from in passing, or fast food purchased on the way home, or simply no plan at all, and we had to fend for ourselves by rummaging through the fridge and pantry. And now–well, Dad and I hadn't said more than hi in passing for days.

When dinner was over, Mr. Peterson started putting away leftovers and gathering the dirty dishes to wash, shooing his wife out.

"I can dry," Nathan volunteered.

Naomi beckoned me deeper into the house. "I'm sorry for the mess."

Entering Naomi's room shocked me in a way I hadn't expected. First of all, it was definitely a *girl's* room. Flowers on the bedspread, colorful curtains, and wall décor that wasn't a single poster held up by tape and a prayer. Instead, she had woven accessories made of some kind of rope tacked up, several old art projects, and a shelf full of records. A few of her clothes cluttered the floor, along with miscellaneous piles of homework and paper, and though she claimed it was messy, I could tell you right away it was cleaner than my room. It definitely smelled nicer. Mine smelled like sweaty football boy, pizza grease, and funky clothes. Naomi always lived with her heart on her sleeve but stepping into her sanctuary was like pulling back the curtain on *Naomi*, and seeing her displayed unceremoniously and unselfconsciously. Photos taped to the mirror above her dresser. A favorite shirt on the floor. Several notebooks and pens, and folders open to sheets of guitar chords and praise and worship lyrics.

She plucked a battered acoustic guitar from its stand, slinging on the strap, leaning on her bed frame. Running her fingers over the strings, she twiddled a few pegs, frowning and muttering before she was satisfied.

I lingered in the doorway, unsure where to put my hands or if I should sit down.

Naomi glanced at me, then chuckled. "You can come in, Zed."

"Uh, yeah." I inched my way over the threshold.

"Here." She slung the guitar over her back and kicked away a pile of clothes and moved a stack of books, unearthing a butterfly chair. "Have a seat."

I sank into the chair, still tense and shy.

"Um. I guess I'll just go, then?" Her fingers moved absently up and down the neck of the guitar, before she strummed a chord, sweet and homey. She leaned on the edge of her bed, kicking one leg out in front, and bending the other at the knee to support the instrument. Intimate in this small room, this haven of her own, her voice filled the space, the slight huskiness winding around me and drawing me in, pulling me under until all I saw and heard was her.

Everything faded away until there was just her, beautiful and honest in her song, and me, wanting too much.

I cannot tell you the words of the song, only that they were beautiful. I cannot tell you the tune, only that it was sweet. I cannot tell you a single note she played, only that she played them and I was allowed to hear.

I was in love with the curve of her calf, the curl of her hair, the cut of her cheekbones. I loved her, certain as the heart beating inside my chest.

When she finished the song, I applauded softly, and she waved me off, laughing. "Hush, it wasn't that good!"

"No, it was," I said, confident.

She ducked her head. "Well, thanks. I appreciate it." She strummed her fingers absently over the strings. "Drawn anything good lately?"

I shrugged. "Nah. Seems like I mostly end up drawing garbage. Or football plays."

"Oof. I know that feeling."

"It's like...There's stuff in my head, but I can't get it on the page."

She grunted in agreement. "There's—so much I wish I could say, but I can't. But sometimes, I get close."

"And when you do, and you get that feeling or that image and it's *close*, right, that's—that's why I do it."

"*Yes!* Yes that's it exactly!" She snapped her fingers and pointed at me. "I know I'm not the best and I have a long way to go, but gosh, I'm working hard and maybe someday I'll get it right!"

"Yeah. Someday."

"Or maybe not," she said bitterly. "The music industry is hard. Will they even see me as someone special?" she said, anger lacing her words as she pucked harshly at her guitar strings.

You're special to me, I wanted to say, but it wasn't the right moment, so instead I said, "You should have more faith in yourself."

"Please," she sighed, and it revealed this deep well of anxiety in her I'd never seen before. "Maybe they'll see I'm different, that I'll be this—this *real* person, you know? That I won't go for all the photoshopping and products and stuff. Or maybe they won't. Like, what if I'm just another blonde girl with a guitar? What if they think I'm some Taylor Swift wannabe? How am I even going to get noticed anyway?"

The force with which she spoke the words frightened me a little, made me want to take a step back, though I remained sitting. I ran a hand through my hair. "You never know..." I ventured. This was a side I'd never seen of her, and I wasn't sure I liked it. I'd never seen her so tense and anxious. I liked fun Naomi better, the Naomi who cheered at football games and giggled in Finn's truck, not this anxious person full of self-doubt. I opened my mouth to offer what probably would have been more platitudes, but Naomi pressed her fingers flat to the strings with a flat plonk, and strummed a chord.

She sang in a wobbly voice, "And maybe I'm alone–unfit for the shapes I'm supposed to slot–who am I? Who am—oh gosh I'm bringing the mood down." She flushed, embarrassed, and I had the split second realization she'd played part of an original song, before she launched into a fast country song, clearly trying to move past the moment.

I let her play, letting her words tumble in my mind, the tiny spark of fear fading. Naomi *was* something special, and I knew it. And if I saw it, surely the rest of the world would, too. But it was clear she wasn't so sure of herself, or of the rest of the world.

Nathan called from the kitchen, interrupting us, asking for help with the dishes. Naomi put the guitar away, and with a toss of her head, beckoned me to follow. Nathan washed while I dried, and Naomi put away, and there was a peacefulness to it. It reminded me of doing chores with my sisters, of how it feels to belong and be at home. I wondered if in twenty years, maybe the three of us would be doing dishes at a house Naomi and I shared. One filled with warmth and light, untouched by loneliness.

When I went home that night, I clicked on the lamp in my room, illuminating clutter and dust, disarray and chaos. Nothing like the beautiful mess that was Naomi. My room was dark and dim, undecorated and empty of memories.

I cleared a space on my desk, opening a sketchbook. In the yellow lamp light, I worked until the wee hours, heedless of the moon rising and setting outside. Pencil dashed over page, smudged, gray, defined here, foggy there. When I finished, I looked at what I'd done, and got a glimpse of everything that could be. Naomi laughed at me from the page, her freckles sharp and eyes glowing. I had captured a bit of her essence, in that sketch, her kindness and lightness and heart.

There was a lump in my throat I didn't understand.

I fell face-first onto my bed and slept like that, over the covers.

In the morning, the drawing was still there, as was the memory of the night before, and that shared, secret song.

16

Autumn deepened and what scant trees we had dropped their brown leaves. Winds picked up, making pass plays difficult, and rains poured down frequently, soaking the fields and leaving our cleats, socks, and pants spattered with mud. I spent several evenings a week at the coffee shop, serving clients that largely consisted of old men talking about the weather, old women talking about their grandchildren, or my friends talking about the old people.

Joe kept a bulletin board of cafe momentos—newspaper clippings announcing the opening of the shop, the first dollar he made, and photos from opening day-to the right of the counter. After our win at homecoming, he tacked up the article about it. He had done this with every article from every game after I started working there (at least, all the winning games). Sometimes they had a blurry photo of one of us in action or on the line or huddling.

When I asked why he did it, he got a speculative look, focusing on the board. "Around here, most towns were built on cattle, oil, or cotton."

I hadn't signed on for a history lesson, but I buckled up.

"We were an oil town. We all came to work the derricks and the shipping and such. Cotton used to be king, and this is ranching country. People drove cattle, raised cattle, sold cattle, shipped 'em."

I winced at the mention of cotton, but then thought of the railroad tracks on the southeast side of town, overgrown and rusted. I mostly knew it as the site where my classmates went drinking or had romantic meetups.

"It was hard, but we were proud." He looked at me, nodding at me. "And that's all gone now, and we're just hanging on. You give us something to be proud about."

I thought again of homecoming, and the rolling orange sea every home game. The clippings on the board, small and gray, looked like the barest hint of nothing. Just paper on a corkboard, fluttering in the breeze from the ceiling fan.

"Yessir," I said. "We do our best. We're in the playoffs."

"I know. And we're all very proud."

***

The arrival of Thanksgiving meant a trip back to Houston, thank God. I didn't know if I could stand another holiday on my couch with my father.

Mom, the girls, and I piled into the car and went to my maternal grandmother's house, where I got to see all my cousins, aunties, and uncles. We spent the day watching football and eating too much delicious food. I hadn't eaten so well since before the divorce. The next day, at Mom's house, I vegged out on the couch—it was still my bed—while my sisters and I binged TV shows from our childhood. Dinner (more thanksgiving leftovers) was reheated and eaten whenever we were hungry.

When both my sisters retreated to their rooms to talk on the phone with a boyfriend (Hailey) and to facetime a best friend (Stella), Mom sat beside me on the couch. She reached out her arms for me like I was a small child again, and I tipped into her embrace. I felt too large for her, like I was this big hulking block about to crush her petite frame. I'd grown since I'd seen her last but we both refused to acknowledge that she hadn't been there to see it.

"I miss you so much," she said into my hair.

"I miss you too."

"How are your friends?"

"They're good, Mom."

"Do you have any...*special* friends?" She patted my knee.

"Not...not really."

She pushed me back so she could look into my eyes. "I don't believe you."

I laughed. "Look, there's a girl, but it's not going anywhere."

"How do you know?"

"Because she's my friend. My best friend. I don't want to ruin that." I didn't meet her eyes.

Mom sighed, letting me lean against her again. "I understand."

"Do you?"

"I had a friend like that, when I was your age."

"Really? What happened?"

"When we tried to date, it didn't work out." She snapped her fingers. "And then we weren't friends anymore, just like that."

I flinched. That was my worst fear with Naomi.

"But just because it happened to me doesn't mean it will happen to you."

"Yeah."

She stroked my hair, her acrylic nails scratching pleasantly against my scalp.

"Mom?"

"Yes?"

"With you and Dad...do you wish it was different?"

Her exhale was long and slow, measured. "I wish...you didn't have to go through that. Your father, he was good to me. But when we had kids...something changed. We both changed. It made things hard. Really hard. And I wouldn't want to have to live with that again. It was like he—well, that's not important." I knew she was censoring herself so that I wouldn't carry resentment back home. "But no, I wouldn't wish for it to be different. Because being with him gave me you. And it gave me your precious sisters. And I wouldn't change that for anything."

I nodded.

"Sometimes, things that hurt us are for the best in the end. And sometimes, things happen that are hard, and we choose to focus on the good parts of them. We have to make peace with things. With the way things are."

"You can't change the past," I said.

"You are very right."

"I wish Dad would change, though."

"Oh, I do too. I really do. I'm sorry—" again, she cut herself off. "Are you eating enough?"

"Yes, Mom. Three meals a day. And plenty of snacks. Dad's not so incompetent as to starve me," I said in a tone of fond exasperation.

She muttered something under her breath. "He has the potential to be a better man. He just never chose to pursue it. But you, my son, you will be a better man. Right?"

I shut my eyes. "Yes ma'am."

"Good." She continued to scratch my scalp.

If only I knew exactly what that looked like. Maybe something like Coach C. Maybe.

***

The next Friday it drizzled all through the game. Cold, soaking stuff that got into all the little chinks in our pads and faceguards of our helmets. A sharp cold wind sent needles of icy drops blowing into our eyes. My fingers ached with it and Nathan's hands kept slipping on the wet ball. Off of concussion recovery, he was thrilled to be back, but what a miserable game to return. What fans we had braved the weather clothed in coats with ponchos over them. Coach grumped his way through the game, rain dripping off the end of his cap. Coach Carlson took the footballs and slid them under his poncho and sweatshirt to try and keep them dry, and to warm them between plays. All through that blue, wet, miserable evening, I thought of Joe, the newspaper clippings pinned to that little corkboard, and how Terrytown was counting on us. More importantly, my team was counting on me to not give up or give in to despair, just I was counting on them for the same.

The only one seemingly unaffected by it all was Luis. Sure, he was as cold and wet as the rest of us, but he kept his wide, easy smile on his mouth the whole time. He was the first to offer a slap on the back and a turn in front of the space heater Mrs. Carlson had hooked up to four extension cords to plug it in at the school. Luis wouldn't have known a mean temper if it reached out and grabbed him by the nose. Even when Caleb Hanson hassled him, he let it roll off his back, like water off a duck, which was pretty accurate for how soaked we were. He never did tell us us what Hanson had said either, though I had my suspicions. Caleb, by my count, was a small minded person. He had nothing intelligent or thoughtful to say whatsoever, at any time. But I digress.

It was a miserable game, but it was important. If we won, we were headed to State. And while that electrified all of us, excitement does not keep bodies warm. We spent every spare moment of the game jumping up and down on the sidelines, sticking our hands in our armpits, being hassled by Doc to stretch and move and stay warm.

When we won, our celebration sounded muted, given the roar of the wind and rain, but I could still tell Luis was ecstatic, throwing his arms around us and shouting in our ears. Naomi, hair plastered to her face and a plastic poncho flapping over Nathan's spare jersey, let his joy infect her, and she jumped and laughed with him, careless of the mud on her shoes and jeans.

After that game, Coach Carlson drove me home. He offered to drive me, then practically demanded it when I started to say something about my skateboard. So I sat in the back of his car, dripping on his clean floorboard, probably still smelling like wet dog despite the hasty shower I took. Mrs. Carlson didn't seem to mind. She smiled at me and asked me about my classes and my homework.

As Coach C continued driving, I noticed he didn't head toward my house. Instead, he went to Whataburger, and waited in the years-long drive through. He didn't even twist to look at me. "What do you want?"

"Uh—you don't have to get me anything."

"What do you want?"

"I really—"

"Son, just make this easy and tell me your order."

"I can pay you back, but a bacon burger would be fantastic."

He waved a hand at my mention of payment, and then got me a large fries and a large Powerade to boot. He knew his wife's order without asking.

She rehashed the game to her husband, asking about players and referees. I didn't know until that night that she knew all our names, our numbers, and our year. I figured she knew our parents, too, at least, for the ones who had parents in town.

Coach listened to her intently, patiently answering every question. As we drove to my house, I could see them holding hands over the console in the dark, almost like they were still teenagers.

"Goodnight, son," he said as I climbed out of the car. "Good hustle tonight."

"Thanks, Coach. For dinner, and everything."

"Anytime."

I opened the door to my house to find my father, snoring on the couch. Three beer bottles piled beside him, along with a greasy pizza box. He blinked awake at my entrance.

"Geez, Zed, you're home late. Where you been?"

"At a football game. Playing. For State."

"Huh. You win?"

"Yes." I moved across the living room, but he called after me.

"Good for you. Uh, proud of you."

I stopped. "Do you want to come to the state game?"

His eyes flicked away from me, back to the muted TV. "I'll see about getting time off from work."

A traitorous leap of hope filled my heart. "Really?"

"God, it's late," he grumbled, and headed to his room, leaving his trash on the couch.

I tucked my chin and fled to my room.

***

The next morning, Luis had posted a photo Naomi had taken—we were all tagged in it, but he and Nathan were in the center, a little blurry. They were both smiling, Luis' arm tossed around Nathan's neck. I was tagged as a hand coming in from off the side, and the back of Finn's head was visible over Nathan's shoulder. Luis filtered it black and white, and the caption was only an orange heart emoji.

Beneath, in the comments, Caleb Hanson had written: *you and your boyfriend sure are cute.* Caleb's brother—a freshman, and apparently just as nasty as Caleb—had replied, *gaaaaay.*

I sighed, rolling my eyes, knowing the exact mocking tone he'd use to say the words.

The post was gone before the end of the day.

.

17

The second week of December was the Texas six man football state championship in Dallas. We were headed to the stadium of the Dallas Cowboys, baby, real pro stuff. A caravan of buses and cars headed out of Terrytown to Dallas the day before, the team staying the night in a hotel.

Multiple games were played that day, but the only one I was worried about was ours. We played second, after the 1A game. Stepping off the bus at the stadium, I tipped my head back to gaze up at the massive building. It loomed many stories tall, sporting at least seventeen hundred blue-and-silver stars. It seemed to me I was but an insect, about to be squashed under the weight of looming prospects: the game, high school, and the future. I was a junior. In two years, I'd be in college. I'd have to decide upon a major that would define my career. Maybe I'd be dating someone. Maybe I'd be close to my sisters again. Maybe I'd finally have told Naomi how I felt.

Nathan jostled my shoulder. "Huge, ain't it?"

"Yeah." What else could I say?

Luis rolled up beside us. "Wow. That's, like, a mile high. Imagine trying to climb that thing."

Finn, squinting, snapped, "Well, we ain't climbing it, we're playing in it. Get focused, boys."

We watched him go, head down with a single-minded determination.

The locker rooms were huge, too, and clean and shiny and a thousand other tiny details I missed as I dressed and stretched. Our coaches bent their heads together over their clipboards, and Doc moved amongst us, stretching limbs and massaging muscles.

When we stepped into the stadium, the noise and lights assaulted us. Ads scrolled endlessly on the LED strip screens throughout the stadium. Over the loudspeaker, songs, announcements, and ads echoed. Above us, the massive four-sided screen broadcasted the players on the field to every fan in the stadium, almost like a pro game on TV. And there was an impressive amount of fans. For six man football, making it to State had drawn a big crowd. Given that two years ago I didn't even know that six man *existed*, I was surprised at so many people in the seats. I looked for orange shirts, for Naomi's curls, but I couldn't find her. Somewhere out there, my mother and sisters were sitting together, watching our ant-like forms move to the sidelines. Somewhere out there, scouts were watching, despite our lowly status as tiny west Texas schools.

I did a second scan for my family but couldn't find them. Dad of course hadn't come, not that I'd expected any different. Expected and hoped for are two different things. But Mom and my sisters were here, and they'd been texting me nonstop, well-wishes and excitement. Mom had asked a billion questions about the rules on the phone last night, and I'd tried to answer as best I could. I knew she'd have on her red lipstick like she always did, and would have forced my sisters to dig whatever orange gear they could find out of the back of the closet. I wanted the game to be good for a lot of reasons, but having my family here to watch me was definitely one of them.

I looked up at the ceiling, so far above us. It was closed, but I felt like I was still outdoors because the space was so large. A camera crew prowled the sidelines, their instruments hoisted on their shoulders, ready to swoop in on us like vultures.

Coach motioned to us to stop gawking and hurry up. "High knees, let's go!"

We hustled to the field, jogging back and forth over ten yards, still gaping at the size and space of the stadium. All through our warm-ups, half my mind was on the game, and the other half was busy being awed at the stadium.

Coach called us together for final words. "Boys, this is it. I want your best today. Everything you have, leave it on the field. For the rest of your life, and the rest of mine, we will remember today. Do not hold back. Do not give up. Do not be afraid." He glanced around at us, hard-eyed and determined. "Make me proud." He nodded his head to Coach Carlson.

"What's the one thing I can't teach you?"

"Hustle," we responded instantly.

"That's what I ask of you today. That you hustle." He dipped his chin, glanced away. "Coach, may I?"

Coach nodded his assent, and Coach C whipped off his hat to pray. The rest of us bowed our heads, but I kept my eyes open, glancing at the orange collars of our jerseys, my teammates hands on shoulder pads. Across the way, my eyes met Finn's, and he nodded jerkily. In his face I saw the fear and the determination we all felt.

It came down to this, a band of brothers on the field of battle. We'd either soar or go down swinging, but we'd do it together.

"Hands in the middle," Coach said, and nodded to Finn.

Something like pride entered his face. "Comets on three," he shouted. "One, two, three, *Comets!*"

Our hands flew in the air, and it was showtime. Luis hopped back and forth on the sidelines, pulling his knees to his chest with each bounce. Nathan bent upside down to stretch, flexing his hands. Finn swung his arms across his chest, slapping his back with each pass, hugging himself. I rotated my hip joints and ankles, squatting to loosen my legs.

There was a tautness in the air, like everyone and everything was waiting. It's always like this, before a game, but today was different. Today, it felt heavier, the silence thicker, all of us coiled like a spring, stretched taut like a rubber band. The thrum of energy radiated through me. I felt like a warrior about to enter battle. Gladiators on the edge of the arena.

Finn went out for the coin toss, along with another senior named Jesus, and Nathan. Finn stood by the white hat, making our call. We won the toss, elected to receive. I went in to receive, along with Nathan, Finn, Luis, Tate, and Alejandro. I cast a look at our team, taking in the tilt of the helmets and glare of the lights and green of the grass. Maybe I'd draw it later.

The kicker raised his hand, the whistle blew. The ball flew low to the ground, rolling the last three yards before Luis dropped on it. Almost instantly, the other team dropped on him.

We huddled for the play, clapping to break the huddle. I squatted in diamond formation, everything snapping crystal clear as adrenaline flooded my veins.

I turned my focus to the turf below my feet, to Nathan bending down, hands settling on the leather ball, adjusting his grip.

"Down...Set...Hut!"

It's go time.

The ball snapped toward us, flying neatly into Luis' waiting arms. He set off at a dead run, and I tussled with a defender in front of me. I heard a yell, turned, and saw the ball fumbling from Luis' hands and into the gloves of the player beside him, who took off toward the goal. I ran, possibly faster than I ever ran before, but none of us were enough. They scored.

Up on the big screen, the numbers changed: 6-0.

They kicked the extra point, which is unusual, but it was still two more points. 8-0.

On the line for our first offensive drive, I set my cleat into the turf. This was professional turf. This was championship turf.

(This was also painful turf, when you fell or slipped. People don't tell you that in NFL interviews. Turf hurts.) Like most of the time, I ran routes. Nathan snapped it to Finn, who pitched it to Luis, who scrambled in the pocket before taking off at a sprint. Little by little, we made our downs.

Nathan bent down for the snap, wide legs and folded waist. Luis made the call, *"set, hut!"* and the ball flew into his hands as if drawn by magnets. He pitched it to Finn. Finn scanned the field, and started taking a leisurely stroll behind the line of scrimmage. I was well on my way down the field, looking back, when he started to run. He blew through the line, past Nathan and Tate, grabbing some daylight, and was away. Though a man was hot on his heels, he jumped into the end zone.

We were on the board and the game was just beginning.

Coach sent in some mixed crew for the PAT, which is to say, not me–freshman and players that don't get as much game time.

I went in as kicker for the next drive. I let the tunnel vision overtake me, lower lip pulled between my teeth. Cleat met leather. Ball rolled, traveled sufficient yards, and was immediately dropped on by a cornerback.

Alejandro, Finn, Corey, Tate, me, and Matteo stayed on defense. And, despite our best efforts, they scored again.

Perhaps this would be a back and forth game, like a tennis match.

Heart pounding, we took the offensive line again. I glued my eyes to Nathan's hands, waiting for the snap. It flew neatly through the air, landing in my hands with a neat smack. I held it out to Finn, who tucked it and ran without pause. I ran a fake, swearing under my breath.

We made the first down.

Again, on the line; again, my heart in my throat. I looked at my brothers lined up beside me. For a brief second, I got a crystal clear view of the embroidery holding the black number to the slick orange fabric of Nathan's jersey. Every thread distinct, sharp. I turned my razor focus to the field, to the play. White blades of turf outlined against green. A bead of sweat trickling down the defensive back's forehead.

Snap. Run. Repeat.

At the end of the first quarter, the score stood 21-14, them.

Coach cracked down on defense at the start of the second quarter, shifting the players around and putting Alejandro on point to do some serious knocking down. He hit hard, to the point we were looking at the possibility of unnecessary roughness.

I was not usually a defensive player, but I rotated in and out with Luis and Finn for speed purposes. Always on the line, always looking for where the ball was going. If I could recover a ball and run it in…well, best not get ahead of myself.

Nathan, on the sidelines, was jumping and shouting as he called their play. We rearranged, scrambling to better positions, stilling right before the snap and stopping the play in its tracks. Alejandro tackled the runner, and Coach C yelled from the sidelines, "Gently! Set him down like a baby!"

And sure enough, Alejandro laid him slowly to the ground, and dropped on top of him like a sack of potatoes.

They pushed on, inching down the field. Even with all our effort, they still made the downs. By the time we reached the last twenty yards my lungs burned. I poured water down my throat, sweating despite the temperature-controlled environment. They still scored.

Our drive.

I lined up in the backfield, waiting for the snap. Nathan snapped it long and true, right into my hands. The play was already in motion, I turned to Luis and pitched it to him, and took off on my route.

The crowd yelled in trepidation. I cast a look over my shoulder.

Luis fumbled, dropped the ball. A player reached for it. Luis dropped on it, covering it with his torso. The player fell on top of him.

Whistles blew, and we jogged to huddle.

Luis didn't get up. He rocked onto his knees, one hand bracing on the ground, the other on his midsection. He lowered to the ground again, rolling onto his back.

"Shit," Finn said, dropping to a knee.

Coach and Doc jogged past, Coach C following at a more leisurely pace.

Luis laid there, unmoving, as the rest of us traded nervous glances.

It seemed a long time that he lay there before being helped up. He raised a hand to us in passing, a little green in the face.

"Just winded," Coach C called in passing. That made sense. He'd fallen pretty hard on the ball, must've knocked all the air out of him.

Still, it was disconcerting to lose any member of our team for any length of time, and we definitely played off, flat-footed and unsure.

We didn't score.

By the time Luis was back in the game, we were back on defense. He wasn't much worse for the wear, but it was frustrating to see his hard work and near-injury go to waste.

On the line, I waited for the snap so I could run. There was a vague ache in my chest—probably from not getting enough oxygen—but my body could ignore that for the sake of the game. My ankle twinged, and I rolled it out. I could push through. For the sake of a championship. For the sake of fighting through this with my brothers at my side.

Under Finn's on-field leadership, we got within ten of the goal. Alejandro muscled through the line, but was brought down on the paint, barely gaining a yard. The whistle blew. Finn threw himself on the dog pile a second too late.

The penalty flag flew, a fluttering yellow arc in the air.

Coach was red in the face as Finn jogged off the field, jaw set.

"You know better, son! I can't have you throwing yourself in for a late hit!"

Coach C grabbed a fistful of Finn's jersey and hauled him away, safe from Coach's wrath.

I gave them all a wide berth and waited for the play. We turned over on downs. Finn seethed on the sideline. Nathan worried in the huddle. Luis looked even-tempered but I could see the stress in his hands as he flexed and squeezed them repeatedly.

We were still trailing by ten.

Finally there was halftime, and we jogged off the field all the way back to the locker rooms. It felt like a million miles of walking and honestly collapsing didn't sound like a bad idea if it meant my legs could rest. I stretched my ankle and calf, hoping the ache would recede. Coach, stern-faced and fingering the brim of his hat, gave brief notes on what's working, and then ripped us apart for what wasn't. We nodded and mumbled, "Yes, Coach," like that would save us from his rage, but our screw-ups only weighed heavier on our minds.

Coach C said, "This isn't over yet. Keep hustling. Don't give the game up as lost before it actually is lost."

We trotted back on the ginormous field, stretching our tired muscles and getting harried by the camera crew lurking in our peripherals. The crowd in the bleachers murmured and buzzed. I guess six man had more fans than I thought.

We entered the third quarter trailing but determined to overtake them swiftly. The yellow lights of the scoreboard taunted us, daring us to catch up.

We came on strong, Luis running in for a score on our first drive. He and Finn ran and jumped to bump shoulders, Finn slapping the back of his helmet.

"We'll get you now, you fuckers," Finn shouted cheerfully.

And for a bit, it seemed we might. We got on the defensive, not pushing them back but definitely slowing them down.

Punt. Offense again. Digging cleats through turf, searching for dirt. We pushed forward. Sometimes the details were crystal clear: the leather of the ball under my palm, the sweat rolling down Nathan's face, the wrinkle between Finn's brows. Sometimes it was a blur, all fog and pain and exhaustion, running forever with no end in sight.

Fourth down, within fifteen yards of the goal.

Coach looked up sharply at me. "Can you kick it?"

"What?"

"We're going to kick it. *You're* going to kick it."

My stomach dropped to my toes, then leapt into my mouth. We've practiced this play a grand total of one time. *Once.* "What?" I echoed faintly, looking around.

Nathan slapped my back, a steady hand. "You got this, bro. Pull out all those old soccer skills."

I swallowed hard. I might do our kickoff, but it didn't make me a pro by any means.

We lined up for the unfamiliar play. Nathan snapped. Finn caught it as I stepped forward, my feet landing hard on the turf.

I caught the glint in his eye as I swung my foot, that bright, dangerous gleam, directed at me.

My foot connected with the ball.

The impact rolled up my calf, my knee. I tracked the ball, desperately hoping it went through.

It arced beautifully, soaring upward, clearing the goalline, still traveling—

It missed by inches. I missed by inches.

The refs waved their arms flat.

I dropped my palms to my knees and hunched for a moment.

Grim, Finn shook his head at me, angry. He'd get over it in a minute, but his anger had nothing on mine.

I trotted to the sidelines, sick.

There was only a quarter left.

Crunch time now. I looked to the stands again, ever and always searching for Naomi. Still couldn't spot her curly hair among the sea of people, but I knew she was there. I wished I could see her face, just to get some reassurance. I could practically see her leant forward, elbows on knees, laser focused on the field.

There were seven minutes of play time left. Seven minutes to fix it or lose it.

We could still win it.

I looked at the scoreboard. We could do it.

For a game that's so action packed, it moved slowly. Play by play, yard by yard, crawling close to the end zone. I waited in diamond formation, sprinting when the snap went. Tussled with a blocker, caught Alejandro muscling up the middle. He disappeared under a writhing pile of jerseys. The whistle blew and the ref raised his arms.

It took a second for it to click in my brain. We scored!

It's a tie game!

The fans were on their feet, screaming. I was nearly bowled over by the force of Finn's hug. We were back in it, folks.

On the sidelines for the defensive play, I watched as Coach signed the play in, Finn and Luis and the boys nodding in understanding. They waited for the other team to get set. Beside me, Nathan looked at the formation. "Ten sweep O," he mumbled.

He's right. It's a play we did on the regular, and because of that our boys stopped it easily.

The next drive, we didn't push them back but we did stop them, defense working hard.

I looked back to the stands, looked at our fans, clad in bright orange. They leaned forward in their seats, some of them standing, hands clasped or gripping armrests.

"Turnover on downs!" Nathan yelled, and I hustled onto the field after him. We had two minutes left in the quarter, surely we could make something of them. If they didn't bother to punt it, they must be feeling desperate. We were on the forty yard line.

On the line of scrimmage, I waited for the snap. The ball sailed gracefully from Nathan's hands and I booked it, running down the sideline. There was a defender keeping pace with me, waiting for me to receive it, but he didn't know what I knew.

It was a fake. Luis was running up the middle with the ball, gaining ground with every stride, until he was brought down at the thirty.

My back ached. The pads were digging into my skin, and it was sweltering under my helmet. My right ankle throbbed incessantly, though I couldn't remember rolling or twisting it.

If we could just make it through this—

I looked to my boys, lining up the snap.

Finn received, fumbled, and swore colorfully as the ball slipped through his hands. Before he could do anything about it, the ball was picked off. Luis brought the man down and the whistle blew.

"Finn—" I started to attempt to soothe him.

Red in the face, he stormed off the field, still swearing.

We moved into the fourth quarter still tied.

Coach kept taking his hat off and slamming it back onto his head, red in the face. He spoke only in grunted instructions and plays. Coach C hovered behind his shoulder, anticipating the moment when he became the "gitback, Coach." But Coach wasn't harassing referees now, he was harassing us.

"Get your heads in the game! I need you in the here and now!" he snapped. "Press in on offense. Defense will keep doing what they're doing. If you see it, call it. Keep driving. And don't drop the damn ball!"

Coach C raised a hand to rest on Coach's shoulder. Coach waved him off as though batting a fly.

"Ready," started Nathan, putting his hand in the middle.

"Break. Comets," we grunted, exhausted.

The last quarter began with an excellent offensive move by Luis, who juked a guy so cleanly and ran so fast that the defender gave up and let him go. He was, of course, stopped by someone else, but it didn't matter. When he peeled himself off the ground, we surrounded him with such jubilance he was shaken by our back-thumping.

I spent much of our next drive on the ground, consistently knocked flat on my back by the defender, who looked about as frustrated as I felt. By the third or fourth time, I'd started to make conversation, but he remained unresponsive.

"Hey, nice to see you again."

"You come here often?"

"This is getting boring. I hope we score soon."

And then we did score, via Alejandro hustling through a crowd to fall inches into the endzone. He was knocked back to the ground by a yelling Finn, who rolled off him to help him back up and slap his butt. Others thumped his helmet or punched his shoulder.

But the game wasn't over yet.

Almost rhythmic now. Huddle. Crouch. Snap. Run. Defend. Tussle. Sweat. Drink. Repeat.

They scored again, naturally, because nothing can ever be easy. Three minutes remained in the game. There was still a chance.

We set up for a running play. I could tell that Finn was tired, running on fumes, but he pushed through, gaining us the down with some extra yardage.

Luis passed it to Tate, who ran it for a small gain, and then we switched it up again for yet another run. While we couldn't get it in, our opponents did, pulling ahead in the tie. Our progress was slow, and time was against us. Though we were gaining ground, no plan was sticking, and our plays didn't gain us more than a couple yards at a time, fighting for every down.

Coach called a timeout. He leveled his fingers at us, singling out me, Finn, Luis, Nathan, Matteo, and Tate. "You." He pointed to Luis. "I want you to run as fast as you can. You." Now pointing to Finn. "Throw it as far as you damn well can." He motioned at Nathan. "You snap it straight and the three of you—" he indicated me, Tate, and Matteo "—clear the way."

We had seconds left. This was a Hail Mary, I supposed. This play had worked before, would it work again?

The ball sailed from Nathan's hands, arcing neatly to Matteo who pitched it to Finn. I ran, looking for ways to cut off Luis' pursuers. Finn took a shuffle step, twisted his hips, let the ball fly. It sailed neatly through the air, a perfect spiraling curve.

My lungs burning, I kept watching, as Luis turned, opening the cradle of his arms.

The ball sank, dipped.

Luis stretched, reached—

The buzzer blew.

The ball dropped to the turf.

I jogged to a stop.

We were so close.

I looked at Finn, uncomprehending. His jaw was set, clenched so tight it was white at the joint. Though he refused to look at me, I could see tears in his eyes. Scoreboard, still displaying our shame, proved the truth of the matter. 64-58.

We had lost.

I couldn't tell you much about what happened after, caught in a fog. I know our Coaches tried to console us, and I know we ate a meal. I'm pretty sure Doc wrapped up my ankle. I'd rolled it or sprained it, ignored it from adrenaline, and kept playing on it. A bad combo. I also think Doc buddy taped Nathan's swollen and purple index finger to the middle one, which we later discovered was broken. I know we shook hands with the other team, because we always do. We had to have showered, hot water soothing sore muscles, but it did nothing to ease the internal pain. I do remember Naomi hugging me, wrapping her arms around me and pressing her body against my chest. I got a face full of curly, coconut-scented hair, distracting me with a funny moment of kinship since so many of my own products were coconut-scented. I remember seeing mom and my sisters, too, their gentle frowns and sorry eyes. They'd come all this way just to see our greatest shame, and now turned around to drive back to Houston, promising to see me again at Christmas.

We slunk home, tails between our legs. The bus had never been so quiet. In Terrytown, we unloaded at the school, hauling gear bags and suitcases.

I threw an arm over Luis, whose eyes were downcast. He lolled his head onto my shoulder, heaving a sigh.

Nathan slapped us on the back. "Hey. Keep your chins up."

"Yeah," I agreed.

Luis stepped away from me, his dark hair flopping over his forehead, his permasmile missing.

Finn hopped off the bus, yanking his bag from the luggage compartment, slinging it over his shoulder, and heading for his truck.

"Finn," I said, watching him go. "Finn!"

"*What*, Zed?" He whirled, glaring daggers at me.

"Just—do you want to get Whataburger, or something?" My voice sounded weak and unsure to my own ears.

"Do I want to *what*? No, I don't 'want to get Whataburger or something.'" He did big air quotes around my words. "I want to go home, and go to bed, and wake up tomorrow and this isn't real." He rolled his eyes, setting off in the direction of his truck again.

"See you later?" I called.

"Whatever," he shouted back.

Nathan sighed. "Let him go."

"He'll come around," Luis said, like it was the easiest thing in the world.

I watched Finn's form grow smaller. His family hadn't come to the game, hadn't been able to afford it. And he'd given up shifts at work to make this trip. We'd all missed two days of school. And for what?

I squeezed Nathan's shoulder. "See you tomorrow?"

"Tomorrow," he agreed heavily, and turned away.

I scanned the parking lot, looking for my dad, but he wasn't there. My last text to him was still on *delivered*. And with Finn gone, I didn't have a sure way home, save walking. The wind bit at my cheeks. Maybe I shouldn't do that. I looked for Coach C, but he was already gone.

I set off on foot to Joe's, knowing he'd run me home. He was nice like that.

As I passed hillbilly row, Caleb Hanson spit a stream of tobacco. It landed on the pavement with a wet smack.

"Heard you lost today."

"Yeah," I said, not breaking stride.

"Man, why'd y'all even try? The football team hasn't been good for years."

I didn't respond. He muttered something under his breath that sounded like an insult. I did not deign to give him the satisfaction of an answer.

"Hey, it's the big man!" Joe said as I walked in the door.

I gave half a smile.

"I was watching on the streaming whatchamacallit thingy. My granddaughter set it up for me. Y'all played real hard."

"Thanks."

Joe looked at me kindly. "Better luck next time, hey?"

"Yeah." I swallowed, sliding into a seat at the bar.

"You want a coffee? On the house, for the man who made it all the way to the big leagues."

"Sure. Thanks."

Joe poured the cup, sliding me one of the mugs we used for the bottomless $2 drip coffee. "You know, we're all still real proud of you."

I nodded, silent. The coffee scalded on the way down, but it warmed me.

He busied himself at the counter, while I sat at the bar and moped.

We were thieves and renegades, just scrappy kids in ripped jeans and t-shirts, and we were on top of the world for the briefest of moments. We were heroes, once, and what were we now? We were solar flares, burning bright, loud, and brief. And like solar flares, we burned out.

***

There was no newspaper clipping about it in Joe's. He said nothing further about it, for which I was grateful. But every time I looked at that board, I had a pang of sadness running deep through me, and I had to look away.

My father, potentially well-meaning but probably thoughtlessly, said, "It's just football."

And I remembered Finn saying in his truck, shaking and intense, "Football is everything. *Everything.*"

***

I went back to my mom's for Christmas. She caught me up on the ride home. Hailey had survived her first semester of college with a little sweat and tears. I'd been to the graduation in the spring, but it still didn't feel real, that she was actually in college. She still held straight A's, and managed a social life with it. But she looked tired, and napped for hours at a time. Stella, meanwhile, was relishing being an only child, at least according to my mom.

"And you, mom?" I asked.

"I miss you, baby."

"I miss you, too. But I'm here now."

She reached across the console to pat my knee.

And what it came down to is who was I, out there, away from my mother, away from my sisters, surrounded by men and boys? When the only girl I really talked to was Naomi and occasionally Finn's sisters? Who am I when my family is split in two and I, already the product of two worlds, was transplanted to a completely new one? Who am I at all?

Eating Christmas dinner together, the four of us, a partial family ripped and mended, I looked at faces that mirrored my own. I could walk into the street and see more people that looked like me than I would in Terrytown. I was well aware of my role in making up half the 2% African American student population. The other half was James Owens, who'd been adopted from Kenya when he was, like, seven. I think for a bit everyone thought we'd be friends, and like, listen to rap music together, but we mostly just slapped fives in the halls and gave each other the bro nod upon occasion. And yet, I missed it. I missed them, my friends. I felt like I belonged there, with them.

Naomi was the first to say Merry Christmas in the group text and I knew those words meant something to her they didn't to me. It was intertwined with her faith, her world, and brought her more of the joy she carried with her everywhere she went. But I was thankful, anyway. She thought of me (our whole group, but I could pretend it was me), on Christmas day.

I kicked Stella's butt in Mario Kart and made ruthless jokes to Hailey about her boyfriend, but it all felt hollow. I felt out of place. I missed my friends, and wanted to play them in Mario Kart, tease Nathan about his mysterious secret girlfriend. I thought of them each in their own homes with their own families, and wished I could have come along.

Bringing home a stray, Naomi had said. If only I could turn up at her doorstep like a stray dog and let her family take me in.

Going back, driving across bare gray plains, flat Texas ground and tired scrub brush, I left the city skyline far, far behind me. I love my mother, and I love my sisters. But my friends, they drew me back, pulled me in.

I would slot into their spaces as easily as I once fit with my sisters. I would be just as welcome at our table in the cafeteria as I was at the battered wooden table in my mother's kitchen. I would smile there even more than I did here.

There's something to be said for friends who become family, for people who choose you every day when they wake up not because of accidents of biology and birth but because they genuinely like you. I was going home, whether I could name it or not.

Some people think Terrytown is the kind of place you spend time trying to get away from. Some people think it's the kind of place you spend time remembering to come home to. Finn is the former. Naomi is the latter. And I—well, I didn't come or go to a place. I went to the people. Not for the red Texas dirt or the green field grass, but for the circle of friends I'd never expected, and I never wanted to let go.

18

The start of spring semester meant we were closer than ever to Finn's graduation; his eventual moving-on from high school, and, by extension, us. And it began as they always do, in the gray of winter, with old slush on the ground from one of those rare West Texas snows, with students trudging down the halls, disappointed the school didn't burn down in their absence. Coach C still taught history, welcoming the football players with fist bumps and high fives. We got the sense that he remembered what it was like to be a teenage boy with a short attention span, with the way he cracked jokes and kept the class moving and dynamic. One time he made us play a game involving throwing crumpled paper at cups balanced on a classmate's head.

    Our first lunch, I found our table and sat down, unreasonably happy to be back among these people. Nathan's hand was in a cast to brace his finger. Naomi had her hair done differently today, piled on top of her head rather than its usual fluffy tumble down her back.

    Luis still brought his lunch from home and today it looked like pork tacos in corn tortillas. When I asked him about it, he said he'd made it, which blew my mind. I fend for myself in the food area most of the time, but that usually meant reheated frozen meals. And then Luis here just up and made himself a whole fancy meal.

Finn slumped into a seat, slamming his tray down with more force than necessary.

"Hello, sunshine," Nathan said, layering on the sarcasm.

Finn shot him a glare.

"Who put salt in your coffee?" I asked, drawing his angry eyes to me.

"Today sucks."

"I'm sorry," I said honestly.

"This whole year sucks, actually, and I'd like to leave now."

We traded glances around the table, over his hunched and glowering form, while he picked at his lunch. Naomi opened her mouth to speak and decided against it, retracting into herself a bit.

"Look, buddy, you can talk to us or you can not talk to us, but don't sit there being angry for no reason." Nathan paired this with a back slap, to take the sting away.

From where he was sitting between the twins, Finn looked at me, the exasperated look of one parent to another that said, *can you believe these crazy kids?*

I indulged him, and raised my brows back.

"It's your senior year, isn't it?" Luis asked, remarkably intuitive.

"Yeah, it's my last year and the last time I get a chance, we lose."

Even now, a month later, it still woke a bitterness in me. We'd tried so hard, and we'd still lost.

"Hey, relax, Finn." Naomi jostled his shoulder. "Take pride in the fact that you made it all the way there! You made it so far!"

He shrugged her off, looking away, mumbling, "'S not the same."

Hurt flashed on her face as she retracted her hand. "Sorry."

"You don't understand!" he burst out. "I thought maybe I'd—get a scholarship, go someplace! And I'm just back here, eating lunch with you all, and waiting to graduate so I can go work a minimum-wage job that I hate and live in a trailer house with my kid sisters!"

Naomi bit her lip and turned her face away.

"It's just senior year," Nathan said placatingly. "You'll figure it out. The pressure's on right now."

Luis pulled Naomi to lean on his shoulder. "Maybe loosen up a bit."

Finn looked at me, his sharp eyes boring holes in my head. "You get it, Zed. Comin' from a big city. There's like—dreams there."

"There's people in high school there, too," I said, unsure if it was the right thing. But I kind of got the feeling I *was* the only one who got it. I knew the feeling of looking over the flat gray terrain and seeing *nothing, nothing, nothing.* I also knew that there were things here I wouldn't find in the city. But I didn't know how to say that either.

"Small dreams are good, you know," Naomi said, muffled against Luis.

Finn scoffed. "Football was my dream." He stood up, yanking his tray away. "This was it." He looked at each of us, lingering on Naomi, and for a moment, he looked remorseful. Then the shutters closed over his face again. "I'll catch you later."

I looked at Naomi, who had sat up at Finn's abrupt exit, looking a little red around the eyes.

She sniffed, smiled, and looked at me. "Well. Isn't he just a ray of sunshine?" she said brightly. "You working this afternoon, Zed?"

I nodded.

"How about we crash Joe's then?" Directing this at the other two, she spread a big smile on her face. "C'mon, I know you both need more coffee in your lives."

"Sure," Nathan said. "Sounds good." But the words sounded hollow.

✱✱✱

It didn't surprise me when Finn's truck pulled up in my drive that night, headlights shining into my window. I hopped in the idling vehicle, unsurprised by his surly look. He was wearing his letterman jacket, received at the end of last semester, an orange *C* emblazoned on the breast. He hunched into the collar of it, scowling.

We drove in silence for a long time, and since I was too busy trying to figure out what to say, I didn't notice we were leaving Terrytown and headed due west. "Where are we going?"

"Outer space."

Covertly looking at his long, bony fingers gripping the wheel, I tried to gauge what was on his mind.

He flicked on the turn signal, headed into the wilderness.

"You're not taking me out here to kill me, are you?"

Finn turned to me with a crazed, creepy smile. "It is time…to make a sacrifice."

"Sure, dude, whatever."

He blew a raspberry and focused on the road. "We're almost there."

"Great." We'd been driving almost an hour and my legs were cramped.

When we finally pulled up to wherever we were—I really hoped we weren't trespassing—I spotted first the cacti dotting a ledge. We were on top of a caprock, or on a road adjacent to the caprock—I don't know, I'm from the city—but there was a drop, and there was rock looming beside us.

Finn motioned me into the bed of the truck and offered me a beer that he pulled from the back seat.

"How'd you get that?"

He rolled his eyes, a motion I could see despite the darkness. "Don't worry about it. Do you want one, or not?"

"Um. No. But if you're going to have one, maybe I should drive back."

"Please. One beer's not going to hurt me." He tipped the bottle back by the neck and drank several swallows.

I looked up at the stars. Clearer out here, they winked at us, diamonds in a velvet blue sky. Despite the chill and the cold metal of the truck, the beauty of it descended upon my spirit.

We settled in the bed of the truck, me still gazing upwards, Finn still nursing his bottle.

The night is anything but quiet, when you take the time to listen. Wind rustled the grass. Bugs chirped and coyotes howled. I closed my eyes and listened to the world, to the sound of Finn breathing beside me.

He chucked the empty bottle into the grass. "You ever feel like you're an alien, and everyone else around you knows how to belong except you?"

I kept my eyes closed. Did I know what it felt like to stand out, to not belong? Did *I* know what that felt like? Too black for my white relatives and too white for my black ones. The wrong shade of brown in the school. The only boy among three siblings. A city kid in ranching territory, listening to a foreign language of weather and cattle and oil. The soccer kid on the football team.

Did I know how that felt? Did I look at the Peterson's and wish I had my family back together? Did I look at Coach C and wish my dad had tried a little harder? How could they all live lives that made sense when I had no idea how to deal with mine? When Finn and I could do nothing more than sit on the edge of the world and ask pointless questions?

All I said was, "Yeah."

***

It's a little embarrassing to admit that I don't know very much about basketball. It feels shameful, like I need to turn in my "man card" or something, but I've never been super interested. I know the basics—put the ball in the hoop—but I knew I'd be leaning over to Nathan about every two minutes to ask him what that foul meant and who had the ball.

About half the football team were also half the basketball team, and there was an element of humor to sitting in the seats to watch the guys I usually played beside playing a different game. Coach and Coach C also coached the basketball team. Just small school things. Although, if I had to guess, Coach was more passionate about football, based on his relaxed posture and less-scowly-than-usual facial expression.

The five of us all sat together in a row, and within minutes, Luis and Finn had headed to the concession stand. I snagged the seat beside Naomi, patting myself on the back for my cleverness. Naomi waved at a group of girls two rows down, and then at the English teacher, and then at the theatre director. Nathan traded "'sup" nods with a couple of the basketball team, and I did the same. I kicked my feet up onto the bleacher seat in front of me. The cheerleaders stood over to the side, sporting their long sleeved winter uniforms, rustling sparkly pom poms.

Luis and Finn returned with their arms full of tiny bags of popcorn, packages of Sour Punch Straws, bags of Skittles, and bottled waters. They passed out their offerings between us, and I snagged the blue Sour Punch Straws (because they are the best and I was feeling a little selfish). Nathan, who wasn't getting his cast removed till that weekend, had to ask for help opening his candy, much to Finn's amusement.

The lights dimmed, and the announcer—the same guy who did the football calling, if I wasn't mistaken—started introducing the starting lineup for the basketball team. The boys in question jogged down the line of their teammates, trading knuckle bumps and high fives as they went.

When our boys won the tipoff, Naomi yelled, "C'mon, team, let's see some hustle!" and clapped her hands loudly.

Nathan leaned back so he could talk to me over the slope of her back. "Now you get to see what she's like during our games."

She rolled her eyes. "Please, I'm not half as bad as Mom."

"Mom is embarrassing. That's why I'm glad I can't hear you guys when I'm on the field."

"You know, one of my favorite things to do is wear some boots with a heel so that I can stomp my feet on the metal bleachers. It makes a huge noise, especially if others join in."

"I can't hear you," I admitted. "It's really hard in the helmet and on the field."

She shrugged. "The point is not that you hear us—it's that we disrupt the competition. And it works—SET THAT PIC!"

I flinched back from her volume, without a clue what she was yelling about.

"It works sometimes, because we've seen them struggling to call the plays," she finished at a normal volume.

"If it works…" I trailed off as she lurched forward to shout again.

"I'm so glad I don't have to witness you act like this," Nathan said again, running a hand through his hair.

She grinned, infectious, and I grinned back.

"Maybe I should give it a try," I said. "Just tell me when to yell."

"Anytime the ball goes through the hoop is a good start," she said, and I turned my eyes to the court again.

By the end of it, I really enjoyed watching someone else play a sport for a change. We lost the game pretty badly, but I yelled just as loud as Naomi for half of it, laughing at myself, so I had a good time regardless. We went to get food after, naturally, sipping on shakes in the corner booth.

Finn took a long slurp of his shake. "Man, the best part of that disaster was watching Camilla dancing."

Naomi frowned.

"Finn—" Nathan began.

"Please, you're telling me you *didn't* take a good look at the cheerleaders?"

"I mean, I watched them dance, but—"

"Don't lie to me, the only reason they're there is so the guys can enjoy them." He leaned back against the seat, smirking.

"Stop it, Finn," Naomi snapped. "You're being gross!"

"Pfft, no, I'm just being a man. A normal red-blooded man who can appreciate a beautiful woman."

"You can do that without—without being ugly about it! I mean, I'm a girl, too, and you don't look at me like that!"

"Yeah but all the other girls are all bitches and hoes. You're… Ugh, you just don't understand."

"Why not?"

"Because you're not a guy, Naomi. Duh."

"That's so—that's not even—" she sputtered, searching for words.

"Can we just drop this?" Nathan asked, trying to lean between them to cut off their line of vision.

"Is this your whole attitude towards women? That we're for ogling?" Naomi cut back in, ignoring her brother.

"Look, I'm just saying that women are pretty and men are specifically geared to look at them. Find them hot." Finn shrugged.

Luis frowned "I don't know—" he started, but Naomi cut him off.

"What about your sisters? Your mom? Do men look at them like that?"

"No, my sisters are just kids! My mom has enough boyfriends that I know men look at her like that!"

"But that's—ugh!" She threw up her hands. "I'm not doing this right now," she huffed, and scooted out of her seat before hustling out the door.

Nathan cast a worried look after her, hesitating a moment before following.

"Don't be gross," I said belatedly, torn between looking after Finn and checking on Naomi. I'd text her later.

"You think the same things, don't lie!"

"I really don't," said Luis firmly. "Have you ever even talked to Camilla?"

"Yes!"

"And what did you say?"

Finn spluttered. "I asked her for her number."

"Nothing else? Do you know her favorite color? What snacks she likes?"

"She likes smoothies!"

"And you know that because…?"

Finn pouted. "She posts on her stories."

Luis rolled his eyes, slowly and expressively. "But you haven't really talked to her. Maybe you should try that first. Then you can find out if you really like her."

"I know I like her!"

"But do you *like* her," Luis said. "Not 'do you think she's hot.'"

"Whatever." Finn blew a raspberry.

Our phones buzzed. It was Nathan, in the group chat, saying he and Naomi were going home, and he'd see us Monday.

Awkward silence itched at me, though Luis didn't seem to notice as he slurped his shake. "Well," he said leisurely. "I think I'll head home. Thanks for the sugar high, guys." And he sauntered out the door, where his mom was just pulling up in her Chevy Tahoe.

This left me and Finn, sitting across the table from one another. "At least you haven't abandoned me," he said bitterly.

"Hmm," I said. "I still don't think you're right."

"Ugh, don't start that again. You want to go for a drive?"

"No…I—I have homework," I said lamely. It wasn't totally true, I just wasn't comfortable.

"Fine. Goody-two-shoes." He jangled his keys. "I'll take you home."

19

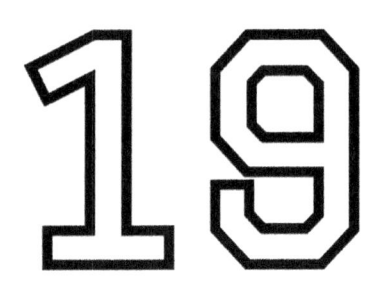

Every teenager wishes they could go on one big adventure, just them and their friends, at least once. Well guess what?—I actually did. That spring break of my junior year, I set up plans to visit my mom. Mom had a sister who owned a condo on Galveston Island. Now, I know Galveston is the toilet bowl of the world, but it's my toilet bowl and I will be taking no criticism, so I don't even want to hear it. So I called my mom, who called my aunt, who graciously agreed to let a pack of teenagers come stay in her house. My mom would function as the adult with brains—Finn certainly didn't count on that front—and my sisters would come along, too.

I broke this news to my friends over a lunch table in February, when it was cold and dismal and threatening snow. They, of course, were delighted. Naomi set about making plans, listing out board games to pack, beach activities, pulling up restaurants on her phone, backup plans for if it rained. Finn offered to drive us, and Luis said he'd talk to his mother about getting us a dinner reservation somewhere definitely too nice for us. Once again, I was reminded that he came from money, and we would likely never understand each other's views of the world. Nathan pulled up a map—ever practical, ever calm. But I grinned and imagined a week with my friends, more specifically, a week with Naomi. Maybe I could finally make a move.

For a while it seemed like Finn might not come—leaving us rideless—but then he said he'd readjusted his work schedule and his grandma would take care of his sisters while his mother was working.

The last week of school before break lasted approximately twenty years, and we had to wait through Sunday (Naomi didn't want to miss leading worship), before we met up at the Peterson's house early Monday morning. We began packing luggage in the bed of the truck with Finn and Nathan yanking on bungee cords to hold it down, a cooler of sodas (courtesy of Mrs. Peterson) in the backseat, where it would get kicked and nudged and smudged by our continual need to put our feet around or on top of it.

Mr. Peterson stood to the side of the driveway, carefully checking over our work "Text me when you get there," he said, but it wasn't an angry directive. It was a reminder, to which Naomi responded with a hug.

"We will. We'll be fine."

He nodded, and stepped back, hands in his pockets.

I climbed in behind the driver, my designated place after so many full-truck-to-school rides. For this drive, Naomi demanded she get the front seat.

"I'm not sitting next to your stinky B.O. for six hours. Plus, I'm the only one of us who can *actually* read a map."

"Hey, I keep a map in my head. You don't do that, you just use the GPS," Finn said.

"I can read a map," Nathan mumbled. She ignored him.

"And who's lost more often?" Naomi countered.

"I never get lost," Luis said, tilting his head whimsically. "I always know right where I am. Here. With myself. Somewhere in West Texas."

"You're lost, like, in the school," Finn grumbled.

"I actually did get lost on my first day."

"No surprise there."

"*How?*" I asked. It wasn't even that big.

"Backseat boys!" Nathan called, climbing in and closing the door behind him.

"Actually, Nathan, can I sit at the window? I'm always in the middle," Luis said.

"Sure." They initiated a complicated switch, involving Nathan arching upwards, cramping his limbs, while Luis slid beneath him over to the window.

"Oh my lord," I groaned, watching them monkey around.

When Nathan sat down in the middle with a thump, Naomi turned around, eyebrow cocked, to ask, "Are you quite finished?" Nathan responded by sticking out his tongue.

"Great, now I can't see out my rearview, you're too dang tall," Finn grumped.

"Just drive, Finn, those three are ridiculous," Naomi said.

"What did I do?" I cried, laughing.

"You exist," she answered, flapping her hand as if that explained everything.

The Petersons waved at us as we backed out of the driveway. Above us, long, gray clouds raced northward, blown away by swift March winds.

Naomi (given aux privileges by right of being in the front seat) started us on songs backed by guitars and stripped-down sounds, which I enjoyed when I could hear it. Finn and Nathan kept up a running bicker about a movie that was released ten years ago. Luis alternated between scrolling on his phone and making random comments about the scenery. ("Cows. Barn. Lots of trees. Ooh, a tractor. Bluebonnets, pretty.")

Like a scene from a movie, we sped (sometimes literally) through the Texas scenery, laughing, watching the sun climb in the sky. We survived on road trip snacks and sodas and gas station bathrooms, just for that day. It was all so transient, and dreamlike, and perfect.

I'm going to remember that drive for the rest of my life, I think. Even as the conversations we had faded, and even as I airbrush it to perfection, I'll remember it. It was the five of us, in a car, driving through the Texas spring. We were living every teenager's dream. Just for one perfect moment.

A day is not very long, all things said. It may seem so, but in the grand scheme, it isn't. A blip, really. Twenty-four hours. A passing breeze. But it can mean so much, in the end.

***

A lot happened that week, most of it involving sand or sightseeing. Those were meandering, lawless days, marked by ice cream and sunshades and endless waves. We stayed up too late and woke later, eating junk food and fighting a losing battle against sand getting everywhere.

My aunt's condo sat about four blocks from the beach, and had once seen some flood damage from a hurricane. But she practically lived there in the summers, and it remained fully furnished with three bedrooms. Naomi shared with my sisters, stowed on bunk beds and a rollaway, and us boys were left to the other room with air mattresses and a pull-out couch. Mom took the master bedroom. The only true hangup was the single shower issue, but my older sister drew up a little schedule of who showers first. (It was a genius schedule, really, not that I'd ever tell her. It ran from youngest to oldest, then oldest to youngest, then split down the middle so everyone had a chance to be the first at some point.)

The first day we went to the beach, hauling a picnic lunch, my mom and sisters coming along. Nathan was the first to suggest sunscreen for the white kids, but Finn somehow got sunburned all over his back by the afternoon. We got ice cream from a little kitschy shop nearby—my choice was a chocolate cone, hastily licking it before it melted away. Naomi chose lemon and raspberry in a cup, because she didn't want it running down her chin.

Nathan, licking vanilla cone into a neat peak, had it smeared on his chin and the corners of his mouth.

I indicated his mess, and he wiped it away with his wrist, shrugging. "I'll just wash off in the ocean."

Finn chose a single scoop of chocolate chip, and I made a mental note to check with my mom about maybe covering a couple of his meals or snacks. Subtly, though, so it didn't needle his pride.

Luis, naturally, had a lurid confection in blue, pink, and yellow.

"Your lips are blue," I said. "And your teeth. And—stick out your tongue. Yep. Tongue, too."

"Finally," he drawled "I'm fulfilling my true role as an alien. Soon I can be accepted into their society."

"You already are an alien," Finn said. "You talk like an alien who once read a book about how to talk to humans."

Luis put a dazed look in his eyes and deadened his tone. "Hmm. Take me to your leader."

Rolling his eyes, Finn groaned for the billionth time, "My back hurts."

On Wednesday, halfway through our trip, we visited the gardens and aquarium. Luis and Stella were making and messing with little bracelets made of rubber bands, something she'd been into recently. I could tell he'd be coming home with three dozen up to his elbow. Hailey was sticking close to Mom, but I bumped my shoulder against hers as we walked in.

"Ew, go away." She made the sign of the cross with her fingers.

"You stink," I returned.

"You were a mistake."

"All I'm saying is, our parents knew you wouldn't be good enough, so they had to have me."

"Ouch! Right in the insecurities!" Sibling greeting ritual completed, she said, "So, Naomi."

"What about her?"

She rolled her eyes. "You're so obvious."

"Buzz off!"

"She's pretty."

"Anyone can see that."

"I'm your older sister, it's my *job* to tease you about it. It's in the Older Sister Handbook we're given at your birth."

"Ugh."

She stuck out her tongue at me, childish as always.

I made a face back at her, pulling my chin into my neck to create a triple chin and crossing my eyes, and jogged to catch up with the boys.

Naomi and Nathan were huddled with their heads close together, murmuring. Finn punched me in the arm as I caught up to him, but when I returned the gesture, he flinched away, whining about his sunburn.

Once inside, I whipped out my sketchpad and started doing lightning sketches of plants, bugs, animals, birds, textures of bark, the angle of light through the windows. I kept Naomi in my peripheral. With her arms loose at her sides, chin tipped up, she looked at everything around her wide-eyed. She let herself get swept up in it, and I loved her for it.

In the quiet blueness of the aquarium, I couldn't see well enough to get clear sketches, so I walked beside her.

"Which is your favorite?" I asked quietly to not disturb the magic feeling of being underwater.

"I like the tropical ones that are bright and colorful. I don't know any of their names. Except Nemo. Which isn't really Nemo."

I laughed softly. "Right. I think the ocean is so beautiful, but so, so terrifying."

"Mm. Big and powerful."

"Yes. Have you seen some of the horror movie fuel down there?"

"Like the angler fish?"

"Yes! Or sea stars? Those are freaky."

"But the ocean also has dolphins. And shrimp! And crabs and turtles and octopuses," she said cheerfully.

"Octopi are terrifying too! They're like, the smartest creatures. They could take over the world if they tried!"

"Yes, but they're so cute!" She clasped her hands under her chin.

"I guess we'll have to see one, then."

When we did find an octopus, it was alone in its tank. Naomi pulled out her phone, trying to find a good angle to photograph. The creature—too many legs, too-bulbous head, and too-intelligent eyes—drifted to the front of the tank, raising and lowering its legs.

"It's—It's posing!" Naomi giggled.

"What?"

"It must know what a phone is. Or pictures. Or something."

"Wow, that's upsetting, I hate that."

"No, it's so sweet! It wants to be a little influencer, an internet star!"

I shuddered, making a disgusted noise.

Finn slammed into me. "What's up nerds, where've you been?"

"Naomi is adopting an octopus."

"Sick. Can I make it ink?"

"No! That means it's scared."

"No joke though, I want actual ink. A whole sleeve, clear up my arm and onto my back." He indicated the places on his body.

"Ouch."

I said, "If you get a tattoo, it's going to hurt worse than that sunburn."

"I'm tough. I can handle it."

"Like you're handling that sunburn?"

"Bro, shut up."

"Where's Nathan?" Naomi asked, finally shifting her attention from the water alien.

"Still looking at turtles," Finn supplied.

I pictured Nathan as a turtle, his shoulder pads as his shell. It made an odd kind of sense, his quiet steadiness, his need for solitude.

That night, as we piled under blankets in the living room to watch Nathan's choice of movie, I drew a little cartoon of him. I enhanced his jaw, his front teeth, made him look how he did when we won a game. I gave him a little fish friend.

I passed him the picture, without saying anything, in the middle of the movie. He looked at it for a moment. To me, he gave a quick thumbs up and a smile. But I saw him smooth it flat carefully before folding it with precise creases to tuck it away.

On Thursday, my mom took my sisters and Luis mini golfing, while Finn, Naomi, Nathan and I decided to go back to the beach. We took it slow, strolling down the sidewalk and leisurely picking a place to set up our towels.

Naomi lay on her towel, paging through a paperback.

"I'm gonna take a walk," Nathan said, jerking a thumb over his shoulder. As he strode away, broad shoulders cutting into the sky, he pressed his phone to his ear. I wondered who he was calling. Probably his girlfriend.

Finn kicked off his sandals and sprinted for the waves, whooping, peeling his shirt off as he went. He drove right into the sea foam, disappearing beneath the blue and reappearing much further from the sand.

I thought about following him for the briefest instant, but instead lowered myself beside Naomi, my toes digging into the sand. For a moment I simply looked at her, in her shorts and tank top, her hair piled atop her head. She had a mole on the outside of her right knee, and a scar at her left ankle, a little arc curving around the bone. Her cuticles were torn and chewed.

When I looked back up, her eyes met mine, and she raised her brows at me.

"Sorry," I said.

"For what?"

"I—" My heart thudded in my ears, and the words burned on my tongue, behind my teeth. *I love you. I think you're beautiful. I'm enamored with your voice and your smile and the calluses on your fingers.* I swallowed hard. "Nothing."

Her smile slipped away, and she swallowed. Finally, she said, "You have beautiful eyes, Zed."

"What?"

"Yeah. They look like Bambi eyes. Big, long lashes." She bit her lower lip. "Just. Really nice."

Naomi's eyes held the center of a supernova, a sunburst, the entire ocean. I had no clue what she saw in mine.

Something slimy slapped the side of my face, wrapping neatly around my nose, reeking of salt and ocean. I slapped the seaweed off my face, sputtering and spitting out sand.

"Oi, you coming or am I going to have to drag you?"

"I'm coming, Finn," I said, but I was still looking at Naomi.

***

By pure serendipity, I got to talk to Naomi alone that evening. We hadn't gone to bed yet, still eating junk food and cheap packaged cookies while talking over a movie. My inner introvert needed a moment alone, so I stepped onto the back porch of the condo that faced the beach. It was dark enough to see the stars, and I loved the way the sky met sea, two endless swaths of blue colliding and enveloping us.

Naomi padded out, barefoot in her shorts and a sweatshirt despite the beachy warmth. She leaned on the railing by me. "Stargazing?"

"Mm," I affirmed.

She turned her gaze upwards, and I, ever in tune with her movements, felt her smile at the sky. "Space," she started.

"The final frontier?"

She chuckled and jostled her shoulder into mine. "I meant that's what's out there. Space. And we've explored so little."

"You think there are aliens out there or something?"

"Maybe. It's so big...the possibilities are endless."

"Yeah. You ever heard of the multiverse theory?" I hoped she didn't think I was too nerdy.

"Where there's like...an infinite number of other realities out there that are different from our own? Yeah. It's cool."

"I love thinking about that. Like, what other possibilities are there for me? What could be different?"

"Yeah. And I don't know how it, like, meshes with Christianity, but the thought that there are other me's out there, living totally different lives from my own is really cool. I hope the Other Me's are doing okay, y'know?" She tucked a loose strand of hair behind her ear.

"Yeah." We were quiet for a moment. "Wonder if we all ever met, in those other universes."

"We have to. I refuse to believe we didn't."

A lump rose in my throat suddenly. I hoped we'd all found each other in those other worlds. Hoped we knew how good we had it, with each other. "Yeah," I said softly.

"Maybe there's a universe where you're like, super famous football players or something. Prodigies or whatever."

"What about you?"

"I'll be your groupie."

We giggled. "Or maybe there's one where we're in a band."

"Nathan can't carry a tune in a bucket," she said.

"He can play the drums. You can be our lead singer. I'll play electric guitar. Tattoos all up my arms. Wear some guyliner."

"Be like—be like the bad boy?" She laughed.

"Yeah."

"Or maybe there's one where I tried out for the Voice, or American Idol. And maybe I won." She said it so quietly, it felt like a secret confession. Like the admission of a private, long-beloved dream.

"You'd be great, of course you would."

She shifted in a shrug. "I'd hope so."

"And we'd all support you and love you, of course. We'd all be there at every show."

She hummed noncommittally.

"And anyway, if you're a musician in one, then I'm an artist in another, right? And maybe I meet you guys at one of my exhibitions. And like, maybe I get commissioned to paint a portrait of Luis, the talented football player. And of course, Finn has to come along to bother him while he's being painted."

"Oh Lord, he'd have paint on the walls."

It was my turn to laugh. "Yeah."

"I just feel like...we'd always find each other, you know? I don't like the idea that we didn't."

The burning lump in my throat was back again. "I know what you mean."

"And maybe it's like—we don't meet until college, or until we're older, or it takes us a long time to get together, a long time to find each other—but we still find each other, and know that we've found good people."

"The best people." I reached over and put my hand on top of hers. Just rested it there, a little lifeline to reality and the knowledge that we were together. "I bet I'd know you anywhere."

"I'd know you, and I'd choose you," she said.

"Choose me?"

"Yeah. Over anyone else, I choose to love you." Her words rang with complete conviction through our little patch of starlight. *I choose to love you.*

I swallowed hard, fighting back prickling in my eyes. "Yeah. Absolutely."

Her fingers shifted under my own. "Zed..."

I retracted my hand, slowly. "Sorry."

"No, I—"

We looked at each other then, in the darkness, like we were going to kiss. Or at least, like I was about to kiss *her.*

And then, forever the coward, I stepped away. Deep in the pit of my stomach, I knew I was making an irreversible choice. I loved our friendship so much, too much, and it would kill me to lose it.

I couldn't love her if there was a chance I'd lose her.

"Naomi, I...I can't." I swallowed hard. "I'm sorry. I- Goodnight," I said. I backed away quickly, stumbling over my own feet.

Her expression shuttered closed, mouth snapping into a line. "Goodnight," she said.

As I went inside I heard her exhale like she was going to cry.

That Friday we biked the length of the island. I avoided Naomi, hanging back to let Finn and Luis race ahead, with Nathan and Naomi in front of me. She drooped on her bike, as Nathan kept pace with her. I slowed my peddling, giving her the space from me she deserved. The sun shone in my eyes as I pedaled, passing touristy shops and beach houses on stilts and rocks steps to the sandy beach below. I passed several cairns of flat rocks, which I found a fascinating expression of humanity's desire to make art, regardless of the medium or setting.

Too soon, I found myself dropping too far back, and had to hustle to catch up, panting. When I caught up, they were waiting for me, propping their bikes on one leg.

"Ice cream?" Naomi said to me.

"Is that even a question?"

"I don't know. There's plenty of questions I need answers for."

I swallowed. "Yes, I want ice cream."

We ordered. As Finn went up to the counter, I stepped beside him. "I'll get it," I said.

"The hell?" he snapped.

"I just—just for fun."

"Fun? I can pay for my own damn ice cream." He slapped cash on the counter, his chin pointed at me like he wanted to fight.

I threw my hands up. "Sorry."

Once I had my cone, I drifted away to watch the rolling ocean, listening to the endless waves and watching the foam dance and toss. I seemed to be screwing up left and right.

Friendship is like that, sometimes. You mess up. And you ask: How strong is your friendship? Can it survive mistakes? Hurt feelings? Can it survive your own stupidity?

Finn—Finn is easy to fix. Give him five minutes to be angry and noisy about it, and he'll get over it. Maybe it's a guy thing. But it wasn't until our drive home that things started to feel right again with Naomi. We left the condo, saying farewell to my sisters and mom. Mom insisted upon a text at our safe arrival home. We settled in for the long haul.

Nathan, copiloting Finn, had a slow country soundtrack running against the rumble of the wheels on the road.

Naomi leaned against the door, her head on the window.

Luis snored on my other side.

I turned my head to her. I considered apologizing, whispering a confession, taking her hand. Instead, I slid her a folded piece of paper.

She glanced at me sidelong as she unfolded it. I had drawn us, as a band, surrounded by stars and little galaxies. I leaned into the cartoonish style, adding tattoos and piercings and instruments. Beneath, I'd added her words: *infinite realities.*

I held my breath, crossed my fingers beneath my thigh.

She smiled.

My heart started beating again.

"I love it. I'm going to put this on my wall."

And all was right in the world again.

20

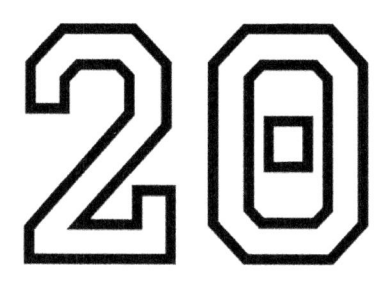

March blew into April. Spring descended upon us with bluster and thunder—and of course the ever present threat of tornadoes. We're basically in the middle of Tornado Alley, and we spent more than one class period sitting in the hall. We did enough homework to keep our chins above water in our classes, dreaded standardized testing, thought longingly of summer. Naomi borrowed Finn's letterman almost every morning while it was still chilly, showing up to math class with the sleeves covering her hands. Nathan kept making mysterious phone calls, and frequently passed on Friday evening hang times. Luis and Naomi prepared for spring theatre things—one act play— and I found myself doodling through classes, doing just enough to pass. We dealt with the usual stressors of grades, standardized testing, teachers giving homework as though they were the only person to assign homework and we had nothing better to do. Coach C continued to teach in class, and he always made sure to exchange a few words with me after class, like he was checking in.

One day in the middle of April, when we got to school, we found that someone had spray-painted the f-word on Luis' locker. The other f-word, I mean, the long one. I'm not going to write it here, but I think you get the picture.

All three of us saw it, Nathan going quiet and concerned on one side, me dumbfounded on the other. Finn noticed last, stiffening the way a bobcat does right before it pounces.

"Who did this?" That was Finn, spitting mad but deathly quiet.

Nathan raised his shoulders. *You tell me.*

"I'll kill him. I'll kill that bastard."

I placed a hand on his arm, the tendons sharp under my palm. My own temples ached with the force of my scowl.

Between Luis and Finn there had always been something heightened, something just on the edge of too intense. Now it was here, in full force, emblazoned on Finn's face. Spelled across his knuckles. Whispered in his ragged breathing. The bookends, the oldest and youngest, the two most talented boys on the team. Whatever it was between them, this friendship, this fierceness, this *nobody picks on my little brother but me,* it was going to blow up, and burn us all in the explosion.

Perhaps language shouldn't be a big deal, especially in a place where locker room jabs fly freely, except under the sharp ears and disapproving expressions of Coach C, but it is. Words mean things, and names mean even more, and they have the power to build us up or break us down.

As a unit, the three of us moved through the hall. The theatre kids were just finishing their early rehearsal. There was Luis, walking through the hall. He kept his chin up, his hair falling in soft curls around his face. He didn't stop to talk to anyone, and no one tried. Eyes were on him, yet he cut through the crowd. If it had been a movie, it would have been the perfect opportunity for a quippy remark, a sharp assurance of himself. As it was, he kept his chin high, and his eyes dry.

Naomi came up to his side and slid her hand into his.

He looked at her, offering a smile.

But for all whispers surrounding him, it could be a normal day at school.

Finn beelined for him. "Luis. We'll take care of them for you, we'll get 'im—"

"Get who?" Luis asked softly.

Finn, confused, stepped back. "Caleb Hanson. Are you dumb? It had to be him, only he would do something that stupid—"

Luis shrugged. "What is there to get?"

"But they—"

"It doesn't matter, Finn," he said firmly. "I'd rather you not get in trouble for me."

"But—" he struggled to process, gripping at Luis' sleeve. "But I can—"

"Finn, no." He looked at me. "You, too, Zed. Besides," he grinned, the same easy wide-mouthed smile he'd always had. "Naomi gave me a muffin. My day is already great." He gently untangled Finn's fingers from his sleeve. "See you later." And he was off, loping through the halls to class.

Naomi stayed with us, hugging her books close to her chest.

"A muffin? Really?" Finn asked.

"It was banana nut."

"Ah, so that explains it," Nathan said. "I do make good muffins."

Finn, bewildered and a bit untethered, leaned back on Nathan, who caught him easily and kept him upright. "He's not even mad. Is he in shock?" He turned to Naomi.

"No. He's more upset than he's letting on right now, but really, I think he'll be alright." She shrugged. "If anyone could survive this, it's Luis."

Inhaling sharply, Finn pushed himself off of Nathan, frowning. "Right. Meet me after, we'll go to his house. See what he actually wants." He moved away to his locker with such determination. A ship plowing through the ocean. A rocket cutting through the atmosphere. Or maybe, a tree, bowing in a storm.

Everyone heard when Luis got called to the office on the intercom. Every eye followed him on his way out the door. He didn't come back.

***

After school, Finn drove us to Luis' house. I hadn't seen him since the beginning of school so he'd probably been sent home. His mother opened the door, brows pinched with concern. After greeting us, she directed us to the game room, where we found Luis draped across a chair and thumbing his phone.

"Luis! My man! What's the plan to mess these guys up, huh?" Finn plopped onto the couch.

Naomi, Nathan, and I arranged ourselves about the room: Nathan settling beside Finn like an anchor; Naomi on top of the pool table, legs crossed, tapping at the ledge; and me on the floor, sitting with my legs splayed across the white shag rug.

"Nothing, Finn," Luis said, still scrolling.

"Please. They can't be allowed to say shit like that about you, man. It's not right."

Luis sighed and dropped his phone onto his stomach, clearly bracing for a long conversation. "It doesn't matter. Guys like them, they say stuff. It's wrong. *We* know it's wrong. They have to figure it out on their own."

"Well, maybe we could help them figure it out."

"No. It's like—look." Luis shifted, shaping his hands like he was holding a beach ball. "Look, bananas are my favorite fruit, right? But Finn hates them."

Finn nodded, making a face. "Mushy," he mumbled.

"But like—he can't stop me from eating them. If he does, I'll probably just keep picking them to annoy him, or whatever. Caleb, he'll keep bullying other people, and he'll just keep doing what he does, and he probably wants us to react, but he's not going to stop just 'cause we try to tell him to." He talked in his slow way, drawling out his story with more precision than usual. No rabbit trails. No side stories. (Mostly.) "You gotta let people make their own choices. You can't go on trying to fix 'em or change 'em, they'll just do what you don't want even harder. You see?"

I snuck a glance at Finn, who looked more baffled than anything. Nathan seemed to be tracking, and Naomi, too, though she was picking at the tassel dangling from the collar of her blouse. For my part, I think I got what Luis was trying to say. Caleb was a bully, and he wasn't going to stop being a bully just because we told him to, or because we told him it was wrong.

"What they did was still wrong, though," Nathan said, rolling his head on the top of the couch to focus on Luis. "They made a bad choice."

"But like—it doesn't really matter. The thing to do is let it go, and leave them be."

"That's like, really zen, dude," Nathan said.

"We can't just—*let it be.* That's not how it works," Finn cried, pinching his brows together. "Bananas are gross, but they are *not* the same as bullying."

Luis sighed. "Well, look. The right thing to do is treat people with kindness. At all times. I've decided."

"Oh, you've decided? And so now the whole world oughta follow your plan?" Finn threw his hands up in exasperation. "Tell me how that works out."

Luis shrugged. "If enough people realize the best way to live is to be kind, sure."

Snorting, Finn shook his head. "Right. Well, that's never gonna happen. Keep dreaming, bro."

"I agree with you, Luis." Naomi dipped her head. "I think you're right. But it's still wrong, what they did. Still bothers me. They weren't acting with kindness. But I guess we can't fight fire with fire." She squeezed her hand over her knee, once, quickly. The only sign of her anger. "And I—I guess I just want you to know I love you. That's all."

Luis smiled, open and chill. "I love you, too."

Finn threw himself off the couch. "Oh, so it's all sunshine and rainbows now? Butterflies and roses? Because Luis said it's alright we're just going to ignore they called him a *fag?*"

Nathan flinched. "Don't think you should be saying that word, bro. Doesn't seem right to me."

Finn blew a raspberry.

Luis, tapping at his phone again, and not meeting their eyes, said, "What if, maybe..." Slowly, so slowly, he shut off his phone and placed it on the seat beside him. "What if, maybe, I was what they say I am?"

"Oh, Luis," said Naomi, sliding off the table. She reached for him. He went, leaning into her stomach and ribs. "Of course that doesn't change a thing." He wrapped his arms around her middle, and she stroked the back of his head. "We're your friends, and we aren't planning on being anything different. No matter what." She cast her gaze around at us, and I nodded back. I was with her. Of course I was.

Finn still looked undone, confused. "You are?"

Luis gently pushed away from Naomi and nodded. "Yeah." He said it softly, with certainty, but his eyes faltered from Finn's face.

"But—"

Nathan put a hand on Finn's arm.

"Cool, bro," I said, unsure if it was the right thing. "'S awesome that you've, like, figured it out."

Luis laughed, even though it wasn't funny. "It wasn't very hard. Hardest part's hoping people still love me."

"Oh, of course we do, of course we do," Naomi said, the words spilling out of her.

Nathan nodded. "Thanks for sharing with us."

Only Finn remained silent and still, separated from us, almost like he was confused.

"You're not—bothered?" Luis asked. "Because, y'know..."

Naomi tilted her head, a funny look on her face, halfway angry halfway confused. "Because we're Christians?"

"Yeah."

"Nope," Nathan said. The twins shared a look. "If you were doing something bad, or hurting somebody, we'd—we'd speak the truth in love, I suppose. But this isn't the same. I might not—well, it's not the time to get into intricacies."

"Not the same at all," she added. "And anyway, it doesn't matter. You're our friend."

Luis tilted onto Naomi, heaving a breath. "Oh my god," he whispered, like it was the first time he'd exhaled a breath he'd been holding for ages.

I looked for Finn again, but he'd left the room. Nathan shrugged at me, and got up to go after him.

I nudged Luis' foot with my toe. "Is that why you're so fast on the field?"

He scrunched his nose in confusion.

"Cause you're outrunning all the haters?"

"Boooo," Nathan called from the doorway.

Luis and Naomi laughed, and relief rolled off Luis in waves. I felt that everything was the same and nothing was the same, but it was alright.

***

When I got home that evening, Dad was also home, which was unique both in its rarity and in the fact that he stood in the kitchen, when normally he'd be on the couch or in his room.

"Hey," he greeted me, rummaging in the fridge.

"Hey," I said warily, unsure of which version of Dad I was going to talk to, having last seen him swearing into his phone about something oil related.

"How was school today, son?"

His use of the word 'son' irritated me—what right did he have to call me that?—but I couldn't pinpoint why, so I replied sharply, "Great. Some kid called my friend a faggot and got away with it."

Dad looked at me fast, eyes narrowed. "Just locker room talk, ain't it?"

"Not when it was spray-painted across his locker by guys who aren't on the team."

"I'm sure there ain't nothin' personal behind it."

"I don't know, Dad, seems about as personal as someone calling me an Oreo. Or a coon. Or what have you. It's the same kind of thing." My face flooded with heat. I dropped my backpack to the ground with a thump.

"No, it ain't the same at all."

"And why not?"

"Guess it only matters if it's true. And your buddy, the gay boy, it's true, isn't it? If you're speaking the truth, it doesn't matter, right?"

"Yes, yes it damn well does!" Nathan's words came back to me: *speak the truth in love.* No, this wasn't the same thing at all.

"Do *not* swear in my house! And don't you take that tone with me."

"You really think it's okay to say cruel things because they're true?" I blazed on.

He shrugged. "You ain't never going to agree with me."

I locked my jaw, swept my bag off the ground. "Thank you for your opinion," I said.

"Well, the school called me about it. The secretary said since I'm your parent she assumed I'd want to know you were dealing with a bullying situation. Small towns," he grunted.

I jerked, angry. He was gone for days at a time, a barely speaking to me, and *now* it was appropriate to parent me? This was my friend we were talking about, someone he would know if he'd bothered to pay attention to my life. Weirded out by the secretary's call—how was it any of her business?—I turned on my heel and said, "Well, everything is fine. My friend is fine."

"Huh. Stay out of trouble, y'hear?"

"Yeah, whatever." I shut the door to my room with a click.

***

The next morning, I skateboarded to school. When I arrived, I spotted Nathan right away, towering head and shoulders over the other kids. He grabbed me as I passed him, foregoing our normal fist bump in favor of dragging me down the hall so we could see in the window of the Coaches' office. Coach C and Coach both sat in the room, along with Luis. Coach C appeared to be doing most of the talking while Coach mostly just nodded every few words.

Luis stood there, looking small in a sweater with the sleeves pulled over his hands. He kept his arms close to his chest, but his spine was ram-rod straight. Coach C put his hand on Luis' shoulder, and he relaxed, chin tilting up.

Coach opened the door and rolled his eyes when he spotted us, unsurprised at our snooping behavior. Luis exited, smiling at us.

Coach C poked his head out. "Morning, gentlemen. Was spying on us to your satisfaction?"

I felt my face heat. "Sorry, Coach C."

"Don't worry about it, son."

I flashed back to my dad saying *son* the night before. Funny how I didn't feel that irritation now. Coach C told us to get to class and shut the door.

"What was that about?" Nathan said, throwing his arm over Luis' shoulders in his familiar big brother style, bracketing the boy between us.

"He just wanted to talk. Told me to keep my head down and my chin up."

"Wise words," Nathan said.

"How would you even do that?" I asked, slipping into a joking tone. I tipped my chin down, then up, raising my brows and frowning. "Seems physically impossible."

Luis grinned as Nathan tussled his dark, sleek hair. "And he wanted to make sure I'd be comfortable in the locker room, and that if anyone on the team said anything to me he'd take care of it. What do you reckon that means?" He cast an arm around my waist and pulled me in, so casually affectionate.

"Probably bench them for a game or two," I said. "I didn't think Coach'd be so...progressive."

Nathan wrinkled his nose at me. "We're a small town, bro, not the nineteen fifties."

"That's not what I meant," I said. "I just meant—he seems so...old," I finished lamely.

"Coach C is good people," Nathan said, which roughly translated to mean he'd drop everything to help out a friend in need.

Luis heaved a sigh. "I thought when they called me in there they were going to kick me off the team. That was so much better than I thought."

The bell rang. We disentangled ourselves just as Naomi sprinted up, her backpack bouncing.

"Guys," she said, almost frantic. "Where's Finn?"

"Probably just late again," Nathan shrugged. It wasn't the first time this year we'd had to seek alternate transportation–Mr. Peterson had driven us.

Naomi hurried on, "I know, he texted me he was running late. But you know who else is missing today? Caleb Hanson."

I tried to connect the dots, even as Naomi had clearly connected the dots *and* finished the color by number.

"And I've been texting him and he won't say where he is or what he's doing."

I scratched my chin. "He could just be like, really late. Or he's skipping. He's a senior, after all."

She frowned at me. "What would he do instead?"

"Drink or smoke, probably."

"I didn't know he'd been doing that."

"Well, he's not going to tell *you*," Luis chimed in. "You're too much of a goody-two-shoes."

She stuck her tongue out.

"He's probably just late again," Nathan soothed. "We gotta go or else we'll be late for class, and that's dumb because we're already here."

The little furrow between her eyes didn't disappear, but she nodded. Her fingers brushed over her phone in her back pocket, then moved to her mouth where she nibbled on her thumb nail. "Right. Let's go." Pivoting on her heel, she was gone.

It wasn't until lunch that we learned what happened to Finn. He showed up late, strolling in like the cat who got the canary, a cut over his eyebrow and bruising under his left eye with bandaids all across his knuckles. He slid into his seat, manspreading as he reclined with his hands behind his head.

"Finn!" Naomi exclaimed in worry. "What happened?"

"Oh, you should see the other guy."

I frowned. "Who *is* the other guy?"

Finn's smile dropped. "Caleb Hanson, dumbass. Who else would I be fighting?"

"You didn't," Luis said, panic entering his face.

"I did."

"Oh no." Luis buried his head in his hands.

"What did you do, meet in the parking lot at three in the morning?"

"Nah, this morning, before school."

"You weren't late at all," Naomi realized, newly horrified.

Now here's a thing that's important to remember. I'm from the city. I saw fights at least once a week back there–the serious kind, not the little scuffles in the hall. I knew exactly how this was going to go down. "Finn," I said, "you need to leave. They're going to suspend you anyway, especially if you fought on school grounds."

"Like I give a shit."

"Finn," I said, more urgently this time. "You're a senior. You're trying to get a scholarship, right? This won't help your case. This is a misdemeanor, man, it's going on your permanent record."

"And the fact that I was defending my friend won't mean anything?" He ran a bruised hand over his head, his hair all shaggy and messy, making him look like a hedgehog or a racoon. Some sort of small, pointy, rodent-like animal, cornered and snarling.

"It won't," I assured him. "Noble fighting is still fighting."

He made a gruff sound, further reinforcing his resemblance to a wild animal.

"How bad is it?" Naomi asked, reaching toward his face.

He shied away, ducking out of reach. "Not that bad."

She bit her lip, unconvinced.

Luis' head was still down, fingers threaded through his hair. "I didn't want this to be—I didn't want—" he mumbled. Standing so fast he tipped his chair over, he scooped up his tray and dumped it in the trash, tray included. The lunch monitor sent an aggrieved look at his back, but he left the cafeteria and didn't look back.

"What'sa matter with him?" Finn asked, tonguing his split lip.

"You did exactly what he didn't want you to do." Naomi had her arms crossed now, retreating into herself.

Nathan poked at the food on his plate. "I understand why you did it," he said. "But you shouldn't have."

Storm clouds gathered on his face, darkening his eyes and making his face red. "I didn't see you doing anything." He slammed his palm flat on the table.

I flinched.

"Catch you losers later. I'm out." Finn stormed away, hands pushed into the pockets of his letterman jacket.

Nathan sighed, shaking his head. "I knew—" he stopped.

"You *knew*?" Naomi asked.

"I knew I should've stopped him," he clarified. "But yes. He asked me to come along."

"Oh my god," she said softly.

"He's going to get suspended," I said. "They both will."

She shook her head. "I'm worried about him," she confessed, blue eyes darting between us.

Nathan nodded his assent.

I thought of him drinking in the bed of his truck, and me, not stopping him.

***

Finn got suspended that day. He texted the group chat,

Suspension for the cool kids. And by cool kids, I mean me.

I wasn't surprised when he pulled up to my house that night. He drove west again, alternating between saying nothing and rambling for long stretches about everything. Everything except what had actually happened. I wondered if his family could afford any sort of fine.

At our spot at the caprock, he killed the truck and sat for a long minute, gripping the wheel. The click of the seatbelt thundered in the silent cab.

He offered nothing, no words, no explanation, as he pulled a blunt out his pocket in the bed of the truck and lit it. He cast a glance at me. I'd never actually seen him smoke, though I knew he'd done it. And now here he was, holding the blunt between his forefinger and thumb like he wasn't sure what to do with it, and looked wrong somehow, like he'd grown a sixth finger.

He handed the blunt to me.

"Dude, I'm not so sure about this." I hesitated to take it, holding it gingerly between two fingers.

"It's just marijuana, dude, it's not cocaine. Relax."

I took a drag. It burned. I coughed.

"You're not supposed to—" he took it back, huffing in frustration. "Like this." He took a smooth drag, chest rising and falling, and passed it back.

The back of my throat burned, and my eyes and nose still watered but I tried again. I hated the flavor of it—burnt, sweet, smoky—and I shook my head. "I don't think that's for me, man. Maybe I'll change my mind, but…"

He shrugged. "More for me, then." He leaned back, humming. "Caleb Hanson had it coming."

"Maybe."

"He's deserved that since sixth grade."

I didn't know about that, about anyone deserving a beating, but maybe he was right. There certainly was no love lost between Caleb and me.

He took another drag, the tip of the blunt flaring orange in the darkness. "You know, you're probably my best friend."

And that, despite everything, made me smile. I had never been Finn's copilot—that had always been Nathan—but I couldn't deny that what we had was special, too. I'd never had a best friend like him. I'd never had friends like any of them. And I didn't intend to lose them, not now, not ever.

"Yeah," I said softly. "You too."

21

I worked a morning shift on my birthday, which put me in an absolutely fantastic mood. Joe, presumably, had no idea it was my birthday, and only waved a hello as he unlocked the door. The morning sky, foggy gray, didn't improve my mood. Nor did the first three vans of moms getting coffee while their kids squealed in the back seat.

But right about nine thirty, Finn's truck pulled into the parking lot. I squinted, leaning over the counter to get a better look through the door, and was greeted by the sight of Luis sprinting up and plastering himself to the door, smushing his cheek, lips, and ear to the glass. Finn popped up over his shoulder, puffing out his cheeks and bugging out his eyes, wiggling his fingers on either side of his head like moose antlers.

I groaned theatrically, but couldn't stop the smile already spreading across my mouth.

The door burst open. "Surprise!" shouted Naomi. She had on flowy yellow overall shorts with a blue and white polka dot tank top underneath. I could see all the freckles dotted up her arms and scattered on her shoulders.

"Hey guys," I said with exasperated affection.

"Did we get you?" Luis asked.

"Yep, you sure got me," I said.

Nathan walked in, orange balloons bobbing above his head. "Happy Birthday!"

Joe hustled in from the kitchen. "Surprise! Oh, I'm late."

"You knew about this?" I squinted at the old man.

"'Course I did. Wouldn't make you work this early on the weekends otherwise, would I?"

I raised my brows. "Uh..."

He slapped my shoulder, shifting his focus to Naomi. "Did you bring that cake?"

"Actually, I did," Nathan said, holding up a rectangular pan. "It's lemon."

"That sounds delicious," I said. "What coffee goes well with lemon cake? Hang on," I pulled my phone out of my back pocket.

"I thought I told you no phones at the bar?" Joe said.

"Um—" I wondered if I'd just lost my job, but Joe slapped my shoulder again.

"I'll let you get away with it. It's your birthday!" He shook his head as he left from behind the counter. "You kids and your phones. 'Course, when I was your age, it was 'you kids and your rock and roll music'."

"Music!" Naomi said, delighted, and whipped out her own phone. A moment later, she hijacked the coffee shop's Bluetooth system to play what sounded like some classic Motown.

My google search turned up very little in the way of lemon cake/coffee pairings, so I decided to make everyone a drip coffee, except Naomi, to whom I would give my free drink of the day in the form of a hazelnut latte, because she liked those. By the time I poured the malformed latte art into a cup and hastily concealed it with a lid, Joe was shooing me out from the bar and gathering the mugs I'd filled with the $2 drip.

My friends wrangled me into a chair at the head of a table, where they placed candles all along the lemon cake, which had a thin layer of white glaze dotted with poppyseeds. Naomi led them all in singing Happy Birthday, even as I covered my face in my hands and pretended to be embarrassed, I was secretly pleased.

We all sat around the table stuffing our faces, though I kept one eye on the door so I could jump up and get back to work if someone came in. Finn was right next to me, with Naomi on my other side.

"This is really good, Miss Naomi," said Joe.

"Oh, actually Nathan made it," she said.

Nathan shrugged. "Just from a box. But yeah, I like to bake."

"Well, whaddya know," Joe said, leaning back in his chair. "My wife, she was a really good baker. Used to bake bread every day, and cook dinner, too. You know, we met in high school."

"I didn't know that, actually," Naomi said. "Were y'all high school sweethearts?" She was focused on him the way she always did when she listened, fully locked in on their face like they were the only person in the room.

Nathan had some of the same mannerisms, but with him, it felt more like he was being polite and respectful.

"Yeah, yeah we were! Got married in..." he thought for a minute. "Sixty-two? Yeah, that's right. She was a cheerleader and I was a football star."

Beside me, Finn twitched and rolled his eyes. He muttered, "Go figure. Everyone here is high school sweethearts."

I sent him a quelling look. "How long were you married?" I asked Joe. I'd never seen or heard of a wife, just his granddaughter.

He paused, mumbled under his breath and seemed to count on his fingers. "Forty-eight years," he said finally.

I was impressed. Forty-eight years was far, far longer than my parents.

"That must have taken some hard work," said Luis.

Again, Finn muttered, "Yeah, it's definitely not because getting a divorce back then was super hard or anything."

"Finn," I grumbled. "Please."

"Oh yeah, hard work. Just remember the husband always gets the last word in any argument, and those words are 'yes ma'am.'"

Again, Finn turned toward me and away from Joe to privately pretend to gag. I glanced at Joe to see if he noticed, but he was looking at Luis.

Luis, for his part, had his hands clasped under his chin. "What's the most romantic thing you did for her?"

"Oh…I don't know. I always made sure to buy her flowers. On her birthday…Valentines, you know, all the holidays. Or just because."

"That's sweet," Naomi said. I could practically hear the gears turning in her mind as she thought up a sweet song.

"Did you always live here?" Luis asked.

"Yep. Never left."

Finn coughed into his hand. "Gross."

I nudged him with my elbow, and made a quick hand gesture to say, *cut it out!*

"Yep, Terrytown might not be the biggest or the richest or the cleanest town, but it's a good place. And you can always tell what's going on. If the oil rigs are still, it's hard times. If they're moving, expect good times to come." He shrugged, face wrinkling to smile. "It's always been that way. And probably always will be."

My phone cut into his monologue, ringing loudly. It was my mom. I held it up. "Do you mind if I—?" I motioned toward the door.

Joe waved me off.

I stepped outside, squinting a bit in the sun. "Hi, Mom."

"Happy Birthday!" three feminine voices squealed on the other side of the line.

"Thanks."

"Are you having a good birthday, sweetheart?"

"You know, I really am." I glanced back inside. "My friends surprised me with a cake at work."

"Aw, that's so nice!" Stella said.

"It was really yummy." I paused, unsure how to go on.

"Did you get the card I sent?" Mom asked.

"Uh, not yet, but I'm sure it will arrive soon." I glanced inside again, wanting to rejoin my friends. Naomi was also doling out more cake and I wanted some.

"Well, keep an eye out," she said. "Let me know when it gets there."

"I will."

"Do you feel older?" Hailey asked in a teasing tone.

"Not really?"

She sniffed, and added in a mock-teary tone, "My baby brother, all grown up."

"Okay, okay," I said.

A minivan pulled into the parking lot and headed for the drive-through.

"I gotta go," I said, already with my hand on the door.

"okay," Mom sounded surprised and a little sad. "Bye sweetheart, we love you."

"Love you!" my sisters chorused.

"Bye," I said, and hung up as I hustled behind the bar. I served the minivan, scarfed another slice of cake, and served another two cars at the drive-through. An elderly couple came in and drank their coffee at a table while watching my friends out of the corner of their eyes. My friends were keeping the noise to a dull roar, at least. They weren't being disruptive. Yet.

Soon, Nathan and Naomi moved to clean up the cake dishes and balloons, and Luis rubbed his belly theatrically and sidled up to the bar to ask me for more baked goods. I told him would have to pay for them, and he pouted at me.

"Bro, you're like, loaded," I said.

"Yeah," he agreed, "but I forgot my wallet at home."

"That makes sense," I said.

He wandered off to pester Nathan about more cake, even as Nathan wiped down the table to rid it of sticky yellow crumbs.

Finn leaned on the bar. "I don't like birthdays," Finn said. "It's just a reminder of all the shit I can't have. Like, am I always going to be stuck here? Will I always be driving my kid sisters around and stocking shelves? Am I already a has-been at eighteen?"

I felt a rumble of discontent. He was so mired in his own self-pity, he couldn't even have a good time at my birthday. "Finn..."

He glared at me. "Don't you start. I haven't gotten a single call or email or anything from a scout or a college or nothing. The only way I'd keep playing football is on a scholarship, and I don't see anyone lining up to give me money."

I finished toweling off a coffee cup and set it among the mug stacks behind the counter. "Maybe there's more to life than football or college," I said cautiously.

"Like what?" Finn scoffed.

I didn't know how to answer, but fortunately, Naomi saved me by flouncing up. *Unfortunately*, what she said was, "Guys, guess what? I got my SAT scores back. I can start applying for college!" She did a little dance to express her joy. "It's equal parts exciting and stressful."

Finn made an ugly face before walking away in a huff.

"Did I say something wrong?" Naomi asked in a small voice.

"He was just talking about college," I said.

"Oh," she said in an even smaller voice.

"I'm sure he'll get over it," I assured her, even as I wondered if that was true.

"Right," she said. She sat at a bar stool. "Did you have a good birthday?"

"Yes. Thanks for doing this."

She waved me off. "I like doing stuff like this."

"It really meant a lot," I said. "I love hanging out with you guys."

"Me too," she said, smiling. "I liked hearing Mr. Joe's story."

"Yeah, it was cool. Couldn't imagine living here my whole life, though."

Naomi shrugged, a fond sort of wistfulness in her face. "I could. A lot of people do live here their whole lives. They get jobs in the oil field and marry their high school sweetheart, and they never leave." She swallowed, looking at the wood grain of the bar.

I wiped coffee grinds off the counter—a constant problem—caught them in my palm, and washed my hands. I didn't want to stay here my whole life. I wondered if Naomi did *want* to stay. I wondered where any of us would be, in ten years. That thought was too scary and I hastily shoved it away.

By the time I returned to Naomi, Nathan was using a blade of bahia grass, picked from outside, to tickle her ear. She was swatting it away and trying to snatch it from him. He held it over her head, a distance she'd never hope to cross, unless she suddenly developed the tree climbing skills of a squirrel.

"We're headed out," said Nathan, as Naomi tugged on his shoulder. His arm didn't budge.

"Give me—!" Naomi snarled, then in a tone sweet as honey, said, "Bye Zed, see you later!"

I laughed, waving goodbye. Luis gave me a big smile and a wave as he headed out the door, but Finn only nodded with his chin. Looking into his eyes, I could still see the anger and pain lingering there as he turned away.

***

"We *have* to go," said Naomi. "You have to go, Finn, it's your senior year."

He rolled his eyes, the busted one still vaguely yellow with fading bruises. "And do what? Stand awkwardly to the side?"

"No, we'll go with you! And it will be super fun. C'mon!"

He rolled his eyes again, picking at the shag rug in Luis' game room. His cut lip now healed and the rest of the bruising faded to a mottled yellow-green, he had returned to school. Naomi desperately wanted to go to prom, hence why she was trying to convince Finn.

I'd never been to a prom, though I'd been to a few other school dances, and they were all the same: awkward dancing, loud music, flashing lights. I didn't particularly care but if Naomi wanted to go, then I was one-hundred percent down for it.

"Look," Naomi said, "I'll even buy your ticket."

Finn slumped, knowing he'd lost.

So we went, all five of us. Finn picked me up in his truck, as always, wearing cowboy boots and his good jeans, which was as close to dressy as he got. Luis came on his own, looking very snazzy in a suit and bow tie, and the Petersons arrived together.

I spotted Naomi first, wearing a yellow dress. Every other girl was wearing either a strapless ballgown or a tiny tight dress that didn't leave much to the imagination. But not Naomi.

She wore a yellow ballgown, tight at the top with wide straps. The skirt fell loose in an uneven, pointed hem. When she spun, it swirled out around her in a star-like shape. Her hair fell in a sheet, soft and flowing, all the rebellious curls coaxed away for the evening.

She looked a little like a princess. She looked a little like the sun.

"You're blonde!" I said, and immediately on the heels of that, "Nathan has a *girlfriend*?"

She laughed. "You haven't noticed? He's been mooning over her all year!"

Nathan walked in, Annabella Gutierrez on his arm. He had the biggest, goofiest grin on his face, and nothing could have wiped it off.

I frowned appreciatively. "Huh. I wondered who he'd been talking to." I looked her up and down. "You look beautiful. The blonde is a good look."

She flushed with happiness, flashing white teeth. "Thanks. Mom said I could dye it after my birthday."

"You look—you look beautiful. I mean, it looks beautiful."

And she was lovely, all radiance and light.

"You should tell her she looks like Taylor Swift!" Nathan shouted. "She'll love that."

"No!" Naomi squealed. "That's not why I did it!"

Luis said, "I think you look like a disney princess. Maybe Merida, because of the curls. But she's a red head. Or maybe Rapunzel? Not long enough. How about Elsa?"

Naomi shook her head and made the sign of the cross with her fingers. "No side braids for me. Remember what happened in the green room?"

"Do I ever," Luis said, getting a shell-shocked look in his eyes. "We went though a whole bottle of detangler."

Naomi grimaced. "Don't remind me."

Luis grabbed her hand. "Dance with me!"

As he pulled her away, I heard her laugh, "I love you, you weirdo!"

The music shook the gym and the lights flashed bright around us. People congregated on the floor, jumping together like it was a club. The five of us joined the fray, Finn being pulled unwillingly along by Luis and Naomi. Nathan kept Annabella in his general radius, putting his wide frame between her and some of the more excited dancers.

As the night grew longer, the girls shed their shoes, the boys their coats.

Finn ground up on Nathan, both of them laughing and batting at the others' limbs. Luis bent over to twerk, grinning at the pair of them. Naomi laughed too, bouncing to me and bumping my hip with hers. She tipped her head back to laugh. Captivated by the column of her throat, I could only smile. She grabbed at me, pressing against me. Her hands found my hips. I reached for her on instinct, one hand on her back, the other on the curve of her hip. Her body was flush on mine.

"Are you drunk?" I shouted over the music.

"No! I'm just really, really happy!" she replied.

I could feel the zipper of her dress under my fingers. The fabric was slippery, fancy. She slapped aimlessly at my shoulders, my waist. "C'mon, Zed! Dance with me!"

I looked at her, at the sparkles in her eyes and on her face, at her blinding grin. She was a bright, bouncing embodiment of light. One of the roaming spotlights illuminated her face briefly, causing her to glow.

I grabbed her hand in mine. "Okay." I joined her in unrefined bouncing, limbs flopping without direction. We jumped, we spun, we laughed. We looked utterly stupid, but I couldn't find it in me to care. Our friends formed a little circle, clapping and cheering, moving to the beat.

Other people on the dance floor doubtless thought we were stupid and uncool, but not one of us cared. We were here, we were friends, and that was enough.

I know the night of prom is supposed to be a rebellious and romantic time, but all we ended up doing was heading to Luis' house and crashing there, piled on couches and blankets in front of the TV, watching movies, and giggling until early morning.

I remember looking around the room at them, still a little sweaty from all the dancing, sleepy and slow in the blue light from the TV. Naomi caught my eye and smiled, a private moment between us. She curled into a ball, her hair rumpled but angelic, like a halo over her head.

On the floor, Annabella curled into Nathan's side, sweet and shy, looking content. And Nathan seemed over the moon, gazing at the top of her head with the kind of tenderness I knew to expect from his continual awkward kindness. Luis, blissed out on extraversion and exhausted, dozed on the floor, a blanket tossed over him. Even Finn, who had been so prickly about everything recently, looked happy, draped across the couch under a throw blanket.

And there was I, alone in an armchair, watching them all. Cataloging the moment. Filing it away—for what I didn't know. For something. For after Finn left for school, maybe, or for the knowledge that, yes, I have friends—real friends, true friends who love me.

If I could time travel, I'd go back to that moment. Just us, sleepy in the living room, together.

22

Finn graduated in May. He walked the stage, took his diploma, and walked off. He didn't even seem pleased. He had no afterparty or celebration (though Naomi wanted to throw one, he refused), just a picture with us and smiles for his sisters, and that was all.

Summer descended in a crushing heatwave, humid and hot. We congregated at Luis' house in the pool or Joe's in the A/C, but we were all getting busier, and it seemed I saw less of them every day.

Nathan was spending more and more time with Annabella (go figure), Finn worked almost twice as much now, and Naomi was spending more time on her music—meeting with teachers online to learn more and songwrite.

I went to Houston for a couple weeks, where it was hotter and humider, and spent the time longing to be back in Terrytown with my friends. My sisters were great, but they couldn't compare to the friendship I had back home. We played board games and watched T.V., ate far too much sugar and potato chips. Though we get along as well as most siblings, I didn't feel knit together with them the way I did with my friends.

Finn showed up the night I got back, two six-packs in a cooler. He drove us out to an empty field, where the crickets chirped loudly and the breeze cooled us ever so slightly.

He put away the beer quickly, until he was lying on his back, humming old country songs under his breath and tapping his fingers lazily in time on his own chest.

I nursed a single bottle, watching him, worrying.

"It's your last summer," he mumbled at me. "'Fore the real world sucks you in."

"I guess."

"Don't get old, Zed, it sucks."

"You're not old."

"Pfft. Please. I'm an adult now, with a job and everything. I'm old."

"Finn, you're eighteen. Have some perspective, please."

He opened his eyes, slurring his words a bit. "I get up, I go to work, I come home, I make dinner, and I drink. I'm old."

I flinched.

"I want to go on the field and throw the ball around. Forget everything else." He burped. "It's like...screw everything, y'know?" He rolled unsteadily to his feet. "'S go, 'm done w' this shit."

I lunged after him as he opened the driver door. "I'll drive," I said firmly, twisting the keys from his liquor-limp fingers.

He raised a hand, and for a moment I thought he was going to punch me, but instead, he blinked, lowered his hand slowly, and scoffed. He marched to the passenger side, slammed the door, and slumped in the seat, never once looking at me.

I climbed in and started the truck.

I drove him home, unlocked his front door, but didn't follow. He could get himself to bed. I was too mad to help. When I got home, I set an alarm to drive the truck back to Finn before he had to get to work (and before my dad would see it. Not that he would particularly care, he'd just be annoyed it was in his way).

It seemed I stared at the ceiling for hours, days. Would he be alright? What was I supposed to do? How could I help? Was there anything I could do at all?

I rolled over, kicking off my sheet. My phone lit up at my touch, half-blinding me. I opened the contacts, scrolled to Naomi's name. My thumb hovered over the call button for a long time.

Naomi [sunshine emoji]. A profile picture of her with her tongue sticking out.

I pictured her waking up, her voice gravelly with sleep, fuzzily telling me hello. What was wrong? Was I alright?

I clicked the phone off, plunging the room into darkness once more.

Best to let her sleep.

***

The next day, four of us congregated at Luis', the white kids slathered in sunscreen while Luis and I reveled in our ability to tan. Naomi floated on a pool noodle, arms draped over, kicking idly to keep from running into walls.

"Y'all thirsty?" Luis asked. He climbed out of the pool, tugging up his shorts, which were light blue and printed with flamingos. They barely came to mid-thigh. He unabashedly loved them.

"Can I have a Coke?" Naomi asked. "Please."

Nathan airily waved a hand, saying in a British accent, "Bartender, fetch me a drink."

Luis dipped his toes in to flick water at him. "I'll be back."

He headed for the house, but instead of unlocking the gate, he climbed over the fence, getting his shorts caught and tumbling in a graceless heap to the other side. He held up a thumbs up over his shoulder, grinning foolishly.

Naomi watched him with a mixture of fondness and exasperation. So, standard procedure for watching Luis do anything.

I nudged her with my foot, sitting on the side. "Write anything good lately?"

She shrugged. "Maybe."

"Care to share?"

"Maybe."

"It's a yes or no question!"

"What if I'm not sure you'll like it?"

Of course I'll like it, you wrote it, I didn't say. Her eyes matched the color of the water around her. Her hair, piled atop her head in the cutest messy bun I'd ever seen, still carried the bleach job. There was a freckle on her shoulder.

What an exquisite creature she was.

Nathan jumped off the diving board. "Cowabunga!" We were showered with water, completely ruining whatever moment was developing.

I slid into the pool, tackling Nathan as he came up for air. We tussled for a bit, attempting to drown each other with friendly violence.

When we finished, he shook the water out of his eyes and hair like a dog, laughed, and said, "Too bad Finn's not here. He'd have been on my team."

"Please," I said, laughing. "We'd've whooped your ass." I hoped Finn was alright, and that his hangover wasn't too bad. He'd driven me back home early this morning with a hungover grimace, then headed off to work.

***

At the beginning of August, Luis texted the group to say he wanted to have a pool party to end the summer.

So, what we do every weekend basically, Nathan texted.

Yes. But like, fancy, Luis responded, and I could hear him say it in his slow cadence.

This was not the sort of party where his mom would be out of town and the entire high school would come over to trash the place. Rather, Naomi and Luis texted a few theatre kids and Nathan and Luis texted some football guys, and our little group showed up a couple hours early to pretend to help his mom set up. Really we just wandered aimlessly about trying to look helpful. "Helpful" meant making requests to Naomi for the party playlist, cracking open soda cans with a satisfying hiss, and dipping our toes in the water while commenting how good it would feel to get in the pool. Luis' mom had out two blenders (seriously, who has two blenders?) and was making virgin margaritas (Finn implied he wanted them not-virgin, but Naomi told him to shut up and be polite), as well as mangonadas. Naomi was the only one of us who was actually helpful, so she cut up mangos at the kitchen island.

People started rolling in just at sundown, starting with Annabella in a turquoise bikini—and from the looks of it, Nathan appreciated it very much.

The football boys jumped in the pool immediately, already starting the game of who-can-drown-the-other-first. The girls from theatre clustered in the shallower end, leaning on the side and talking, their hair up in buns. Somebody found a volleyball and started a spontaneous game of "don't let the ball touch the water."

I was on the porch, taking a Dr. Pepper break, when Annabella came up, wrapped in a towel. We said nothing, just exchanged the look and nod you trade with those you don't know super well but have a connection to nonetheless.

Naomi came from inside, pulling a sundress over her head to reveal her yellow two piece. I missed the first part of their conversation because my brain was busy just shouting *tummy thighs back YELLOW* but I tuned back in for Annabella saying, "Oh yeah, we have early band practice every day this week."

"Ugh," Naomi said.

"It's better than marching in the heat," Annabella pointed out.

"Oof, yeah. Sometimes I think about living somewhere else, just for the weather." Naomi grabbed a soda, raised it to me in a toast. "Bet the heat's worse Houston, Zed, huh?"

"Me? Oh, yeah, I guess. But it's really the hurricanes that are the problem."

Naomi blinked at me for a second. "Wow, I never even thought of that."

"I mean, my house wasn't ever flooded or anything, but yeah. It can get really nasty." I shifted my weight from foot to foot, having brought the mood down.

"Wild," Naomi said. "I got another flier from a college. I don't even know how they're getting my address!"

"Probably the SAT or whatever. Where's this one?" Annabella asked.

"This one's from SAGU. And another from Mary Harden Baylor."

"Those Christian schools are really coming after you."

She shrugged. "It's because of the scholarships I applied for."

"You're getting a head start," I said, sudden anxiety rising because I hadn't done anything in the way of college applications yet.

"It's in my nature," she said. "Chronically early."

"She's even early to the early morning rehearsals! Shows up looking all chipper with her little coffee, way too happy for first thing in the morning." Annabella wiggled her fingers as though she were Naomi saying hi first thing in the morning.

"Oh stop," she said. "I just like mornings."

"Nobody else does! You're just crazy! Zed, do you like mornings?"

"Um. Not without coffee," I said, thinking of the few morning shifts I had worked at Joe's. They were...not fun, to say the least.

"See?"

Naomi protested. "I just like being up in the mornings! The birds, the sunrise! Not all of us can be night owls. Some of us are just built different." She framed her face with her palms.

Nathan sprinted up from the direction of the pool, dripping wet. "Come on, Annabella, please give me a hug."

"No, I just got my hair dry—!" She failed to evade him, he swooped her up and carted her off as she kicked, both of them laughing.

Naomi shrugged at me, and raced to the pool, leaping off the side in a golden flash to send up a spray of water.

I followed slowly, finding Finn on the far side of the pool, dipping just in his feet in. He had a can in hand. "Wish this was a beer," he said.

I scoffed. "Really? Right now?"

He made an ugly face at me.

"Sorry."

"I'm just so tired, Zed. Sick and tired of—this." He gestured at the kids in the pool with his can. "I'm supposed to be going to college or starting my life or whatever, and instead I'm hanging out with a bunch of high school kids."

"Ouch."

He shrugged. "It's true."

"Yeah, but…we're your friends."

"Ah." He took a long drink.

"It's true, Finn. We're your friends." *I'm your friend,* I wanted to say. *I'm here for you.*

He dropped his head, hair falling over his forehead, backlit by the pool lights. A portrait outlined in sorrow. "Life sucks," he said. He reached over and shook my shoulder, jostling me back and forth. "Thanks."

"Anytime. I'm—"

"That's enough out of you!" His jostle turned to a shove, and I fell. Before the water closed over my head, I heard the sound of his sharp laughter.

***

Two days before school started, I awoke to my phone ringing. It was Nathan, but before I could answer it, the call ended.

Missed call, read my notifications.

Missed call.

Missed call.

Missed call.

From Nathan, Naomi, Coach C.

I blinked at my screen, uncomprehending.

Someone banged on the door.

I stumbled out of bed, pulling on a t-shirt as I went. I opened the door, glaring in the sunlight.

Naomi stood on my doorstep, trembling. "Zed," she whispered.

"Naomi?" Still befuddled and half-asleep, I motioned for her to come in.

She shook her head. "Zed, it's Finn." She swallowed, bobbing her head as she spilled out the next words. "He's dead."

"*What?*" The word tore from me, strangled.

She sniffed, the tears falling fresh over her cheeks. "He was d-d-drunk driving, and they—they found the car this morning." She hiccupped.

I did the only thing I knew to do and pulled her to me. She sobbed against my chest, violent, jerking affairs that shook her whole body. I swallowed, scanning an unseen horizon. Dead? Gone?

Finn?

I waited for tears, but none came. Instead, I felt numb, tired, split down my middle and unable to sew myself up again.

Naomi curled against me, hair tickling my neck and chin.

This wasn't real. I was still asleep. Any minute now I'd wake, or I'd see a giant purple slug rolling down the street, or a flying cow.

Naomi backed away from me, wiping her nose on the back of her hand. "Sorry, I've…" She waved at the wet patch on my shirt.

"Oh." I hadn't noticed. "Finn…his sisters?"

"I don't know. We only just—we just got the news. We thought it was better to…tell you in person." Her eyes, red-rimmed and tired, wouldn't meet mine.

"I don't know." I said nonsensically, and sat on the floor of the entryway, my legs suddenly deciding they were done doing their job for the day.

"If you want, you can come with us," she offered. "We're going to Luis'. Just to be somewhere. Together."

I nodded. I needed to dress, but my clothes were all the way in the other room. And my toothbrush was in the bathroom, practically miles away. And I just wanted to sit here, for just a minute.

Naomi reached down, and took my hand.

Our fingers locked. At any other time I would have been rejoicing.

She was crying again.

We trudged to the car. Nathan was driving, which shouldn't have surprised me, because he always was the most level headed in a crisis.

At Luis' house, I sat on the couch in the game room, unsure of how I got there, clutching a crumpled bottle of water. Across the room from me, Nathan sat similarly, teary-eyed, staring into space.

Naomi wept silently, tears rolling down her cheeks. And Luis simply looked like the saddest human on the face of the earth, his lower lip out a bit, the corners of his mouth weighed down.

The room was dim, cold.

And Finn wasn't there. He'd never be there.

Finn was dead.

.

Have you ever felt an absence like a presence?

SENIOR YEAR

23

His funeral was on a Wednesday morning. We were all there, all four of us. I couldn't stop myself looking around the room and doing a mental tally. Nathan, Naomi, Luis—Nathan, Naomi, Luis—

I suppose technically all five of us were there, since we were putting Finn in the ground.

Mr. Peterson did the service, the sanctuary filled with solemn-faced, black-clad people. It seemed the whole town was here.

Idiots, I seethed. *Hypocrites. Fakers. You didn't care while he was alive. You only care now because he's dead, because he was young, what a tragedy. But he was falling apart for an entire year and you didn't care.*

Finn's mom, looking like a light wind would blow her over, tottered in the front row, her chin pinched, eyes red and dry.

The girls clustered around her. I couldn't look at them. It hurt too much.

Annabella had come with Nathan, holding his hand in silent support. He was tired and ragged-looking, sad. They sat two rows away from me, in their own little bubble.

Luis sat with me, fat, crocodile tears rolling down his face in a steady stream. Every so often he'd sniffle, hiccup, or sigh, but that was all. Just soft, continual weeping.

And then there was Naomi. Naomi who owned so very few black things, wearing a black dress reaching her ankles. Naomi, makeup smeared at the corners of her eyes from tears, her pale skin more pallid than normal. The blonde of her hair now streaked with brunette at the roots, she had it pulled back into a tight and severe bun.

Mr. Peterson talked about things being wrong in the world, about how this wasn't the way it was meant to be. He talked about who Finn had been, how hard he had worked, how much he had loved his family and friends. It was all past-tense and final, as though I didn't feel like Finn would burst from the coffin shouting, *Surprise! Did I get you? You big wussies, crying over me.* Mr. Peterson talked about hope, about knowing that there is a world beyond this. He left out the parts where Finn was sharp-edged, hard-nosed, sometimes cruel. He left out the drinking and the smoking and the accident.

It was Finn, but it wasn't.

Finn was fierce and loving and determined and loyal and strong and sharp. He was cuss words and drinking and screaming song lyrics into the wind out of the window of his truck. He was sweaty smiles on the field; playful tussling off it. He was many, many things, and I wanted to remember him the way he was, all of him, even the ugly parts.

The casket was closed, and after the ceremony, some of us lingered, sitting in the pews in reflection. Naomi stood and walked to me, looking like a willow swaying in the breeze. She dropped into the spot beside me and leaned on me, like a tree falling under its own weight. I wrapped an arm around her shoulders as she began to cry, big shaking sobs that wracked her whole body.

"It's not fair," she whispered. "It's not."

Pretty soon Nathan was there, too. He took the pew in front of us, turning to look back. He patted his sister's knee, and she grabbed his hand.

We sat in silence for a long time. Why does grief love silence? I don't know. Perhaps it is because sorrow must be acknowledged and welcomed and accepted before it will ever go away. Perhaps talking simply drowns it out. You have to make grief your companion, have to realize you will carry it with you for the rest of your life. If you wouldn't have ever stopped loving the person, you will never stop grieving their loss.

This is the way of the world now. The four of us and our grief.

***

School held a memorial for him, though I don't recall it. I'm sure kind words were said, but I don't remember much from the first weeks of school. It's all in a fog, a confusion of resetting the world to recognize what it looked like now. Things change. Life goes on.

I went to football practice, a senior. Expected to be leaders, Nathan and I knew we'd be the unofficial captains. We'd been here long enough, played together well enough.

And yet. And yet.

Even though he wasn't going to be here anyway, I kept looking for him. Kept thinking I saw him on the line or in the bleachers or walking across the field. Kept hearing his voice call plays. Kept looking for his number among the jerseys. No one wore it anymore. Probably no one ever would again.

His ghost was everywhere, in the halls on the field, on hillbilly row where all the trucks parked.

But everyone else seemed to have forgotten. People sent us pitying looks in the halls, whispering behind their hands to one another. It was only gossip, not real concern or grief. Aside from our little group, I didn't think anyone else was looking everywhere or wondering what he'd say if he were there. Finn had never been the sort of person everyone loved, the sort to make people adore him and smile when they said his name. But God, we had loved him, our group, and he had loved us so fiercely it was scary. And though he never seemed to fully understand it, we loved him, too.

***

Our summer slipped into fall, one rainstorm and orange leaf at a time. I felt old while on the field, watching freshmen come in and learn the game. They were so young, round-faced, and awkward-limbed. Their voices still cracked sometimes when we broke the huddle, they still had braces on their teeth. Had I once been so small?

We started our fall season with a win, an auspicious sign. I stood on the field with Nathan on one side and Luis on the other. Before the game started, our announcer took a moment of silence for Finn.

"And he'd think this was the silliest shit and we needed to just play ball," I muttered, only loud enough for them to hear.

They laughed silently, shoulders shaking with the force of their stifled giggles. Sometimes, grief is laughter, too.

Nathan snapped to Luis, who threw to Tate, who ran it in for a score. I ran back to the sideline so the freshies could go in for a PAT. I didn't join in on the back-slapping jubilee. We had a game to play.

Nathan met me there, ducking his head to mumble a guess at the next opposing play in my ear. He'd be right, of course, because he always was. How he didn't see his own genius, I'd never know.

Naomi sat in the front row of the bleachers wearing Nathan's away jersey, within easy waving distance. I snuck a glance her way between plays. She was the magnet that pulled me in every time.

At school that day, she'd worn a long, colorfully patterned dress over a long-sleeved turtle neck. Her newly touched-up blonde curls cascading over her shoulders. "Are we hanging out this weekend?"

Nathan tilted his head, conveying something to her via twin telepathy.

"Oh, that's right, you have plans."

"With *Annabella*," Luis cooed, then mimed gagging in my direction.

Naomi rolled her eyes. "Okay, you two?"

Luis shrugged. "Dunno. Might be headed to Dallas with my mom."

Naomi gazed at him speculatively for a minute, then looked at her lunch tray.

"I'll hang out with you," I said quietly. "My dad'll probably be gone. We can chill at my house. Watch TV or something."

She squeezed her lips to the side. "Sure, okay."

I had a game to play, I couldn't be bothered worrying about her coming over. It was a short game—we forty-fived them in the third quarter. I scored two touchdowns myself, and I was very proud.

As soon as I got home, I cleaned. Chucked out all the greasy pizza boxes, threw my smelly football gear in the washer.

In the morning, the first thought in my head was, *Naomi is coming over today.* None of them had come to my place before, though I'd been to all of theirs. Finn and I weren't the hosts– that was Luis, or the Petersons, or Finn's truck, I suppose.

I wondered what had happened to his truck. Was it totaled? Did his mom have it?

Naomi showed up in her family van, parking in the drive. She had on a yellow sweater, and I couldn't help but smile when I saw her. "I cannot get over how beautiful this is," she said.

"Gorgeous," I said, without thinking. "I mean—"

She tipped her head up to look at the sun. "This is the perfect sort of day. I want to go on an adventure."

I ran a hand through my hair, probably frizzing and messing the curls. "It's Terrytown."

"I *know*, but that doesn't mean we can't be adventurous." She put her hands on her hips. "I want to learn how to skateboard. Can you teach me to skateboard?"

How is a man supposed to say no?

So I hauled out my board, demonstrating how to push off and glide. "Uh—here." I thrust it at her, and she took it, putting it on the ground and resting one foot on it.

As soon as she stepped fully onto the board, it slid out from under her and she dropped to her butt on the concrete.

I jogged after my board, and by the time I returned, she was already up and dusting off her pants.

With the board in front of her again, she reached out hands to me, flexing her fingers. I hesitated a moment before grasping hers, tightening my forearms as she tugged on me to balance. The tip of her tongue sticking out, she rocked back and forth, and finally tapped her fingers against my palms to let go. She pushed off again, tumbling off quickly, but once again bouncing upright with a smile.

It took several tries, but soon she was able to keep her balance for a short distance. Arms held out wide and face determined, she pushed off, wobbling as the board slowly moved forward. She drifted a short way, kick-pushing again when she slowed. She looked over her shoulder at me and grinned.

I smiled back, trying to hide the way she made my heart pound, my throat tighten, and butterflies flutter in my stomach. Still, after all this time.

She coasted a bit further before drifting to a stop and hopping off. "Your turn."

I took the board and stepped onto it before it was even fully on the ground. Kick-pushing, I rode down the sidewalk, pivoting neatly to turn back around. I circled her, making a face like it was so easy, no effort required. Showing off? Maybe. Anyway, it made her laugh.

"Try again," I said, holding the board still for her. She stepped up, wobbling. "Okay, great. Just keep your balance." I put a foot on the board behind her, keeping it steady. I brushed a hand against her waist as I tried to step up, but our combined effort overbalanced us, and we tipped to the side, falling in a heap. "Are you ok?"

"I'm great, she giggled, rolling to her feet.

I fetched the board, and again, we tried to double balance, her in front and me behind, but again we couldn't balance. This time, we were more ready for it, and I hopped off before we totally collapsed.

"Wait, let's try this," I said, a plan forming in my mind, and I held the board steady as she stepped on. Taking a quick breath, I put both hands on her waist and gently nudged her forward, walking behind the board.

She laughed, stretching her arms out wide for balance. "I'm flying, Jack!"

I picked up speed, jogging gently. This was harder than I expected. I was so focused on keeping her from falling that I couldn't even be too excited about holding her by the waist.

She squealed, failing her arms for balance.

"I've got you," I reminded her. The wind pushed at our faces, sending Naomi's flyaway hairs into my mouth. She relaxed into my arms finally, giggling as we made it down the street. At the end of the street, I stopped us and brushed my sweaty hair off my forehead, relieved we hadn't fallen.

"That was amazing," Naomi breathed, eyes bright.

I smiled at her. "I'm so glad you liked it." I grabbed my board and we walked back up the street to my driveway.

"Show me your tricks?"

"Uh, I don't know about that," I hedged. There wasn't a skate park here, and I was horribly out of practice. But, never one to give up an opportunity to be cool for Naomi, I stepped on the board again, pushing to gain speed. I approached the sidewalk, and popped a neat ollie to hop the curb.

Naomi clapped and laughed.

"Uh, that's all," I said lamely.

"Still cool," she said, and I was satisfied with that. "I wanted to tell you," she started, trailing off. She crossed her arms over her chest. "I got accepted to Denton Christian University."

"Oh yeah?"

"Yeah, it's in Denton. Obviously. But I think I'm going to go there." She straightened, lifting her chin.

"It's a good fit, I guess?"

"Yeah, they have a really good music and theatre program."

I nodded. She seemed a little sad about it, like she wasn't sure how I'd take the news. "I think that's great," I said sincerely, and she smiled.

It was a small and simple moment between us from that fall, the first fall after. We spent only the afternoon together, watched some TV and did the thing teenagers do where they scroll through their phones side by side, show each other funny videos, and call it hanging out.

I still loved her then, nearly three years after I'd first seen her. I wasn't the same gangly boy I'd been, and she certainly wasn't the same girl, but I still felt for her just as much as I always had. But sitting there next to her, I still felt how the time had passed. We weren't right for each other; or maybe we were, but it wasn't the right time. I would take what I could get before she was gone, too, lost to college and time.

24

Our final season slipped by, days bleeding into weeks into weekends into games. A lot of it passed in a blurry fog of grief and exhaustion. Naomi and Luis were, of course, in the fall musical, and Nathan and Annabella spent a lot of time together. Sometimes I felt a bit untethered, without a match. Without Finn, pieces were missing.

I braced my ankle before every game, as it never fully recovered from the odd sprain or roll. (Doc said I didn't rest enough. Not sure how I'm supposed to rest when I have to walk around school and skateboard to get places, but I digress. At least it wasn't a broken bone.) It wasn't a serious injury—no broken bones, unlike Nathan and his finger—nor was it a concussion or a career-ending injury. It was just a fact of athlete life: you hurt yourself for the love of the game, for the love of the sport. We won game after game—in heat, in rain, on turf and on grass—until suddenly, we were in the playoffs.

One playoff game took place at a little school further west of us, where the field was positioned directly next door to a cattle barn, and boy, it sure smelled like it. The field was pockmarked with holes that would turn your ankle if you weren't careful. I wrapped my braces extra tight.

The sun sank low to the horizon, effervescent orange.

"Maybe it's a sign," I said to Nathan, indicating the bright sky and our uniforms.

"Paint the town orange," he said and knuckle bumped me.

Luis, punching my shoulder pad lightly, sang something about "out of an orange colored sky," and grumbled we don't know good music.

"No wait, that's Nat King Cole," I said. "My mom loves him."

"A lady of taste," he agreed.

"Line *up*," Coach C called, and we yanked on helmets, hustling to run a brief warm up and passing drills. We broke into groups, Nathan leading one group in passing, while Coach C supervised the other half of us in blocking. Then we swapped. In the last few moments before the game, while we stretched and hopped and massaged muscles, Nathan called me to the side to snap to me a handful of times. The first was too high and the second wobbled oddly, but the next three flew straight and true, landing in my hands with a gratifying *smack*.

"Thanks, bro," Nathan said, smacking my hand. He tossed the practice ball into a pile of miscellaneous gear.

"Looking good."

"Gonna be a good game tonight," he said, and swished some water in his mouth before spitting it back out onto the dry, dusty ground. He bounced on his toes. "I can feel it."

I agreed. The tension that snapped in the air, present before every game, felt extra taught. Something was going to happen.

Coach called for a huddle and Nathan gave us our pregame speech.

On the starting line, Tate, Nathan, and Alejandro crouched. Behind them, Luis, Matteo, and I waited in a tight V-spread. Nathan snapped. Luis caught it. He tossed it in a perfect arc into my waiting hands, and I tucked it tightly. I wove through the defenders, sensing the guy creeping up on my right shoulder. He wrapped me up and I fell, extending as far as I could. Just short of a first down. The second play, Matteo handed off to Luis, who scrambled us over the line, and the cycle started over.

Nathan was right. Something felt good tonight. Coach called the plays, sending a runner in to relay it. We knew our routes. Even the freshmen were getting it, hustling their asses off for the sake of the game. We ended the first quarter leading by three touchdowns.

I didn't want to get lazy, but I figured we could maintain it.

There were no locker rooms here—we'd all wiggled into our uniforms on the bus—so we sat in the endzone, sipping on water and Gatorade. Our water boy—still Alejandro's little brother, now in seventh grade and playing on the middle school team—carried the little caddy around. And as always, we ended the huddle with, "Ready? Break. Comets!"

Coach put in some of the freshmen to start the second half, but he pulled them when our opponents started to score. I thrived in the running lane, letting speed flow through me and push me onward. There's a way to just drop and relax into the rhythm of it, and I loved eating up the ground beneath my cleats.

That is, until I stepped in a hole. With my bad ankle.

I tumbled, head over heels, letting out a yelp. The whistle blew.

Nathan appeared in my view, offering a hand. I took it, hauling myself up, bracing on his shoulder. I tested my weight, a twinge spiraling up my calf.

Doc walked to me, in no great hurry. He could see I wasn't broken or bleeding, which is usually a good sign. He took me from Nathan, and walked with me back to the sidelines, where I tumbled onto the single metal bench. He prodded and rotated my ankle in slow, gentle motions, and offered me some ice.

I'd told him about it at the start of the season, and he was the one who told me to get a brace for it.

"I think you're out for the game," he said, gently prodding the swelling that was already rising.

"Dangit. This is the second time," I said, throwing my hands up in annoyance.

"That's the way of it. Stay off it this weekend and you'll be fine by Wednesday. But only if you stay off it," he said, waggling a warning finger at me.

I nodded, resigned to my fate. Suddenly a spectator, I watched my team run plays I knew in my sleep. How different from my usual, narrow view through a helmet. How different from how I'd spent the last year constantly on the field. I'd gained so much skill from the kid I'd been when I first hopped the fence to join conditioning in the middle of July. With the throbbing in my ankle, and the lack of tension from our comfortable lead, my mind drifted.

For the millionth time, I wished Finn was here. Unruly hair, sweaty face, spiky smile. What would I say to him? What was there to say?

"I'm sorry. I miss you. I wish you were here. Why did you do it?"

A cheer went up from the crowd. I whipped attention to the scoreboard. We forty-fived them! I hopped up, winced, then sat right back down again. Nathan jogged to me, smiling, and hauled me up to limp through the shake-hands-good-game line.

***

At home that weekend, I iced my ankle and propped it up on the coffee table, watching college football. When there was a knock on the door, I hobbled over, and unlocked it. It was Nathan. He had a package of cookie dough and a DVD.

"Hey," I said, bewildered.

"Hey." He shouldered past me. "Where's your DVD player?"

I pointed vaguely, supporting myself on the wall as I tottered back to the couch.

"Sweet." He set the DVD by it, then made for the kitchen, me hobbling after him. He punched buttons on my oven—mostly unused, save to reheat pizza, and even then I usually opted for the microwave—and puttered around, finding the one metal cookie sheet.

"Let me help you with that," I said, reaching for the cookie dough.

"Uh-uh," he said, sliding it out of my reach. "Go sit down."

"You're in my house, dude!"

"Sit down."

I didn't.

"Well, fine, here." He tossed me a chunk of raw cookie dough, which I nabbed midair, and stuffed in my mouth. And *then* I went to sit back down in my nest on the couch, where I'd piled up my things all day: empty plate, sketchbook, random food wrappers. Nathan hummed under his breath in the kitchen. I decided to put the movie in—the football game was kind of boring and there were too many men on the field anyway—and got it set up in the player.

Nathan came in and settled on the couch like he had done it a million times, cracking open a soda as he did before passing one to me. We never hung out at my house. It was too small, too messy, too sad. The definition of a bachelor's pad, really. Even the fridge was sad, empty of most things save milk, ground beef, and beer.

"Where's Naomi?"

He waved a hand. "Theatre party thingy."

"Oh. She mentioned the other day she's going to major in theatre."

"Yeah, I'm pretty sure she's going to Denton Christian University, you know, the little one? They have a really good music and theatre program."

"She said something about that the other day. You made up your mind yet?" Nathan had been talking about trade school or a gap year, but I hadn't heard definitively.

"Nope," he said, popping the P.

"Don't have to have it figured out yet."

He shrugged. "I'll get there." A sip of soda. "Annabella's going to do nursing, so she's going to Tech to get that settled."

"That's not too far."

"Still feels far. Thank God for cell phones."

I hummed in agreement.

"Start the movie?"

"Sure."

Of course, five minutes into the opening, the oven beeped, and Nathan brought out a beautiful tray of warm chocolate chip cookies. When they were cool enough to handle, I bit one clean in half.

"Oh, these are amazing."

"I added a little cinnamon in the dough. Plus topped it with a little salt. I think it really levels it up, you know?"

"For sure."

We unpaused the movie, making comments about the story, the special effects, the performances.

"If somebody killed my dog, I would also go on a murder spree," Nathan said.

"You don't have a dog."

"Hypothetically. I'll have one one day."

"What kind?"

"Oh, something big and sweet, probably a mutt. They're the best dogs."

"Agreed. I don't like the little ones."

"Ew, no."

It's nice to have a friend with whom the conversation flows easily and unobstructed. No worries about causing offense, no concern about whether their feelings are hurt. There was no need to rush things. No need to worry he was comfortable. He had a way of coming right in and making himself at home. Nathan has always been my most steady friend, someone to rely on and count on and trust.

So, when the conversation turned to Finn, it was natural. It was gentle.

We'd switched to playing video games, he hunched forward a little, elbows on knees, while I leaned back, slouching into the corner of the couch with my controller balanced on my tummy.

"I was thinking about Finn last night," Nathan said casually, though it felt a bit like a confession. "During the game."

"Oh yeah?"

"Remember how he used to get all bouncy when we were doing well? Hop on his toes?"

I snorted. "Oh shoot, yeah. He could never play poker."

"Heck no."

"It was like he had no facial filter, or something."

"You always knew exactly what he was thinking. And sometimes—gosh, I wish he could keep it together. You know how many refs he pissed off cause he was glaring bloody murder at 'em?"

I shook my head, laughing. "Oh gosh, yes."

"And that one time he got in a fight—man, if he'd paused to think for *one second*—"

"Right? No impulse control. When I picked up his sisters with him those couple times, he always bought me a shake too, even though I know he couldn't really afford it. No impulse control there, either."

"Yeah. Man, I miss him." The light that had entered his eyes dimmed a little, dipping into sorrow.

"Me too."

We quieted, punching buttons.

"You know," Nathan said a minute later, "I bet he would have made a really good coach. If he'd gotten it together and worked on himself a bit, he'd'a been so good with young kids. Or big kids."

"Mm. Yeah. Give him some time to stop yelling at refs and he'd be okay."

"I mean, Coach yells at refs all the time."

"You know when the hat comes off, it's about to get real."

We laughed, and something tight in my chest loosened a bit.

"Do you think he would have ever gotten it together?" I asked softly.

Nathan heaved a sigh, the sound heavy. "I don't know. He was always so…yeah, I don't know. I'd like to think so."

I nodded. "I wish things could have been different."

"Me too, Zed, me too." Nathan looked away from me, clearing his throat. "But. I hope he's getting to score goals in heaven. Or throw a football."

"You think there's football in heaven?"

"There better be! I want to play football with Jesus."

I laughed. Jesus or no Jesus, if heaven was a place where there was endless joy, then heaven for Nathan probably involved football. And if Finn was there—if such a place even existed—then there was probably football there for him, too.

I liked that idea.

"Hey," Nathan said, with the air of a person about to bestow a profound truth. "If an emu showed up in the driveway, do you think you could take it down?"

***

Our final playoff game, cold and miserable, stayed tight and fast the entire game. Rain fell steadily, soaking our uniforms and skin. The coaches hunched beneath ponchos, peering at the field partially obscured by rainfall. It was a running-heavy game, as sometimes the passes were lost in the dim and wet of the storm. Despite the rain, we played a good game. Nathan led us through the plays, a steady rock in the buffeting wind. We won by only two touchdowns.

On the bus, still damp and shivering, I looked at Nathan beside me and Luis across the aisle.

"Guys," I said, over the rumble and shaking of the bus, "we're going to state."

Luis unhooked an earbud and scrunched his brows at me. "Yeah, I know. Did you like, miss the whole game or something?"

"No, but—"

Nathan looked at me too, teasing. "You're just now noticing?"

I rolled my eyes. "Yeah, I've been asleep since the start of the game. No, you idiots, I guess it's just now sinking in."

Nathan shrugged, leaning his head back against the seat. "Yeah, bro, it's pretty cool."

Luis gave me a thumbs up and put his earbud back in. I caught a brief strain of something boisterous and showtune-y.

I turned my back, looked out the window at the endless black expanse. Maybe Finn would have understood, except no, he wouldn't have, because this was about the absence of Finn. We were going back. Without him.

It felt like we came full circle, like fate. It felt like I was living with Finn's ghost over my shoulder, begging me to fix the mistakes from before, whispering to me that it was a chance to redo, to reclaim. To win it for him, in his name. And to win it for myself.

***

As the year before, we drove to Dallas, missing classes. As the year before, we stayed in a hotel, and like the year before, the stadium loomed over us, massive and imposing. Unlike the year before, Finn was missing. I'm sure some of the boys got up to shenanigans in the hotel that night, but Nathan and I went to bed early, lost in our own pregame thoughts.

"Want to watch crappy T.V.?" Nathan asked.

"Sure."

He clicked on the T.V., flicked through channels, catching snippets of dialogue. When we landed on a rerun of *The Incredible Hulk,* he looked at me for confirmation, and when I grunted affirmative, he set the remote aside. I watched with only half my brain, sometimes scrolling on my phone, sometimes staring sightlessly at the wall or the comforter on the bed. I drifted off like that, Nathan's presence solid and reassuring, his steady breathing lulling me into sleep.

25

I wake.
Eyes open, inhale a gasp.
The game, the game, the game.
The itch lives in my fingers, my knees. *Let's go, let's go, let's go,* it throbs, urging me up, onward. I want the game to be *now;* want to be on the field, cleats digging into turf; want sweat running down my jaw, leather under my fingertips, mouthguard clenched between my teeth. The hours leading up to the game move like a herd of cattle–which is to say, slowly.

And yet, when we arrive under the bright, glaring lights, it feels too immediate, too soon. I am not ready to do this again. I am not ready to do this without Finn.

I turn to Nathan and Luis. Nathan has his jaw set, head already in the first quarter, mapping plays and sizing up the other team. Luis, however, looks stricken, pained, gazing up at the massive screens above us. He's watching a player list scroll by, our names among them. He catches me staring, flashes his bright, dopey grin, but it doesn't quite reach his eyes.

The air is weird, flat-tasting from being circulated inside. The fields I play on are outside, hot, textured, and alive. This has the quality of a dream, airbrushed and too bright.

Tate and I flank Nathan as we go in for the coin toss. Three seniors. Three boys who'd been playing together for years. Nathan speaks for us, chooses tails, elects to receive. It is right that he's standing there. It is right that he's our unofficial team captain. He stepped up in his quiet way to lead in Finn's absence, to guide us through our grief and a difficult season.

I square my shoulders, proud to be beside him.

We huddle, and Nathan shouts encouragement, his face stretched wide. "We have put in the work, and it will pay off today! Do not give up today! Do not stop pushing until we get to the end! Give it your best, your very best!" He takes a breath, panting, and continues, "We are here for one reason: to win! What are we here for?"

"To win!" *For us.*

"I said, *what are we here for?*"

"To win!" *For Finn.*

"Ready? Break! Comets!"

I do the kickoff, and for a moment I am transported back to a year ago, watching this happen again. If I just turn and look, there he will be, smiling, pulling on his helmet, cheerfully taunting the other team. For a moment, he's there with me, telling us we're going to win, this time it's going to work out. And then he's gone and I'm left without him. I take a deep, cleansing breath.

As we take our starting positions for what is probably my last game of six man ever, I look to Nathan, crouched at the center. He holds the ball steady, not a hint of nervousness on him. I glance at Luis, big hands open to receive the toss from the snap, eyes locked on Nathan, breathing steady.

I look at my teammates. Tate. Alejandro. Matteo.

My friends. My brothers.

If I had time, I'd scan the stands for Naomi.

I exhale, echoing in my helmet.

Nathan snaps. I run.

We're off.

Our team is good. Our team is *really* good. Something clicks into place today and we glide through the plays smoother than the bearings on my skateboard. We pull ahead by thirty-five in the first quarter. By the second quarter, Coach is sending in our freshmen to run offense. At halftime, we bounce around the locker room, preemptively celebrating.

"Gentlemen," Coach C says, causing us to settle. "The game isn't over yet. Don't rest on your laurels too soon."

Coach grunts and draws some plays on the whiteboard. He talks us through a game plan for the second half.

"And we aren't going to forty-five them," he finishes. "It's bad sportsmanship. We don't need to rub their noses in it. But for god's sake, stop going easy on them!"

Nathan and I trade glances. Coach will never let us rest as long as he thinks we can win.

Coach C nods in agreement. "I've seen you being good men on the field today. Keep it up. I saw you helping up players, refraining from trash talk. That's what I want to see. I'm proud of you."

I straighten my spine, jostle Nathan's shoulder. He gives me a nod. I know we're both thinking of Finn in that moment, wondering what he would have said right then to make us all laugh. Probably something about Coach C being mushier than a ripe banana, or something.

***

Never once do we lose our lead during the second half. Our opponents know it's a lost cause but they never give up, I'll give them that. Every hit comes just as hard as the last, every play executed just as swiftly and sharply as the ones before. They keep us on our toes, for sure, trying new plays and formations. They score, but every time, we answer with a score of our own. But as the seconds tick down at the end of the fourth and final quarter, Nathan snaps it to Luis, who takes a knee, and we've done it. We've won.

Our team floods the field, orange jerseys streaming into a bouncing throng. I yank my helmet off and throw myself at Nathan and Luis, jumping up and down in tandem, yelling wordless joy. Coach C's smile splits his face, eyes crinkling. He offers his hand to me to shake. I reject it and throw my arms around him instead. He pauses for a moment, but wraps his arms around me, patting me on my back and ruffling my sweaty hair.

I glance to the stands, looking for my mother and sisters, who I know are there. My father is not. It doesn't surprise me, and oddly, it doesn't really even hurt anymore. It just is. I finally spot Naomi, a tiny figure in orange, jumping up and down. I wave at her frantically, and she waves back. I spare a moment to think of Finn, bittersweet twining with joy. I hope he's proud of us. I hope he's cheering in the afterlife.

"We're state champions!" Luis yells in my ear, fisting my jersey to haul me to the sidelines. Nathan is grinning, one hand already on the water cooler handle. I grab the other, and we shuffle behind Coach, giggling stupidly.

The water cascades over him, cold and icy, and he says a few words I won't repeat. We sprint away, laughing, even as he yells after us, "You hooligans!" (Or maybe it was, "You jackasses!") But he says it with a smile.

We're state champions. We can get away with anything.

26

I spent Christmas in Houston with my mother, and New Years in Terrytown with my friends. I wore my letter jacket with pride—and in the Houston weather, it was all the coverage I needed. We toasted in the new year with sparkling grape juice from Naomi's parents, and leftover Christmas tamales from Luis. Finn wasn't there to sneak us booze. We missed him, but the feeling wasn't so overwhelming anymore. All of us lounged on red leather couches in Luis' game room, laughing. Annabella tucked herself into Nathan's side, pink-cheeked and smiling. Naomi wore earrings that sparkled when she moved, and she'd done something pretty to her hair, bundled it up somehow with tendrils escaping to float around her like a halo. I got the sense that if I ran my fingers over the edge of her angelic form, she'd dissipate, vanish from the world like magic.

She brought her guitar and played late into the night—or rather, early into the morning. We sang everything from "American Pie" to "Don't Stop Believin'" to most of George Strait's discography. Later into the evening, I asked her to play something she wrote.

"Ugh, I have to hear this all the time," Nathan groaned. "Over and over the same seven chords all day."

"You don't have to listen," she countered. "You can go do something else."

He rolled his eyes. "I'm playing *video games*. What else am I supposed to do?"

"Go outside."

He gestured to the window. "It's twenty-two degrees out there."

"You'd play football anyway."

He hesitated. "Okay, that's true, but I'm not just gonna—"

She drowned him out with her guitar strumming.

It's hard to explain now exactly how that song felt. The way is caught at my heart and yanked, unlocking those little painful bits of grief that we all kept hidden away most of the time.

Lost somewhere in outer space. What does it matter if we're in the same place?

When she finished, I felt the heaviness in the room. We all knew it was about us, and it was about Finn.

"Sorry, I—I brought the mood down."

I shook my head at her. "No, it's—" I couldn't think of anything to say around the rising lump in my throat.

"Let's fix this," she grumbled and removed her capo to launch immediately into "Brown Eyed Girl."

Whatever spell she cast on us was broken, and we kept singing our way into the new year.

***

January. Bone-chilling cold. Our trophy sat in the place of honor in the case at school. I admired it on our first day of classes. Our last first day. I drifted through classes, barely focusing. Senioritis crept up on me, but I couldn't find it in me to care. My grades were good enough to get me accepted into most state schools. I won the state championship. I didn't need much else in life.

I found myself thinking of Finn, more than I have in a long time. He was always there, lingering at the edges of my mind.

But that day it was like I couldn't shut out the thoughts, couldn't push them away.

I walked out of school halfway through the day. It was chilly, the sky gray and hard. Frozen grass crunched beneath my feet. I plonked myself onto the bleachers and stared at the empty field. I'd never play on it again, I realized. I knew that, but sometimes you can know something without really *knowing* something.

I slumped there, on the bleachers, the metal cold against my thighs even through my jeans.

I heard the clanking steps before I saw her. Naomi lowered herself onto the seat beside me. She didn't say anything, just sat there, tucking her hands between her thighs to keep them warm. She had on Nathan's letter jacket over her own fleece pullover.

Finally, I looked over at her, rummaging through my exhausted brain for something funny to say. "You come here often?"

She smiled, giving my line more credit than it was worth. "Oh, only every day."

"You'd think I'd've seen you before." I heard the cadence of my own voice, marked the way "I'd've" pronounced "Ida," evidence of the marks West Texas left upon me. I wondered if I'd ever shake what this little town had done to me, what this place had given me and what it had taken away.

She shook her head, dropping our little charade. "What're you doing up here? We have class."

"Could ask the same of you."

"I'm looking for you. That's my excuse, what's yours?"

I took a breath. "Do you think he'll ever leave us?"

She hissed through her teeth.

Glancing over, I saw her eyes shut, lashes pressed to cheekbones. "Sorry."

"No," she said, reaching for my elbow. "No, don't be. It's—I miss him today, too."

I nodded. Something about this day, this beginning of the end, the umpteenth last-high-school-thing I'd have, made me miss him more sharply. I'd stopped seeing his ghost everywhere long ago. Instead, I felt his absence even more, in the moments when our friends didn't automatically leave space for a fifth person; when the football team didn't say his name during practice; when I saw his sisters and mom in church all together. He was disappearing and I desperately wanted to keep him here, an artist laying atop their chalk drawing as it rained.

"Do you think it gets any easier?"

She exhaled through her nose. "Daddy described grief to me like this: It's a big ball, and it's in a little cube." She used her hands to shape a cube or container. "There's a button on the bottom of the cube, and every time the ball hits the button, you feel grief, or pain, or loss. When it first happens, the ball is huge, and everything makes it push the button." She paused, swallowed. "But as time goes on, the ball shrinks, and it bounces around the cube, and it hits the button less." Her hands relaxed and fell to her lap again. "But the ball still hits the button sometimes. It can happen anytime, from anything. Grief never…it never really goes away all the way. It's a process."

"That's a weird metaphor."

She slugged me in the arm. "Shut up."

I chuckled. "I get it though. We're always going to miss him, aren't we?"

"At least for a long, long time."

I sniffed, pretending the moisture in my eyes was from the biting wind. Standing, I offered her my hand. "Want to get a coffee?"

"Zed, it's the first day of school. We cannot ditch, we'll be in so much trouble!"

"Okay, after school. I'm working anyway."

She cocked her head, cheeks pink from the cold. "Fine." She slapped her hand into mine and hauled herself up. "Let's go back to class."

And so we did.

***

It became a bit of a tradition, coffee after school. Not every day, but on days I worked or days she wasn't busy, she came to the coffee shop and did her homework or scribbled in her leather bound songwriting journal. I loved watching her, drinking in her shape as she worked. She leaned over her journal, eyes far away, a thoughtful furrow between her brows. She twined curls of hair around her finger, whispered words to herself, tapped her lower lip with the end of her pen. She was so beautiful it hurt.

And every time, the words swelled to fill my throat: I love you. I'm in love with you. Do you love me too?

And every time, I swallowed them down again and again. I wouldn't trade what we had for anything. She was my best friend. I refused to lose her. I was too scared of what might happen if she rejected me, and even more scared of what might happen if she accepted. It was too late now, anyway.

Nathan, when he came to visit the coffee shop, always got black coffee, plain. He didn't focus well there, so he would tinker with his fantasy football team, and scroll through the fall's stats on the six man football website. We traded theories on Marvel movies and talked about comic books, or rehashed Nathan's options for the future.

"Yeah, I think it'll be a gap year. Or–I don't know." Nathan buried his hands in his hair. "I can't decide."

"Waiting might be better?" I offered. "Because you can change that decision but if you head straight to trade school, you're locked in."

"Yeah, but is it better to get started sooner? I don't know."

I slid a muffin across to him. "Here, try this. Let it assuage your anxiety."

He took a bite. "S'fine. A little dry."

"I didn't bake it."

"I don't think you *can* bake."

"I know how to work the oven!"

"For warming up pizza, maybe."

"Oh, like you can do better?" I lightly swatted him with a towel.

"I can! I've cooked for Annabella!"

"Oh, for *Annabella*. Because she's your *girlfriend*. And she's so much more special than me! Don't you love me?"

"No. Give me more coffee."
I laughed, and topped off his cup.

27

As winter melted into spring, I dragged myself through my final semester of high school. Senioritis hit me pretty hard. It hit all of us, actually, and we blew off our homework more often than we should. Nathan and I survived English class, and Luis and I struggled through Algebra, and Naomi seemed to float through all her classes simply on the power of her smile.

After last year, I kept a watchful eye on Caleb Hanson, especially now that Finn was gone. He was, at best, an annoying blip throughout the school year. He mostly kept to himself, except when he wanted to bother whoever his latest target was—Luis, Nathan, whoever. He'd stopped picking on Nathan eventually, probably because Nathan got taller and more muscular. Luis, on the other hand, got pestered regularly. He never fought back, though I wished he would. He banked on the power of kindness, I suppose.

When the twins approached their eighteenth birthday, Naomi approached me with a plan.

"I want to get Nathan a special gift this year," she said, conspiratorially, leaning over the bar at Joe's.

"Oh?"

"I need to go to Dallas to do it. Mom won't let me go alone, but she can't go with me without Nathan getting suspicious. Will you come with me?"

"That's suspicious anyway," I pointed out.

"Not if we have Luis distract him."

"Luis is the worst liar I've ever met."

"Luis has already agreed to help me. He's taking Nathan to Six Flags."

"Nathan likes roller coasters?"

She waved that away. "He'll be fine."

"But Six Flags is in Dallas," I pointed out.

"And? Dallas is huge. He'll never know. We'll turn off our Snap locations and everything."

"So I guess I'm going to Dallas."

"Yep," she grinned.

"Delightful," I deadpanned.

"Roadtrip!" She whooped, throwing her arms into the air. From across the room, Joe raised his eyebrows at us, and smiled.

***

Naomi picked me up early in the morning, when the sky was still pale and the gray clouds still blushed yellow with sunrise.

"I just feel like...he needs something special this year. Something good. Y'know?"

I did know. I felt the same way. "Well. Glad to be your adventure buddy for the day."

She nodded, messing with the aux cord. "How do you feel about my DJ-ing abilities?"

"I mean, I'd prefer it if you kept your eyes on the road. Can't DJ and drive."

"You're hilarious." She handed me the tablet she shared with Nathan. "Open up Spotify."

"Okay."

"You're going to DJ under my instruction. DJ by proxy."

I tapped open the account she shared with Nathan. How they ever made that work, I had no idea. If I had to share with my sisters, as much as I loved them, I'd probably go insane. "Okay."

"Okay, there's a playlist. It's in the folder 'Naomi's faves.'"

"Yep." I swiped past a number of playlists with interesting names such as "two a.m. feelings party" and "inspo for thingies."

"It's called 'multi-genre jam session.' Open that one."

I found and opened it. A cursory glance at artists revealed old and new artists such as Fleetwood Mac, U2, and Dodie Clark. This sure would be a heck of a playlist.

"Okay, shuffle it?"

"Yep." I tapped the green icon, and the first song by the Lumineers came on.

"Great. Thanks."

I watched the telephone poles tick by us. She kept one hand on the wheel, using the other to grab for her thermos. The road stretched before us, flat and endless.

There was no way to tell the time or that the miles even moved, save the hash marks on the road sliding beneath us.

I studied her profile–her hair tied atop her head, the slope of her nose, the freckles on her cheeks. I etched it in my memory, the way she smiled as she sang along, eyes glued to the road. I'd draw this in pastels: yellows and grays and pinks.

I shut my eyes and leaned my head back against the seat. Being with her was a sort of ache. Everything I wanted was right there, and I knew I couldn't have it.

"What're we getting him anyway?" I asked.

"We're getting a signed football from a member of the Cowboys team." She left out the name because she knew it would mean nothing to me. "And several comic books that I think are legit. Like, they're the ones he wants. I think."

I nodded.

"That's why you're here, by the way. I don't know enough about comic books to pull that one off completely."

"Okay."

She passed me a list of comics. "Here. We're going to several stores."

I looked at the list. "This is a good list, but can I revise it?"

"Sure."

I did, making a mark here, an addendum there. The song changed again.

"You know, I'm surprised you don't listen to more Taylor Swift."

"What?" She laughed.

"My sisters love her. Blonde girl with a guitar? It's totally your thing."

She wrinkled her nose. "I think she's kind of overrated."

"Wait, what?"

"I mean, I like her older stuff, but she's sold out for the pop scene. All she writes about the boys she's dated."

"But wait, I thought she wrote all her own stuff?"

"How do *you* know so much about her?"

"Hey, I'm...secure in my masculinity. I can admit she's a competent artist. She's got like a billion fans, my sisters included."

"Okay, Zed, sure, she's fine." She rolled her eyes again.

I laughed at her, so full of fondness I couldn't stand it.

We spent hours driving around Dallas, store to store. Naomi stopped at a guitar store and drooled over the acoustics and gadgets. We strolled through a couple book stores, ate lunch from a local place, and got coffee at a little hipster cafe with bare brick, an open ceiling, and Edison bulbs everywhere.

"Do you think this is what college is like?"

"What?"

"This," she continued. "Going places, doing things. Feeling free?"

I shrugged. "Maybe." I was going to a state school, probably Sam Houston or Tech. Naomi was already accepted to a private Christian university in Dallas, and Nathan had eschewed college altogether, planning on going to a trade school for electricity or plumbing.

"I'd love to do homework here," she said dreamily, slumping onto the table. "I'd get so much songwriting done. The atmosphere, the vibes—perfection!"

I hummed noncommittally. College seemed so close, yet so far. I still had months of high school left.

"I wish...I wish there was a way we could all stay together. Wouldn't that be amazing?"

"What?"

"Like, what if we all went to the same school or something. All of us, together."

"Yeah," I said quietly.

"It wouldn't work, obviously, I mean, we're all going to do different stuff and Luis is younger anyway...but I can dream, can't I?"

"Yeah. I know what you mean."

Sometimes, people come into your life, and you know that you'd choose them again, over and over. You know, that no matter how, or when, or where, if you met them for the first time all over again, you'd still choose to be their friend. That's how it was with us. That's the way it should be.

***

Coach made Luis run track again that year. In prior years, it was something Nathan and I had done, though we never competed in the meets. It was mostly to keep in shape. As seniors, we didn't have to anymore, much to Luis' chagrin. I went to support his meet one evening, as it was on our track. It was windy, but not outright cold, so I wore my hoodie and sat in the bleachers to watch the teams mill around. Luis ran in three events, the 100m, the 200m, and the 400m. After his second event, he had enough of a break to join me on the bleachers. As he approached, several other kids from school called out to him in Spanish, and he responded in kind, laughing as he did so.

He plonked down beside me, rubbing at his thigh and calf and stretching his ankle.

"'Sah, dude," I said.

"'Sup," he said.

"Any PRs today?"

"Nah, not today. I'm feeling off, y'know?"

I made a sympathetic face. "Yikes. That's not good."

"It's not like I've got the yips or anything, just that I'm feeling off."

"It happens."

"Yeah. It's bad when it happens on game day, though."

"Right."

Luis chugged from his water bottle. We watched the varsity girls run the 200m on the track. A couple of girls–a cheerleader and a band kid–walked past us and as they did, they glanced at us and whispered to each other behind their hands.

Luis rolled his eyes. "I can *not* wait to get out of here."

I looked from him to the girls. "Were they–were they talking about you?"

He shrugged. "Could be, could not be. But probably. I'm the only kid here who's, y'know, *out*. So I'm like an exotic animal or something."

I looked away, thinking of how I'd gotten some stares in my first few days at school. "I get it."

"One day, I'm going to live so far away from here." He stretched his arms behind his head and leaned back on the bleacher.

I heard an echo of Finn in him, and assessed his face. "Where're you going?"

"New York. Get into NYU, study theatre, try out for Broadway, get a boyfriend...maybe not in that order." He spoke faster than normal, excitement seeping through every word.

"I hope it works out for you," I said, and I meant it genuinely.

"New York is like, the promised land," he said slowly. "Like, allll the queer people are there, and Broadway...and really really good bagels. Mm. Bagels. I want a bagel."

"Houston's not so bad either," I teased. "Besides, the Mexican food sucks anywhere that is not Texas."

"Bro, I *am* Mexican, I can make myself good Mexican food anytime I want. Maybe even convert some of those folks up there to it." He shoved my shoulder.

I laughed, shoving him back. "Maybe convert them to good barbeque while you're at it."

"Mm. Now I want ribs."

"Brisket."

"Ugh, yes. I'm craving it now, but I can't have any till after the meet. Thanks, Zed."

"You're welcome."

He whipped out his phone. "There. Texted mom. Now she'll have to make me something yummy." He leaned back on the bleachers, elbows on the seat back.

"Your mom's not here today?"

"Nah, she had a call. Besides, there's not much to see. It's just a bunch of people running."

I hummed. "My dad never comes to anything."

Luis snorted. "Mine either. And I don't really want him to."

"Really?"

"He's kind of a pain. Mom says she's a lot better off now without him."

"Huh." I thought of my own mother. Did she feel the same? "My dad's...kind of a jerk."

Luis snorted in understanding. "I get that."

"I miss my mom, though. You're so lucky you get to stay with yours."

Luis got a soft little smile on his face. "Yeah. She's the best."

I wished for a second Luis and I had actually talked to each other more before this. But there had always been Finn, who needed me to listen to him, who needled Luis every chance he got. There had always been Naomi, the person Luis confided in, who meant so much to me.

I spotted Caleb Hanson heading toward us, stomping up the bleachers. I made a disgusted noise. "Don't look now, but asshole at two o'clock."

Luis groaned.

"Hey, cutie," Caleb said, his tone making it explicitly clear "cutie" was supposed to be an insult.

"Hey yourself," said Luis pleasantly, but I saw the tension in his shoulders.

"What do you want?" I said flatly.

Luis glanced at me, and then back to Caleb. "Look, if you're just going to say something ugly and then leave, can we skip to the part where you leave? Or do you keep talking to me because you like me? It's like you're obsessed with me or something."

Caleb looked taken aback. "Why would I be obsessed with you?" he finally spit.

Luis shrugged. "I don't know, man. You tell me."

"Whatever," he growled, and stomped away, bleachers clanging as he went.

Luis and I traded a glance. "Well, that was nice," Luis said.

"Do you think he'll stop?" I asked.

"Nope," Luis said cheerfully. "But at least he'll maybe think twice!" He punched me in the arm. "Catch you later, I've got another race coming up." He left me, floating like a butterfly from person to person, group to group, on his way back to the pavement. He made everyone think he was their friend. And he acted like he was everyone's friend in return. And yet, I wondered: how much of it was a front? How much of it was just acting—and coping—until he could fly somewhere that was more ready for him?

I was ready for graduation. I was ready to get closer to Houston and my mom. I wasn't ready to leave my friends.

28

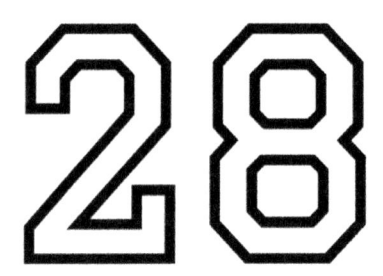

Every year the seniors took a trip. Usually just a weekend trip within a day's drive, skipping Friday classes to come home in time for Monday classes. Our trip was to Carlsbad, New Mexico; more specifically, to the caverns there.

Nathan and I snagged seats together on the bus, though there wasn't a need to panic. There were only fifteen of us on the bus, along with a couple of chaperones. Five kids weren't coming along; the gossip mill said two were in trouble with their grades and were told they couldn't attend, two couldn't afford it, and one wasn't allowed by her very strict parents. Naomi and Annabella sat in the row ahead of us.

Naomi popped in her earbuds and leaned against the window, head rocking gently with the motion of the bus.

"She ok?" I asked Nathan.

"Huh? Oh yeah. Just being a little moody." He shrugged, clearly not too worried. "She gets like this sometimes. Sisters."

I grunted.

Annabella rested her chin on the seat to grin at Nathan. "I have snacks," she said, and held up a Ziploc of cookies and candies in colorful wrapping.

"Ah, you're my favorite person ever," he said, and cupped his hands to receive what she handed him.

She raised her brows at me, questioning, and I nodded. She handed me a bunch of Mamba candies and a chocolate chip cookie.

I chewed on the candy, savoring the sugar. Outside, cattle pastures and scrub brush filled the scenery.

"Hey, want to guess a riddle?" Nathan asked.

Annabella nodded. "Fire away."

"Okay, you're in a box without doors or windows, but you have a mirror and a table. How do you get out?"

"A box..." she chewed on a pinkie finger. "I can crawl out the top?"

"No, unfortunately."

Naomi pulled out an earbud and let it dangle down her front. "Are you doing riddles again?"

"Yes."

"Oh lord, you're insufferable," she groaned, rolling her eyes. "Great big nerd."

"I am a nerd," he said, unashamed.

"Don't play into his games, Annabella. You'll regret it."

"Can I knock a wall down by smashing it with the table?"

"Oy," Naomi groaned again, putting her earbud back in.

They continued to chatter on, until Nathan finally conceded to giving her the answer. "Okay, so you look in the mirror, you see what you saw, you take the saw, cut the table in half, two halves make a whole and you crawl out the hole."

Annabella stared at him for a moment, open mouthed. "You asshole, I hate you!" She punched him lightly in the arm.

"I'm going to have to remember that," I said. I'd use it on Stella. She'd hate it.

Naomi laughed, "I told you he's the worst. Are you sure you want to date him? You're not secretly dating him for a community service project?"

"I'm sure," she said, giving soft eyes to Nathan.

I gagged violently.

They continued to talk together but between the candy and their sappy looks, I decided I'd had enough sweetness and tuned them out.

I tapped Naomi on the shoulder. "You ok?"

She twisted to look at me and heaved a sigh. "Yeah. I just keep thinking of Finn, you know? He didn't go on his senior trip."

"Oh yeah." I hadn't known, but it made sense. Probably too expensive. I hadn't really even addressed the issue with my father, instead making mom talk to him about it. Was that cowardly of me? Maybe. He exhausted me.

"I wish he could be here."

"Same."

"I wish that all the time, but I really wish it right now." Her eyes were soft and distant, turning to the landscape passing us by.

"Yeah."

We arrived in Carlsbad right after lunch time, stopping to eat at a fast food joint. Then, in the parking lot of McDonalds, we discovered Luis in one of the chaperone cars. He hopped out of the car, grinning widely.

"Bro, what?" said Nathan.

"Sah, dude," Luis said, and held up a hand to slap fives.

"What're you doing here?"

"I'm here to see caves, obviously," he said.

"How'd you manage this?" I asked

"Well, my mom decided that since it was you guys' senior year, and since we're such good friends, and I've always wanted to see the caves..."

Behind Luis' shoulder, I made a circular "hurry up" motion. Nathan suppressed a smile.

"Anyway, she said she'd be a chaperone, and I could skip school to come with you."

"And they're going to let you get away with it?"

"I mean...my mom is the biggest financial sponsor of the theatre right now so...yeah."

Naomi's mouth dropped open. "You didn't tell me your mom was the reason we got new microphones!"

He shrugged modestly. "Didn't seem important, honestly."

"Oh my gosh." She tucked an arm into the crook of his elbow. "I'm so glad you're here."

We spent the afternoon roaming the Carlsbad Museum. I was mostly interested in the art exhibits, but I appreciated the ones about the culture and history of indigenous peoples of New Mexico. We worked up an appetite walking around so we grabbed dinner before heading to the caves to watch some bats.

My friends and I had clustered together all day, almost inseparable. And did my heart thrill a little every time Naomi called me her "field trip buddy?" Maybe. That's none of your business.

It wasn't peak bat season yet, so there weren't hoards of bats that you see on the brochures, but there were enough to entertain a group of high schoolers I captured the images in my mind. The little black bodies silhouetted against the orange hued sky; Naomi's wide eyes watching them go. Annabella pressing herself close to Nathan. Luis slouching against a fence post, smiling wide and easy.

At the hotel, we were given strict instructions not to leave the rooms, but everyone knew we'd be hanging in each other's rooms anyway. At eleven o'clock, there was a knock on the door, followed by giggles, and Nathan and I stepped out to see the girls and Luis in bathing suits.

"Are you coming?" Naomi asked, her eyes alive and smile bright.

"Of course I am," I said without thinking.

"We're going to get in trouble," Nathan said.

"Please, they'll never know!"

"This is a bad idea."

"What are they going to do? Send us home? Kick us out of school?"

"Daddy will ground us."

"So we won't tell him."

Annabella, sans contacts for the first time since I'd met her, pushed her glasses up her nose. "It'll be okay," she said gently. "Mrs. Martinez said we could."

"They are never going to let her chaperone again," I said.

"They're too desperate for chaperones," Naomi said. "They're always desperate for volunteers. Now come *on*, before somebody sees us!"

We hustled down the halls to the pool, giggling the whole way. The pool room was humid and smelled of chlorine. Our laughter echoed as we jumped in. The lights in the water turned the whole room a vague turquoise green. Naomi leaned back and lifted her toes—painted yellow—from the water. With a yelp, she disappeared beneath the surface, and Nathan hastily swam away. When she appeared, wiping water from her eyes, he was a safe distance away. Seeing the look on her face, his smile dropped and he ran from her. Annabella, on the side, laughed at their performance, kicking her feet in the water. Luis floated on his back, kicking his feet in the water and putting his hands behind his head. He languidly swam that way down the length of the pool and back again.

For my part, I lounged on the side, paddling my legs gently, and leaned my head back on my shoulders with my eyes closed. The twins kept on doing family therapy—by which I mean splashing water in one another's eyes and grappling—and I kept on listening to the sound of their voices, reveling in the knowledge that they were real and alive and here, and they were my friends.

I felt like we were in the last quarter of a game, watching the seconds slide by, watching the game come to a close whether we willed it or not. Soon we'd graduate, and what then? Where would we go? Who would we become without the others at our side?

Naomi paddled up beside me, water drops falling from her eyelashes. "Hi." She folded her arms on the side and laid her chin on them. With her eyes closed, I could see every freckle on her face. With them open, all I could see was the endless ocean blue of her eyes. She had a freckle right under her right earlobe.

I wanted to draw it. I wanted to kiss it. Maybe, if I leaned forward—

Nathan grabbed me round the shoulders and threw me over his back like a sack of potatoes. I beat uselessly against his broad back, but he prevailed and hauled me to the deep end to attempt to drown me. This forced me, naturally, to retaliate, and climb his back to push his head under. By the time we called truce, coughing and spitting with eyes chlorine-red, Naomi had gotten out of the pool, patting her hair dry. Our moment was long gone.

***

The next morning, we headed directly to the caverns. They opened up from the ground like a yawning earth creature, a cool breeze rising from the hole to waft lightly over our faces. Our tour guide led us deeper and ever deeper, winding on downward switchbacks, getting darker, until we were fully underground and sunlight was but a distant thought. Yes, it was beautiful, stalagmites rising and stalactites falling. But maybe I have a dirty mind, because I found myself distracted by the phallic nature of some of the rock sculptures. Once I saw it, I couldn't unsee it, so I was left looking around at the natural rock formations thinking endlessly *dickdickdickdick.*

Nathan held Annabella's hand under the cover of darkness, whispering to her. Luis's mouth hung open as he stared upward at the ceiling, the way it dipped and rose so high it disappeared into darkness. But Naomi—she seemed to be drinking it in, inhaling the imagery and atmosphere. Her face took on a focused, mesmerized look, and I had a feeling she was storing up this moment to write it into a song.

I nudged Luis. "Hey," I said in an undertone. "Dicks."

He sniggered.

"I'm walking around like, that's just a giant rock dildo!"

"Stop," Naomi complained from in front of us, and moved away.

Nathan let go of Annabella to drift back to us. "You know what Finn would do if he were here?"

"What?"

He nodded at stalagmite protruding from the ground nearby. "He'd grab one of these to jack it off."

We shared a laugh, tears rising in our eyes as we pictured Finn making gross faces and crude noises. He was right, and we knew it.

As though he'd heard us, the tour guide raised his voice. "As a reminder, please do not touch the rock formations, the oils in your skin can damage them."

"Oh, he'd definitely grab one, just double fist it," I said.

Luis bent double to give a full-belly laugh.

"C'mon, we, we gotta do it in his memory," I managed between giggles.

"I don't want to, like, damage it!" Nathan protested.

"I—I know, I don't really either."

"I'll do it," Luis said, and reached over the rope barrier. "For Finn," he said, and ran a finger over the stalagmite. "That's all."

"For Finn," I agreed. "May he forever be remembered by dick jokes and innuendos."

"Amen," said Nathan solemnly, before we burst into laughter yet again.

Our tour included a segment in a huge cave called "The Big Room," and we were told that's where we'd see how dark the underground really is. They turned off all the lights, and we were plunged into utter darkness. Can't-see-your-hand-in-front-of-your-face darkness. There was a rise in noise, gasps and squeals. In the darkness, a hand seized mine, so suddenly I let out a yelp. It was a perfectly manly yelp, thank you.

Naomi whispered, "I don't like the dark."

I squeezed her hand. "It'll be okay."

"I still sleep with a nightlight," she confessed, laughing at herself.

"Cute," I said.

When the lights came on she dropped my hand, and wouldn't meet my eyes. I felt the loss of her touch immediately. I squeezed my hand into a fist to keep the memory of her fingers there. I spent the whole day trailing Naomi, hoping for the same thing to happen again, hoping for something—anything.

My poor heart felt worn out for loving her.

We rode home that day, several of us drifting off in the bumpy bus. That night, laying in bed and still feeling like I was moving forward at 60mph, I pulled up Naomi's Instagram and liked the photos she'd posted of the caverns. We'd forgotten to take a group photo. She'd posted one of herself and Annabella posing all cute, and one of herself and Nathan, only seen from nostrils up, the stalactites above them.

I rolled out of bed and grabbed my sketchbook. I filled the pages with the cave structures, with Luis stroking the dick rock, with Naomi's freckle under her ear. With Finn, seen through the lens of imagination, sticking out his tongue as he grabbed the rock with both hands, the tour guide frantic behind him. The image brought me joy, and I laughed to myself and his ghost in my room.

.

29

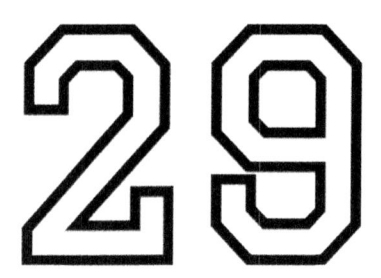

The twins turned eighteen, celebrated with a party at their house. Nathan loved his present, naturally. He gave Naomi a set of guitar picks in a special case, and a set of new strings (apparently those are expensive).

Signs went up for prom around the school, big, tacky, and covered in glitter. The theme was "Star Studded," and there were pictures of movie stars cut out and glued to each sign, along with copious amounts of glitter glue stars. It was horrible and yet I loved it. Naomi nudged me as I wrinkled my nose at one. "We're going, obviously."

"Obviously," I agreed.

Nathan was taking Annabella, and he even did a cute little promposal for her, involving cupcakes spelling it out. He'd baked the cupcakes himself (because of course he did).

Luis was going as friends with a girl from theatre named Viki who kept her hair cropped short and played clarinet. They were going as Ray Bolger and Judy Garland, specifically as their Oz roles. There seemed to be some inside joke there, but I don't think I was meant to get it. I think it was a gay thing? Something about "friend of Dorothy."

When there were two weeks left until prom, while she was at the coffee shop, I finally spit out what I'd been wanting to ask Naomi. I was rinsing out a mug when I oh-so-casually asked, "You wanna go together?"

"What?" She looked up at me, the little furrow between her brows indicating confusion.

"To prom."

"Like...together together?"

"Yeah, like together. As friends." I cringed. No, not as friends, but I'd happily take it.

"Oh. Yeah. As friends." She kept her eyes down at her paper.

"Cool. What color is your dress?"

"Pink. Like a pale pink."

"Cool." I thought perhaps there was more to say, more to ask, but she didn't say anything more, so neither did I.

We gathered at the Peterson's house in April. Annabella was already there when I arrived, her dress a warm orange. Nathan wore a suit with a silver-gray vest and an orange bow tie that complimented her dress. They'd be fun to draw like that, to bring out the colors.

I sat on the ottoman, knees apart. "Are y'all supposed to be celebrities or anything?"

Nathan laughed. "No."

Annabella flashed white teeth at me. "I'm a comet, and he's a star. The theme is *star*-studded."

A smile split my face as I understood. "That's awesome."

And then Naomi came out of her bedroom. It wasn't exactly like a teen movie, where she comes down the stairs and we all stand and gaze at her in awe, but I was certainly struck by her beauty, and I did rise to my feet.

Her dress was pink, fell all the way to her feet in layers, and the sleeves were wide and long. Silver stars decorated the upper part of the dress, and her blonde hair fell loose and light around her shoulders and head.

"You look—" I started, but did not finish. "Corsage," I mumbled instead, and held out the pink chrysanthemum to her.

She took it, laughing. "I almost wish I could bring my guitar."

"Guitar?"

"I'm Stevie Nicks," she said, clearly proud of herself. "I made the dress myself."

"That's incredible." I was sweating so much; I could feel it gathering on my collar and slipping down my ribs.

"Time for pictures!" Mrs. Peterson called, and shooed us toward the mantle to pose like a cliché of every awkward teen movie.

When we arrived at the school, the gym was still a gym, but now there were glittery decorations and pink punch and dimmed lights. The four of us found Luis and Viki, and we all ate snacks and drank punch and laughed at the chaperone's awkward dancing and our classmates being silly. The DJ played top 40 pop songs, and older songs, and all the line dances we all knew. A few scattered slow songs, mostly two-step, because it was West Texas. Naomi and I sat these out, though I kept thinking I should ask her. But no, that would make things weird.

Still, there was one thing I could do for her.

"Alright ladies and gentlemen, I have a special request for you," the DJ said through the speakers.

As the opening notes of "Songbird" by Fleetwood Mac began, Naomi's eyes grew wide.

"Huh, wonder who did that?" Luis said in his slow way. He slid his gaze to me.

"I love this song!" she exclaimed.

"I know," I mumbled. She didn't hear me, but I caught Luis giving me a long, hard look.

"This is so sweet," Naomi said, pressing her hands to her chest.

She stood right at the edge of the floor, swaying back and forth. Several couples shuffled on the floor, mostly leaning on one another and swaying back and forth.

I took a step forward, and froze. My hands clenched, sweating.

Nathan extended a hand to Naomi. "Would you like to dance?"

"You know I do," she said, but there was a catch, a huskiness to her voice.

Nathan looked at me over her head for a long time. He pulled her onto the floor and danced with her, making her laugh in the way only he could, with inside jokes and silly faces.

I knew I'd missed my last chance.

***

Graduation approached. I applied for colleges, though it felt amorphous and vague, not something fully real. Naomi was slowly consumed by one-act play, a shortened version of Alice in Wonderland. They'd done Wizard of Oz in the fall—Naomi was Dorothy, naturally, and Luis played the Tinman. I'd seen it twice. They'd invited the elementary school kids to be munchkins, and the middle school kids acted as crows and flying monkeys and stuff. The small child picking his nose during "Lollypop Guild" had been my secret favorite part, though I'd told Naomi that my favorite part was her, naturally. I'd been subjected to "Somewhere Over the Rainbow" far more than I ever wanted to, and by the time she actually performed it, I probably could have sung it myself.

I finished classes, dragging myself over the finish line like a lazy slug. Senioritis hit us hard. Luis complained about how much further away graduation was for him and how he couldn't wait to get out of this town.

I related, sort of. I'd spent three of the best and hardest years of my life here. And I loved it, despite everything. But I was ready to seek other horizons, other places. Places with exciting skylines and more than one four-way stop, and an abundance of grocery stores.

The last week of school, I swung by Coach C's office. I knocked on the doorframe of the open door, and he looked up over his glasses. "What can I do for you, son?"

"I just wanted to say…thanks." I almost left right there and then, but Coach C took off his glasses and set them on the desk.

"Well, I appreciate that. What for?"

"It's been really great. Being on the team. And in class."

"I'm glad to have been a part of a positive experience. Come sit down. Do you have plans for after school yet?"

I sat in the one leather chair in front of the desk. "I haven't decided between Tech and Sam Houston."

"Your folks are in Houston, aren't they?"

"My mom, yes." I realized that if I'd been with my mom, she would have helped me get a gift for Coach C. Regrets, regrets.

"You plan to be close to them?"

"Hopefully."

"Good luck to you. Have you chosen a major yet?"

"Not fully—maybe art or graphic design. I'll probably be undeclared for the first semester."

"As long as you have a plan. Don't waste your parent's money, that's all undeclared is."

I laughed. "Of course."

"And there's a lot you can do with graphic design. A lot of organizations need social media and that sort of thing."

"Right."

"Well, don't be a stranger. You can call me anytime, son."

"Okay, thanks Coach." I stood to go.

"*Anytime*," he repeated, giving me a little nod.

I nodded back at him. Softer, I repeated, "Okay, Coach. I will."

The day we graduated, our little trio stuck close together. Until they lined us up by last name, I kept an arm looped over each twin. When your school is as small as Terrytown's, graduation is much shorter than average. There were only twenty people in the graduating class.

My dad came to graduation. So did my mother and sisters. They sat across the way from each other, and didn't even pose for pictures. I couldn't find the energy to care. I took pictures in groups; with Tate and Nathan, with the Petersons, with Coach C. Nathan gave me a fistbump and a lopsided smile and said, "Ready, break. Comets!" I laughed. Naomi snagged me for a selfie, grinning so brightly I was blinded.

To me, she had always been the sun.

And then it was summer, and I worked, and packed, and planned to move. We still went swimming at Luis', but it was different now. Everything was on a timer, everything was slipping away. June and July evaporated.

I worked my last shift at Joe's, and was glad of it. I hadn't exactly hated working there, but I would be happy to have no more early mornings or having to deal with entitled old people. As I wiped down the counter for the last time, Joe appeared from back, smiling.

"Thanks for all your hard work," he said, passing me an envelope. My name was scribbled in jagged print. "I wish you the best, getting educated. Education is so important."

"Yes sir." I ran my thumb over my scribbled name, feeling weirdly fond.

"It's the way up in life, you gotta get educated, get a good job."

"Yes sir."

"You study hard, now. No slacking off." He put a hand on my shoulder, looking into my eyes. I could see his warm affection there.

"Yes sir. I will," I said, smiling crookedly.

He slapped my back. "You're a good kid, Zed."

"Thank you."

"Come back anytime. You're always welcome. I'll have a free coffee for ya!"

"Okay. I will. Thank you." I meant it.

"Alright then." With one final pat on the back, he pushed me toward the door.

Terrytown would never be a place I was coming home to. I wasn't really trying to get away from it either. It existed and marked my high school years. It had claimed me as its own for a time. It had changed me. For me, Terrytown would be the place I'd gotten my first scars. The first heartbreak. My first best friends.

My friends, how precious and wondrous they were.

We all got together for one more hang out at Whataburger. We talked about everything and nothing, about winning the state championship, about going to Galveston, about the first time we met. About Finn. Memories spilled from our lips, stories retold and jokes rehashed. The time Finn got ketchup all down Nathan's shirt. Luis and Finn seeing who could spit watermelon seeds the farthest. Smuggling candy into movies. The one time Finn let me drive his truck right after I got my license. Board games that ended with Nathan and Naomi bickering, Finn yelling about cheating, Luis and I studying the rules. Football games. The trips to Big Spring and Carlsbad. All of us trying to squeeze years of loving one another into a few hours.

And then time was up.

"I guess this is goodbye," Naomi said wistfully.

"No, not goodbye. You'll be back, don't be dramatic," said Luis. He put on an exaggerated pout.

"We're theatre people, we're always dramatic." She hugged him gently, with that unabashed affection they always had.

"You'd better come back in a hurry, cause I'm still here."

"Yeah, but—it's different," she said, stepping back.

He shrugged. "Gonna miss you."

I nodded.

"I love you guys," Nathan said quietly.

I nodded harder. I pulled him in for a bro hug, slapping his back with a thump. Luis hugged me tightly, without restraint. His gangly arms wrapped all the way around me and squeezed.

And then there was Naomi. She looked up at me, misty-eyed. I pulled her to my chest, conscious of the press of her body against mine. I stayed like that, allowed myself to wallow in the moment, inhaling the smell of her and drinking in the feel of her. Naomi was my best friend, and I loved her far more than I could ever put into words. And in those final moments, I exhaled, and I chose to let it go. To let her go. We were going our separate ways. That was the end of it. In some ways, I realized, I'd made a choice a million times over. I had chosen, over and over, to remain silent. To let things be as they were. She was my best friend, and I never wanted to lose that. Never wanted to see a wedge drive between us for any reason. But I'd made the same decision–at the beach, at prom, in little daily moments. Maybe in another universe, in another life, we'd have been the right person for each other. But not this one.

It tore inside me, this screaming torrent of unspoken love. But I let it flow, let a few tears fall from my eyes.

I swallowed, stepping back from her.

She sniffled, gave me a nod.

I memorized her every shape, the curl of her hair, the sprinkle of her freckles, the slant of her mouth. The way her shoulders curved inward, the brightly colored loose top she wore. I carved it into my mind to keep forever, to remember forever, to hold forever.

Naomi,

Naomi,

Naomi…

Finn.

And suddenly I was standing in a cinderblock dorm room, staring at the bunk bed and bare walls, wondering what the hell was coming next.

FRESHMAN YEAR

30

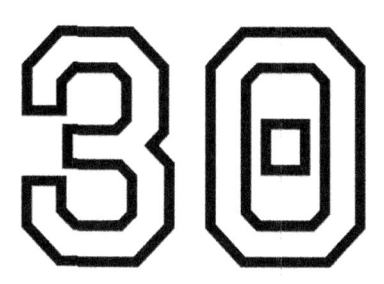

No one tells you how college changes you. No one tells you that you fall apart and remake yourself, that freshman year is really hard, that you'll probably change your major. I felt like I was on a treadmill that kept going faster and I was barely keeping up. Classes, assignments, professors. Bad cafeteria food. Days when I survived on caffeine and sugar alone. A roommate with whom I sort of coexisted. I struggled with graphic design, design theory. I lived for the times I could draw whatever I wanted, the moments of free time.

    I wore my letter jacket every day it was below seventy. I wore it like a security blanket, the C over my heart. Football had been so much of who I was for so long, I wasn't sure how to let it go. I wasn't sure who I was without the field beneath me and the ball between my hands. I worked to reclaim my identity as an artist, as a person. Someone not attached to a group of four other people; someone who wasn't recognized as *friend of the dead kid.*

    I called my mom every week, suddenly drawing closer to her than I'd ever been. I needed to; I had to ask her about laundry and cold medicine and advice for cooking food in the microwave. I texted Hailey a lot, too, about how to get extra credit and how to talk to professors and random memes.

I made new friends; not a group like I'd once had, but scattered individuals from classes, from my dorm, from intramural sports. I was physically closer to my mom, now, too, and went to her house for breaks and weekends.

Our groupchat dwindled, though we shared memes and stories and swapped greetings and happy birthdays. Sometimes Luis would send a story from home, but even he seemed further away than ever. Nathan texted me often, since he took a gap year. He was working full time waiting tables in Big Spring. He absolutely hated it, but sometimes he would share a funny story or complain. He did like the look of his bank account, though. And his managers liked him, because he was on time, polite to customers, and didn't steal from the register (which honestly, the bar was on the floor–what the heck, y'all). We hopped on the Xbox for some multiplayer games of Overwatch. We'd talk while on headset, constantly interrupting ourselves with cries of "Help, help! I'm dying! Shit!"

From Naomi, I heard very little. I thought about her often, but I resolved to let it all go. She was majoring in theatre at that little Christian school in Denton, and it seemed like she was happy.

I spent Christmas with my mother and spring break on a school trip. We went to Rome for an art tour. I almost completely filled my phone with photos–not of the art but of the streets and landscapes, things I wanted to sketch. It wasn't until summer that I finally made a trip back to Terrytown.

I stayed with my dad, and he ate a whole meal with me, grilling me about college. In his face, I could see the regret, the confusion. The wonder at who this man was in front of him. I had changed, and he knew it.

Hunched over the table at the Mexican restaurant, he said, "And I guess you'll be staying in Houston mostly?"

"Yeah, it's closer to school."

"Right." He nodded. "And you don't know when you'll be back up here?

"Not right now, no."

"Huh." He looked away from me.

Part of me hurt. Part of me yelled at the injustice: he spent so long dismissing me, and now he wanted something? He was still my father, after all. "Dad?"

"Yeah."

"Why—why didn't you ever come to my football games?" The words come out softly, lacking anger.

"I mean—I was always so busy—"

"Not even the state championship." I searched his face. I wasn't asking him about football, not really, and he knew it.

"I—I *wanted* to, but I just couldn't...figure out how. Sorry."

I pinched my lips together and looked away. It was the only apology I'd ever receive, most likely. I wasn't sure I could find it in me to forgive, not yet. Maybe someday. It's complicated, and I think it always will be.

I did, of course, stop by Cup O' Joe's, and Joe himself personally made me a latte. He still had the clipping from our state championship win pinned up, a little faded. He asked about classes and if there were any pretty girls, and how my grades fared.

I motioned to the chalkboard menu. "I see you have some new items."

"Yes! Suggestions of my granddaughter."

I smiled. *Pupkin Spice Latte. English muffin, tosted. NEW! Arrowpress coffee.* Every single one of them, misspelled, somehow. If I'd still been working, I would have been annoyed. Since I was no longer working, it made me *almost* nostalgic. Almost. Maybe a little fond.

Joe, like this town, frustrated me, and yet I still had a soft spot for him.

But the real reason I was coming back to Terrytown was to see my friends.

Sorry bro, I'm busy moving to New York!

That was Luis. But the twins responded and said they'd be there, that we could get together for a little bit.

We met at the Mexican place in town, which was weird after years of casually showing up in homes, driveways, trucks, Whataburger. We sat at a booth, the twins on one side and me on the other.

We swapped stories about college or work, our adventures, our new friends. Pauses came often, and they sat tight and heavy between us. It was stilted, awkward, the space between us growing pronounced. Something seemed to have changed between us.

Nathan seemed suddenly more adult, his comments softer, more thoughtful than they ever were. He talked about budgets and classes and the apartment he was signing for. He and Annabella were still doing well, and she was planning to graduate early. I felt small, next to him, and very young. But he'd always been more grown up than the rest of us, always carried seriousness in the set of his shoulders and honesty in his heart.

And there was Naomi. Wonderful Naomi. She talked about songwriting, about music, about her classmates and friends and roommates. About her shows and this guy she'd dated. (Did it hurt? Yes. But I kept it to myself, thank you. I am mature like that.) She always knew everyone, and college hadn't changed that. She told us she had auditioned for a competition for musicians her school did. She said she'd let us know when the performances were. Auditions were in the spring, competition in the fall. She was happy.

And I told them about graphic design and art, about my classes and my friends. It came out haltingly, slowly, nothing like it used to be. I told them I missed them, which was true. I told them I was perfectly fine, which was not.

Those are memories I prefer not to dwell in. I like to think more about when everything was right in the world, when everything was easy.

That was the last time I saw them, in person anyway.

The universe is always expanding, from where the stars were flung when time began. So it was with us: gradual, incremental, drifting. Black holes gradually getting deeper. Space between the stars.

We drifted apart, as is the natural wont of college students. You move away, you leave high school behind, you form new bonds. You grow and you change, and they grow and they change, and when you meet again, you find you don't quite fit anymore, so you let each other go. And it hurts a little, it aches quietly, but it's the way things are meant to be.

I settled into the swing of college. I got a job, I took a creative writing class, and found out I actually like using my words sometimes. I started running, letting my shoes eat away the miles. It wasn't football, or soccer, but it was enough for me. Oh, and I changed my major. I called Coach C about it. He answered with a "What can I do for you, son?" and I smiled, and poured my troubles out to him easily. Graphic design wasn't working, I said. I was depressed, I said. I was thinking of changing things, but I wasn't sure which way to go. He listened, and asked what made me not just happy, but fulfilled. He asked about what I'd always wanted to do, as a kid. And he asked how college was and what I was up to. He always answers when I call. If he's not busy, he says, "What can I do for you, son?" If he is busy or distracted, he says, "H'lo?" But he's never too busy to answer me.

After we hung up, I headed to the registrar's office. I clicked some buttons, answered some questions. Looked at class lists.

Walked out with a new major.

In high school, the best parts of it had been my friends and football. And the best parts of football were the team and the coaches. Coach C—a man I respected more than anyone in the world—had been so important, in his quiet way. What if I could be the same?

I'm going to teach art in a high school, maybe assistant coach on the side if they let me, and I'm going to give back. Everything that I received, I'm going to give back tenfold. I am an artist. I will be a teacher. I used to play football, but now I run. I still wear my letter jacket, still put the C over my heart. Football, Terrytown, and Finn—they will always be a part of me. But they aren't all of me anymore. I am myself; I am who I am meant to be.

I love my friends. I wish them all the best. I think about Finn often, and I wonder if he watches us from the afterlife. I like to think he makes fun of us, with our boring educational and studious lives.

You know, back at the beginning, I told you this story was about football. But now, really, I think it's about them. It's about our little group of friends, and how hard we worked for each other. It's about her. It's about the girl who got away, except not, because I held her and I loved her, but just not quite the way I wanted to. Maybe I could have, maybe we could have dated and been in love, but I think it's better this way. I think a small part of me will always love her, and that's okay.

I still go driving, late at night sometimes. I go out of town, to a pasture or empty field. I try to find the stars. They're different here, than in West Texas, dimmed by light pollution and humidity. But it's out here that I feel closest to him. To Finn. When I see the stars late at night, I remember him, grinning bright in the darkness, shouting he was king of the world. And for a moment, he's here again. He's not so far away. The grief has faded with time. It's less sharp and raw now, less like an open wound. It's more like the way my ankle aches on cold days, or how it gets sore if I push myself too hard when running. It's still there, and I think it always will be.

I will always have a place in my heart for him.

When people hear about Finn, they always say some of the same stuff: *I'm so sorry, that's horrible, that must have been so hard*. They're right, but it never quite captures it the right way. Because I'll tell you the truth: I would choose them anywhere, love them in any time, any place. I would do every single heartbreaking second over again if it meant I got to meet them and love them. I wouldn't change a thing, not even Naomi and me. We loved, and we lost, and we grew up. I would *walk* into love with them, not fall. It was a choice I made, eyes open, feet steady. I hope they would do the same for me.

Ready? Break.

Comets.

A band of thieves in ripped up jeans got to rule the world

A boys of fall playlist

May we all	Florida Georgia Line, Tim McGraw
The Boys of Fall	Kenny Chesney
half of my hometown	Kelsey Balerini
Castle on the Hill	Ed Sheeran
Infinity	One Direction
Renegades	X Ambassadors
Long Live	Taylor Swift
I Lived	OneRepublic
This Town's Been Too Good To Us	Dylan Scott
Famous Friends	Chris Brown
Small Town Saturday Night	Hal Ketchum
I Wonder Do you Think of Me	Keith Whitley
Drive my Soul	Lights
Superposition	Young the Giant
My Town	Montgomery Gentry
Good Old Boys Like Me	Don Williams
Truck Yeah	Tim McGraw
Red Dirt Road	Brooks & Dunn
Down on the Farm	Tim McGraw
Find out who your friends are	Tracy Lawrence
Please Notice	Christian Leave
Our Town	James Taylor
Find Yourself	Brad Paisley
She's Like Texas	Josh Abbot Band

Author's note and Acknowledgments

In November of 2020, I sat in the bleachers of Baird, Texas (I didn't know it existed either), and watched my brother's team win the six man football independent championships. On the sidelines, my brother joked around with his friends and teammates, and I thought, "Oh. I want to write about *that*." The next summer I found Zed waltzing onto my page and making himself—quite firmly and sarcastically—right at home. It took me nearly four years, but I finally got to a place where I could put this story into the world. I never thought my first book would be about six man football. I never thought my first book would be anything other than fantasy, my first and true genre love, where I fully intend to return. But here we all, and *Boys of Fall* is a real book, in your hands.

It's taken quite the journey to put this book in the world, assisted by many people. First, there are the research resources without which I would've been lost. Below are the materials I found helpful on my creation journey.

Six: A Football Coach's Journey to a National Record, Rasmussen, Marc, 2011.
Where Dreams Die Hard: A Small American Town and its Six Man Football Team, Stowers, Carlton, 2005

Friday Night Lights, Bissinger, H. G., 1988
Texas 6, produced by Jared L. Christopher, 2020, which at the time of this writing is available on Paramount Plus.

    Now, for those of you that actually read acknowledgements, here come all the thank-yous.

    First, to my editor, Jadyn McClendon. You took this story and were first a cheerleader, and then pushed me to make it better. It wouldn't be where it is today without you. Thank you for taking a chance on me, and for pushing so hard near the end; for putting up with my frequent Gollum screeching "My precious!" about things that weren't really that important, and for calling out my Herman Melville sentences. See, I put one there just for you! All mistakes remaining are 100% mine, and have nothing to do with Jadyn in the slightest.

    Thanks to my community online and in real life, to every person that told me they were excited and wanted to read it, especially to the acquisitions department of my local library and all the friends who said "Wow! You're writing a book! That's so cool!" Y'all gave me the endurance to push through. Knowing that someone wants to read my words means so much.

    I owe a huge thanks to my family for their endless support of this story. I pestered my brother and father endlessly for rules, plays, lingo, and stories. Some of the incidents in this book take their inspiration from things that actually happened on my brother's team (Go Heat!). So thank you, Eli, for breaking things down for me like I was five years old. Thank you for your endless encouragement and support. Thank you for reading an early draft and saying it was good. Thank you for letting me tell this story. I cannot wait to never write about sports again.

    Thank you, Daddy, for hunting down about thirty country songs for the playlist. Thank you for correcting and assisting my understanding of small town life and small schools. Thank you for your encouragement and advocacy, and for letting me ramble at you about it for forty-five minutes straight while trapped in a church van. Thanks for cheering me on.

Thank you, Mom, for first being the person who taught me to write, and thus set me on this journey. Thank you for answering my questions about punctuation and grammar. Alas, I still cannot spell, despite your best efforts, and commas still make me want to bang my head on the wall. My red pen and I thank you for your help. (Look, even that sentence is in proper grammar. You're welcome.)

Thank you, Desi, for drawing a beautiful cover just as I pictured it. I knew from the start I wanted your art on the cover. I wanted your work to be the first thing people saw about this book, and I adore it. It's more than I could've ever hoped for. Keep sparkling!

Thank you to my love. You read the worst version of this story, even though you don't like sportsball. You listened to me complain and gripe and cry about formatting, and offered patient support, even when I told you it might cost more than I thought. So many cups of tea and coffee and cold-brew, so many home-cooked dinners, so much quietly letting the housework go undone (or stepping up to cover for me) while I was on a deadline. You saw the heart of this story, and you hold the heart of me. All my love always.

And finally, thanks to the Lord, to whom I give all the glory.

—Katie Gage, September 2024

A note from the editor

Dear reader,

Welcome to the wonderful world of Boys of Fall. You have laughed. You have cried. You have lived the life of Zed and his crazy friends. This world existed in the mind of someone with a great story to tell and I couldn't be more excited to share it with you. It takes a village to make that story into a tangible thing that has made its way into your hands but it's the best kind of village that has brought it to you–one not unlike Zed and his friends. The people who brought you this story and this world are dreamers like Zed, ones who wish for everyone to find the light in their life even when the darkness comes to snuff it out. Hold onto your dreams, hold onto your light, hold onto your friends.

Sincerely,
The editor

About the Author

Katie Gage is an Indie author living in East Texas with two cats and one husband. She loves baking, reading, hiking, reading, sci-fi/fantasy, Star Wars and did she mention reading?
If you're interested in keeping up with Katie, follow her on Instagram @cozylifeofkatie, or checkout her website, KatieGageAuthor.com.

Thanks for reading! Please add a short review on Amazon or Goodreads and let me know what you thought.

Printed in Great Britain
by Amazon